Their Perfect Omega

MAYA NICOLE

Copyright 2022 © Maya Nicole
All rights reserved.

All rights reserved. No portion of this book may be reproduced in any form without permission from the author, except as permitted by U.S. copyright law.

For permissions contact: mayanicoleauthor@gmail.com

The characters and events portrayed in this book are fictitious. Any similarity to real people, living or dead, businesses, or locales are coincidental.

Cover Design by Maya Nicole
Edited by Karen Sanders Editing

❋ Created with Vellum

AUTHOR'S NOTE

Omega Match is an omegaverse reverse harem romance series of standalones. That means each of the main characters will have a happily ever after with three or more men. Recommended for readers 18+ for adult content and language.

Contemporary omegaverse has non-shifting alphas, betas, and omegas. Alphas have knots and omegas go through heats, but they do not turn into wolves.

Content warning: As a dog lover I feel I need to say this. There is a pet dog in this book and he goes through some things. He does not die.

CHAPTER ONE

Kara

I was committing a felony. There was no doubt about it. The headline was as clear as the dark highway in front of me: *Former perfect omega steals dean of students' car.*

In my defense, Ella had left her keys on the counter in her apartment that she'd given me a spare key to. She was practically giving me permission, right? She'd even taught me to drive and taken me to get my driver's license.

A driver's license didn't erase the three words no omega wants to read in their email: *No Match Results.*

It had been a month since those words knocked me off my feet, and I was in a weird transition period where

I needed to decide if I wanted to find an omega-friendly job or start attending fall match events. Unfortunately, I'd added *lose my ever-loving mind and steal someone's car* to that list.

Omega Match was a government-run matching program that paired newly graduated omegas with packs of alphas and was the current bane of my existence. After months of meet and greets, we listed our choices in order of preference, and the system matched us similarly to how newly graduated doctors matched into residency programs.

Top omegas always matched with the best packs... except for me.

I'd done everything right since before I'd even emerged as an omega. Having a pack was all I'd hoped for and wanted. What had been the point of all the late nights studying, practicing my skills, and worrying about how I presented myself in public and around alphas?

I was twenty-two, freshly graduated from the most prestigious omega academy on the west coast, winner of four *Omega of the Year* awards, yet I was pack-less.

And now, I was a car thief.

My fucks had gone right out the window like my match results. The matching was done and now I'd have to wait until the fall when the packs weren't as plentiful or as desirable. I tried not to dwell on what could have been.

The farther I got away from the omega compound,

the more relaxed I became. The omega compound might have been a highly secure apartment complex for unmatched omegas, but it was no contender for a determined omega.

With a tall, spiked fence and beta security guards always on watch, I'd still managed to drive out without issue. Between the shift change, the baseball cap I wore over my curly hair, and the cover of darkness, it had been easy to leave. Too easy.

How many other omegas had snuck in and out without our babysitters knowing? I'd lived there a month and hadn't heard a peep in the common areas we shared. But I wasn't surprised; omegas didn't trust one another, and they wouldn't want a goody-two-shoes such as me to rat them out.

Who's the goody-two-shoes now?

The only one I ever hung out with was Ella Monroe, who had been my dean at Elite Omega Academy. We'd become quick friends when I had moved in across the hall from her. I think she knew I needed someone, especially after my twin sister moved a thousand miles away with her pack.

I looked in the rearview mirror to make sure the police and Omega Protective Services weren't chasing me. It was only a matter of time before OPS found out I was missing, but by the time they did, I would be long gone.

The speaker in the car dinged, and I jumped. "Take

the next exit to I-5 South," Siri's monotone voice directed me.

I smiled, checked my mirrors, and left my disappointment behind.

Driving a thousand miles in two days was beyond crazy, especially when my driving experience was limited. I was newly licensed, and Ella had let me drive between the academy and the compound several times as practice, but that hadn't prepared me for the highway or everything that went with it.

I was extra cautious, checking my mirrors twice before changing lanes, staying in the slow-lane, and taking a lot of breaks. That didn't change the fact that this was by far the stupidest thing I'd ever done.

Leaving Washington had been easy, and Oregon had been a breeze since they filled up my car with gas for me, but once I hit California, I was a little intimidated. Thank the knot gods for the internet, otherwise I would have been one of those people that spilled gas all over the place.

I'd stopped at night at cheap motels, not wanting to risk giving my ID to anyone. I was on heat suppressants and scent blockers to minimize the risk of attracting unwanted alpha attention, but there were evil people in the world, and if the wrong person knew I was an omega, I might have found myself in a bad situation. As an extra precaution, I'd picked up some cheap perfume at a gas station to spray the car and myself with.

After two long days, I made it to Kayla's house in one piece and parked five houses down. If OPS or the police came looking for me, I didn't want them to see the car right out front or in the driveway.

Kayla had been texting me all day, so I knew she was home. Her pack was on a week-long business trip to New York City, and she'd stayed behind to work on her plans for a quilting business. I didn't know why she hadn't gone with them since they were bonded now, but then again, she was stubborn as a mule.

I turned off the car and grabbed my purse from the passenger seat. I wasn't looking forward to the trek uphill with my large suitcase, and I looked into the backseat at the two Squishmallows I'd brought with me. "You, my friends, will have to wait. Mama only has two arms." I changed my voice to a higher pitch, pretending one of them was talking. "What happened to no man or Squishmallow left behind?"

The sound of a vehicle caught my attention, and I turned forward. A shiny black SUV with fully tinted windows turned right in front of me into the driveway leading to a gate. I'd parked about a car length back from where the curb dipped for the driveway. Ella's car was nice, but it wasn't Hollywood Hills nice.

The SUV idled, waiting for the gate to open. The idea that someone famous was inside excited me, and I squinted, trying to make out any figures inside. Was it even legal to have windows that dark?

The passenger door swung open and a man in dark blue jeans and a tight gray shirt got out, his phone grasped tightly in his hand. His strong jawline was covered in stubble and his short black hair was faded expertly on the sides.

Holy fucking hell, I couldn't breathe. My heart lodged in my throat and my vision went blurry for a second before zeroing in on none other than Alvaro Estrada of N'Pact, the most popular boyband in the world. Not only could the four-man band sing, but they could move like they were pulled right off the Magic Alpha stage. It was unfortunate they didn't strip down to their underwear like the Magic Alpha dancers did.

N'Pact were all alphas, and this made them not only highly appealing to omegas, but betas as well. Even though betas couldn't bond with alphas, that didn't stop them from imagining they could.

A weird, possessive growl bubbled in my throat. I didn't like the idea of betas throwing themselves at alphas. It was hard enough finding a good pack to be a part of without beta women and men encroaching on what was ours.

Breathe, Kara.

Alvaro was on the phone, his other hand pulling at his hair. His frown was intense and the lift in his shoulders made him look like he was ready to explode. The

SUV had already pulled forward, leaving Alvaro to pace up and down the driveway.

My heart fluttered as he ran the hand that had been yanking at his hair down his face before pinching the bridge of his nose. He looked so tense and upset that I wanted to offer to massage his shoulders.

Bad idea.

I didn't know why I was so surprised to see one of the band members in the flesh; Kayla had told me they lived down the street. They had even helped her out before, but I never imagined I'd spot one.

My hands shook as I fumbled around in my purse for my phone so I could take a picture of him. Maybe I could get one with him? No. That was a bad idea. He was in an intense conversation and was an alpha. They all were. Even if they were famous, I couldn't risk being around unbonded alphas. If something went awry, I'd be in even deeper shit with OPS and so would they.

I was acting like a knottybopper, but I didn't care. This was a once-in-a-lifetime encounter.

My fingers brushed across the edge of my phone in the pit of my purse, and I pulled it out, throwing the bag back into the passenger seat. I looked back up just as Alvaro kicked at a bush before he walked quickly up the driveway and disappeared.

It was for the best. If he caught me snapping a picture of him, he might come kick the car, or worse, call the police. With a sigh, I grabbed my purse and begrudgingly got out. I sniffed the air, hoping to catch his scent, but all I could smell was the cheap gas station perfume I'd spritzed all over myself.

I grabbed my suitcase and overnight bag from the trunk, locked up, and trekked up the hill. Despite only being five houses away, the properties were wide, so it was quite the walk after lying on the couch binge-watching television shows for the past month.

I was heaving by the time I finally made it to my sister's gate, and I pressed the call button on the intercom. It rang once before a man picked up. "Kayla? What the heck are you doing outside the property? I knew we should have brought you with us." Of course Beck had to be the one to answer. He was fiercely protective of my sister and would rip anyone to shreds for even looking at her the wrong way.

"Hi, Beck! I'm here to see Kayla." I smiled up at the camera and took off the baseball hat I was wearing. "It's a surprise." I was met with silence. "Hello?"

"Do you have permission to be here?" What he really meant was did OPS let me come to a major city with no escort.

"Are you going to let me in or not? I think there's a pack of alphas hunting for omegas headed this way."

"You're just like your sister." He growled something under his breath. "I'll unlock the front door for you. If Kayla isn't inside, she's out by the pool."

The gate opened, and I entered, sagging with relief as it closed behind me.

I'd made it. Consequences be damned.

CHAPTER TWO

Alvaro

There was no organization I hated more than the World Pack Health Organization. Well, except for Omega Protective Services, but that hatred was buried so deep I'd need an excavator to unbury it.

Because of OPS, our pack health had to be evaluated every year to ensure we weren't showing any signs of becoming feral alphas. It was a fucking joke, and for the past three years, we'd dutifully done as we were asked. It was an invasion of our privacy, and now they wanted to do it every six months because we were high risk. The only thing that was at risk was their asses from me shoving my foot up them.

The gate closed behind me, and I walked to the SUV where Cal, Avery, and Tate were already grabbing our bags out of the back. We'd been in New York for the past three days doing TV appearances, and I could see the exhaustion in the slump of their shoulders and the dark circles under their eyes.

And now I was going to have to tell them we had to deal with visitors tomorrow.

Jonathan, our beta, locked the doors as the trunk clicked shut. "You guys need anything else?"

"We're good. Go see your girl." I clapped him on the back, and he headed for the side fence where there was a walk-through gate to the house next door. No one knew we owned both properties, but it was necessary for us to function as a pack. We hated sharing our space, even with our betas. Jonathan and his wife, Anya, had been instrumental in making sure we didn't fall apart since we didn't have an omega.

My chest hurt even thinking about what could have been. We'd fucked up, and now, despite all the fame and fortune, we were miserable.

Tate elbowed me in the stomach, snapping me back to reality. "What did they say?"

I followed the three of them inside, not wanting anyone to overhear. We never knew if someone could be lurking around or have a microphone sitting on the top of our wall. Jonathan was responsible for doing sweeps of the property daily to make sure it was secure, but nothing was foolproof.

Our dog, Gizmo, had been a big help in deterring fans and paparazzi from attempting to come onto our property, but if someone was determined, they'd find a way.

"After the police were called last weekend for that party, they want to assess us every six months now." I ran my hand down my face and took my bag from Avery. "They think we're spiraling and are going to become a risk to all of the omegas we don't even have access to."

Cal groaned and dropped his bag in the middle of the entryway, kicking off his shoes right next to it. "Then they should let us be in the match again. Problem solved."

Gizmo trotted around the corner, his nails clicking on the hardwood floor. I dropped my bag next to Cal's and squatted down to greet the Rottweiler. He was so much more than just an added layer of security to our property; he was a comfort.

"Who was a good boy while we were gone?" I butted my head against his and rubbed his ears before standing. "They're coming tomorrow."

"Tomorrow?" Avery grunted and snapped his fingers, calling Gizmo to him. "That's no notice."

"On the bright side, the house is clean. Anya is the best." Cal left his shit in the middle of the entryway and walked into the living area, plopping down on the large L-shaped couch. "I don't know about you guys, but I'm beat. Still might go out later after a nap."

Tate kicked his bag and shoes to the side. "The house isn't going to stay clean for long now that your messy ass is here. Maybe we should lock you in your room to keep the house clean."

Ignoring Tate's jab, Cal put his feet on the coffee table and turned on the eighty-inch television mounted above the fireplace. "What time are they coming tomorrow?"

I sat down in an armchair, putting my bag at my feet. "They wouldn't tell me. The only thing they said was they were assessing all areas; cooperation, judgment, emotional regulation, and reaction."

We all looked over at Avery, who had walked across the living room to the floor-to-ceiling windows looking out at the backyard and the city. Out of the four of us, Avery was the worst off. He'd gone from a smiling, carefree alpha to a brooding one overnight. He was really living up to his last name, Payne, that everyone called him by when we were in boyband mode.

Three years ago, we'd matched with an omega, but she hadn't even been with us a full twenty-four hours before she rejected our pack. One day, we were submitting our match application, and the next, our newly released single became an instant hit. None of us expected it to happen, but the matching was done, and we welcomed our new omega.

Or tried to.

The first day she arrived we'd had a performance and we'd stupidly taken her along with us. We hadn't anticipated the sheer number of people trying to get into the club, and when we arrived, it was pandemonium. None of us were prepared and we certainly didn't have the security or safety plans in place that we had now.

She'd been separated from us before we'd even set foot in the venue, and she had OPS on the phone before we noticed she was missing. We thought we'd been ready for an omega—and we had been—but our situation changed overnight and now we were facing the consequences.

Avery still had Gizmo next to him, petting his head absently. "I'm fine."

Cal snorted. "Will you be fine when they stick an omega's scent in your face, Payney boy? Maybe if you didn't go crazy from it, they'd take us off the blacklist."

Tate smacked Cal on the back of the head as he passed behind the couch. "You're one to talk. How many betas have you slept with since the last assessment?"

My pack was falling apart, and I didn't know how I was going to fix it. We were under so much pressure from the record label, fans, and the world that it was hard to focus on strengthening our pack bond. Jonathan and Anya helped some by seeing our basic needs were taken care of, but it wasn't the same as having an omega. There was no innate need for betas, and even if we had fifty, it wasn't enough.

We needed an omega, but we weren't allowed to have one until we left the spotlight permanently, and that was a few years away due to our contractual obligations. But was it worth it? Some days, I wanted to say fuck it and deal with the financial and legal fallout from breaking our contracts.

"You aren't going out tonight, Cal. Not the night before our assessment." I stood and looked down at him. "Is that clear?"

Cal rolled his eyes and crossed his arms over his chest. "You aren't the boss of me."

Here we go.

My temper flared, and I grabbed him by the front of the shirt, yanking him to his feet. "You aren't going out," I growled. "This isn't just about you."

He shoved me half-heartedly with a growl. "Fuck you."

Gizmo barked at us, and I let Cal go. I hadn't asked Avery if he'd trained Gizmo to break up our spats, but anytime things got heated and the dog was around, he'd bark or put himself between us. Without him, we'd probably already be a dissolved pack.

Tate ran a hand over his face. "I think we should all go to our rooms for the night. I'll order us some pizzas."

Sounded like a plan to me.

Not saying another word, because I didn't trust myself not to rip Cal's head off, I grabbed my bag and went up the stairs. Sometimes the best thing for all of us was to separate. Being together was just a reminder that we were falling apart.

CHAPTER THREE

Kara

The second I stepped foot in Kayla's house, I felt a wrongness about being in her space. The scents were overwhelming, and I pulled up the neck of my tank top to cover my nose. I'd never experienced anything like it before, even when visiting my parents.

I set my bags against the wall so they were out of the way and the sound of the deadbolt locking made me jump. There was no turning back now.

Kayla had matched with a pack of professional Alphaball players who also had multiple businesses that made them millions and millions of dollars. They'd recently entered billionaire territory and their house showed it.

The expansive living room was sleek but inviting and looked right out to the Los Angeles skyline. It was probably breathtaking at sunset and at night. I walked through the living room and to the windows. The backyard wrapped around the side of the house with a small amount of grass. Most of the outdoor area was taken up by concrete and an infinity pool.

Kayla was laying on a large pool float in the pool, a tray with cans of soda and snacks next to her. She really looked like she was working hard on her business plan.

Snorting back a laugh, I knocked on the window, not wanting to scare her too badly. She didn't move, and I went to the open door, stepping outside onto the patio. "Kayla?" She was either sleeping, had her EarPods in, or both.

I moved toward the pool, letting my tank top fall back into place, and squinted as the bright sun hit my eyes. I'd left my sunglasses in the car, not thinking I'd need them, but after scenting all of Kayla's mates in the house, I probably would be spending a lot of time outdoors.

"Kayla!" I said louder, stopping at the edge in her line of sight. I couldn't tell if her eyes were shut under the sunglasses she had on.

I got down on a knee, reached into the pool, and splashed water at her. She jerked away, her body flailing like she was underwater. The float was so big she at least wasn't at risk of falling off.

Ew. Did she have sex with them on that thing?

I scrunched my nose as she sat up and looked in my direction. Her mouth fell open in shock and then she squealed my name. She put her EarPods in the tray and rolled off the float into the water.

As soon as she trudged up the pool steps, she flung herself at me, and I didn't give a shit that she was sopping wet. This was the longest we'd ever been apart, and damn, it felt good to hug her again.

"What the hell, Kara?" Kayla squeezed me so tight that it hurt. "What are you doing here and why do you smell like a bunch of flowers jizzed all over you?"

"Well, the short version is I stole Ella's car and spent the last two days driving here." I cringed as she stepped back, her mouth hanging open again. "I bought perfume at a gas station to cover up my scent."

Scent blockers worked decently enough, but with all the stress of not matching and committing a crime, I had been perfuming more than usual. Enough that it would attract an alpha's attention if he happened to walk a few feet away from me.

"You... stole her car?" She had a tight grip on both of my upper arms. "Do our parents know?"

I raised an eyebrow, and her shocked expression turned into a grin. "Don't start. I'm already worried I'm going to be picking up trash along the highway."

Kayla looped her arm through mine and led me to

the outdoor sofa under the awning. "They wouldn't make you do that. How did you even manage to steal Ella's car and get away without anyone noticing? Or, oh shit! Did they chase you? Wait. How did you even drive?"

"All of the omegas are going to hate me even more when they beef up security. I think the guard was half asleep and didn't even really look at me. He just thought I was Ella and didn't know she'd already left town." I doubted they looked at the security footage very often if there wasn't a reason to and, for the most part, only Ella would notice that I was missing, but she wasn't there.

"But you drove. You don't have a license." She went to a mini fridge in the outdoor kitchen area. "Want something to drink?"

"Water would be good."

"Phew. I was starting to worry you'd been body snatched and were going to ask for a soda." She grabbed two bottles of water and a towel from a cabinet before coming to sit next to me. "Driving? How?"

"I just got my license last week. Ella had been teaching me." I took my bottle from her and took a sip. "It was easy."

"Of course it was. You didn't tell me." Kayla watched me with a hurt expression as I took another sip of water. "I'm so happy to see you, but I'm worried about you, Care Bear. It's unlike you to do something like this."

I sighed and slouched down on the couch, putting my neck on the back cushion. The truth was, I was disappointed and scared. Disappointed that I couldn't handle even the slightest bit of a roadblock and scared that I would never find my place with a pack. I hadn't been uncertain of my future before, but now that I was, I was losing my mind.

"I'm sorry I didn't tell you I got my license. It wasn't even that exciting since I don't have my own car, and well… I didn't want a big deal made about it." I shut my eyes, stopping the tears. "My apartment was just a reminder of what I didn't have, and I needed to get away. Ella gave me a spare key for the summer while she's away so I could use her kitchen gadgets and streaming services. I saw the car keys on the counter, and something snapped."

My apartment wasn't a home because I hadn't made it one. I had no intention of staying long.

Kayla put her hand on my arm. "You know none of this is your fault. I don't know how many times I have to tell you that."

"I know it's not, but my brain doesn't care. I had a plan. I worked hard to be the best and some bitter omega couldn't handle that," I spewed. "And Omega Match just said we're sorry you didn't match, now be on your merry little pack-less way." I opened my eyes and let the tears that had been building fall freely. "It's not fair that I worked so hard and a stupid program can make me feel so… so unwanted."

Omegas used to be able to work for Omega Match until one decided she wanted to destroy it. She had admitted to messing with Kayla's matches, but she hadn't admitted to anything else yet. I knew the second the investigators had talked to me about my match list that the deceitful omega had most likely tampered with mine too.

If she'd been able to mess with Kayla's, she certainly was capable of fucking other omegas over too. At least it worked out well for my sister, even though she didn't want a pack in the first place.

"You aren't unwanted. I just know you're going to find the perfect pack this fall." She moved closer and wrapped her arms around me. "Maybe once you get things cleared up with OPS for this little unauthorized road trip, you can transfer to a compound down here."

Los Angeles has a decent enough academy, but the one in Washington was named Elite for a reason. Packs traveled from across the country for the opportunity to meet the graduating omegas and have the chance to match with them. The compound I lived in was highly sought after because the omegas were also invited to the academy's meet and greets.

"Fuck OPS and Omega Match." I sat up, breaking the hug.

Kayla gasped because I never spoke badly about anything to do with being an omega or our governing bodies. But I'd been holding it in for a month, and now that I was reunited with my sister, I couldn't hold it in any longer.

I stood, my grip tight on my water bottle as I began

to pace. "I hate that I can't say a word about it. I don't see why we even have Omega Match if it doesn't protect omegas like it's supposed to. Who knows how many employees have been paid to change match results or were pissed at an omega and messed their list up."

"I'm sure they're putting things in place to prevent that from happening ever again." Kayla patted the seat where I'd just been sitting. "Are you done? Your face is turning red and you're starting to smell like burnt chocolate, even over that awful perfume."

I plopped down next to her. "I'm done. Sorry." I turned to bury my face against her shoulder.

She sighed, wrapping an arm around me. "Before we found out about all the tampering business, remember how you would reassure me that everything was going to work out?"

I nodded, trying to calm myself down. She was right about me starting to smell like burnt chocolate. My scent rarely took on the bitter smell, but it was happening more and more frequently.

"You're going to match with a great pack, whether it be this fall or next spring or whenever. You're Kara motherfucking Sterling. Boss ass bitch and *the* perfect omega for a pack. You've been working nonstop since we went to kindergarten and this whole thing is even more reason for you to take a break and relax." She pulled back, and her glossy blue eyes stared back at me, mirrors of my own. "Sometimes being perfect means letting go of what's holding you back."

I wiped at my cheeks. "Nothing is holding me back except Omega Match."

"You're holding yourself back, Kara. All the anger and self-loathing is eating you from the inside out, except now it's leaking out of the wounds." She looked at my hair. "And your hair… are you making a nest with it?"

"I wanted to look more like my twin." My hair was piled on top of my head in a frizzy bun instead of down or in a ponytail of well-defined curls. "When did you become so wise?"

She rolled her eyes and huffed out an exasperated breath. "I've always been wise. I just needed four alphas to really bring it out."

I looked out across the backyard and at the gorgeous view. The sun was starting to set, and the sky was turning pink. It was a mostly clear day—surprising for Los Angeles—and I could see the faintest hint of the ocean far in the distance. "That is some ocean view."

"Tell me about it. Can you believe they have that listed on Zillow? A house up the street also says it has an ocean view. What a joke."

We fell into a fit of giggles, my mood already lifting. Being here with my sister was exactly what I needed.

With the copious amounts of Mexican food and the two bottles of Twist Knot wine Kayla and I consumed later that night, I was surprised we'd made it to the living room to pass out.

The smell wasn't so bad inside now, but I didn't know if it was because of the de-scenting spray Kayla had sprayed or the wine muddling my senses. De-scenting spray was the best, but how had she even gotten any? Oh, that's right. She was a billionaire now.

Groaning, I rolled off the sofa and onto my hands and knees. I needed to pee, and I wasn't about to ruin a couch that probably cost as much as a car. I reached over and patted my sister's head. She was passed out cold, a pillow clutched against her chest.

She really was the best sister in the world. We didn't always see eye to eye growing up and our priorities in life were vastly different, but she was my other half. The yin to my yang. The Cheech to my Chong.

I giggled and smacked my hand over my mouth. As if I'd ever smoke weed.

Using the ottoman coffee table to push myself up, the empty wine bottles clinked together on the tray. Kayla didn't even stir. She'd always been a heavy sleeper, and I bet that pillow with her pack's scents all over it made her even more dead to the world.

My lower lip wobbled; I wanted a pack.

I somehow found my way to the bathroom, only running into the wall once or maybe twice. At the academy, there'd been a strict no-alcohol policy—which no one followed—because omegas could not handle their liquor, especially on heat suppressants.

Ugh. Heat. I didn't even want to think about it or I'd really cry, and drunk crying was the worst.

Instead of full-blown heats that were painful without an alpha, they were mild, and toys were enough to be satisfied. It wasn't good to stay on them long-term, though, and since I'd started them right after my first heat at sixteen, it was time to plan on going off of them for a heat cycle. Only it wouldn't be regular since the first heat after suppressants was ten times worse. And with no alphas?

Great. Now I was angry again.

I finished in the bathroom and went back to the living room. My suitcase was open next to the couch, my clothes spilling out. After the first bottle of wine, we'd decided to change into pajamas and have a sleepover in the living room. I didn't remember much after that besides late-night food delivery and nearly choking on a chip laughing so hard at a movie we had been watching.

My mind went back to heat suppressants.

Fuck. I haven't taken mine today. Or was it already tomorrow?

I grabbed my purse and took out my phone. It was just after midnight and my pill reminder had been buzzing at ten-minute intervals for the last four hours. Well, wasn't that just perfect.

After clearing the alarm, I put my phone on the side table and dug into the zippered inner pocket for my pills. Only it hadn't been shut and the damn things must have fallen into the cavernous void at the bottom of my bag.

Not wanting to wake my sister, I went into the dining room which was separated from the living room by a centralized wall with a double-sided fireplace. I preferred an open-concept floor plan, but Kayla said she liked all the privacy she got here.

I dumped my entire purse onto the large table and squinted down at the contents. It was long overdue for a clean-out, but where the hell were my suppressants? I knew I had them because I'd been taking them.

Shaking it again, my heart started to pound. Where the fuck were they? There was no way I could go through a heat here at Kayla's. I'd have to go to OPS to get a spot at the compound and then they'd know about my transgressions.

Stay calm. They're here somewhere.

I ran my hand inside again, and not finding the blister pack, I bit my lip to stop myself from crying out in frustration. Everything else that was supposed to be in my purse was on the table, including my perfume blockers. I grabbed the pack of those and punched one out, swallowing it without water.

Taking a calming breath, I tried to remember when I'd last seen them. I took one the night before for sure because I'd started a new pack and I put them right in the zippered section for safe keeping. But had I zipped it closed?

My apartment keys caught my eye, the N'Pact

keychain practically blinking in neon lights. Oh, shit. My purse had tipped over in my car when I'd been trying to get a picture and I was sure that's where they were.

I was already four hours overdue and couldn't wait until morning, so I went back into the living room, slipped on my flip-flops, and grabbed the key to the car. I didn't want to leave Kayla with the front door unlocked and I had no clue where her key was, so I went around the back.

It was a gorgeous night, the perfect temperature for a late-night stroll. Was it safe? I had no clue, but it was less safe starting my heat when I had nowhere to go and only one of my toys with me.

The gate loomed in front of me, and I waited for it to open for me. When it didn't, I let out a frustrated growl. It opened earlier when we'd grabbed our food from the omega-friendly delivery driver.

There was a small red light where the locking mechanism was, and I examined it closely. Were we locked in for the night? That was a bit extreme and excessive. What if there was an emergency?

I marched back toward the house, but then stopped, bending down to pick up a rock. I was not about to wake up my sister or climb a ten-foot wall to go get my pills. So, I did what only a drunk girl could.

I smashed the hell out of the lock.

CHAPTER FOUR

Kara

I could now add vandalism to my growing list of criminal offenses. If anything, the Thomas pack should have been thanking me for showing them just how weak their fence was. After five smashes, the gate beeped and opened. I'd have to worry about how to shut it when I got back.

With the muddled state of my brain, I felt safe enough walking down the street despite the time of night and the lack of light. Large shadows from the streetlights being partially blocked by trees ran the length of the street. It wasn't completely dark, but just enough that no one would see me unless they were close. A few dogs barked as I passed by the houses on the way to Ella's car, and it made me wish I was with a pack so I could have a dog.

I'd been nervous it would be towed, but the car was right where I'd left it. Opening the passenger door, I cursed as the pack of suppressant pills fell right out into the gutter. They were in a plastic sleeve and the gutter was the cleanest I'd ever seen. But then again, this was the crème de le crème of rich neighborhoods. Residents probably employed someone to make sure their gutters were clean.

"Don't forget us, Kara, dear! We've been waiting for you to cuddle us for hours," I said in my Squishmallow voice.

"Oh, Jane Doe. I would never forget you and Princess Leia. I'm sorry I didn't come back sooner but we were having too much fun." I shut the front door and opened the back, grabbing them by their ears. Jane was a blue deer and Princess was a pink chicken, and they were my favorite ones because they reminded me of me and Kayla.

"Ow! First, you forget about us so you can get drunk, and now you assault us!" Princess squeaked. Everyone had their quirks, and mine was having conversations with stuffed animals. It was no different than talking to a pet.

"I don't have pockets for my pills or the keys, so deal with it or you can go in the trunk for the night." I shut and locked the car. "You should be grateful for my hospitality."

A motorcycle revved its engine and the faint squeak of N'Pact's gate opening made me jump, and I dashed behind the car.

My Squishmallows were beside themselves with excitement. "Oh, my! Are we going to see another N'Pact member? Riding a motorcycle? So sexy. Va va voom!"

"Shhh." I warned myself, ducking as a sleek motorcycle darted out and headed down the road way too fast. "Geez, where is he going so late? Maybe for a booty call?"

The words felt gross in my mouth, and I twisted my lips in disgust. Most omegas would agree that the thought of alphas sleeping with betas made us all slightly unhinged. Biologically, we were born to be with each other. Sure, betas could be with us too, but the deep-seated need alphas and omegas had for each other couldn't be replaced by even one hundred betas.

Brake lights lit up red at the end of the street and then the motorcycle was gone. Had he even shut the gate? I couldn't see the top part of it poking up past the shrubs and wall.

I'd just take a quick look to make sure. The motorcycle had left in a rush. They might have gone out the gate before it had even opened all the way.

I quickly walked the short distance to the end of their driveway and looked in. I was surprised there were tall hedges running along the driveway, so the house wasn't visible. I bet they always had knottyboppers and paparazzi bothering them.

One of my Squishmallows spoke up. "Well, aren't you just like them now?"

Headlights turning down the street caught my attention and my eyes widened. A police car with its lights on but no sirens was headed right for me. If they saw a woman in their pajamas with stuffed animals, they'd surely stop or call in for another officer.

The gate started to close, and before I could even think about what I was doing, I ran through it and onto N'Pact's property. And by ran, I mean I almost fell and dropped my Squishmallows, catching myself on the tall bushes. Luckily, I had my index finger through the keyring, so I didn't drop them.

What was I doing? Did I really just commit *another* crime? Did the three strikes law apply to omegas?

A giggle burst from my lips, and I barely managed to pick up my Squishmallows and shove them against my face to stifle it. I'd just take a quick peek at their house and then leave. It was no different than me going on the internet and looking up pictures.

One thing was for sure, I was never drinking Twisted Knot wine again; it was deceptively delicious.

Walking as quietly as I could since I was wearing flip-flops, I passed the tall hedges and took in the gorgeous three-level house. The driveway gradually sloped downwards toward a parking area and two double garage doors. Thanks to my Zillow obsession, I knew this house had an underground parking area, big enough for eight cars.

One of my favorite things to do was to look at houses on Zillow and this one had caught my eye when I was perusing the neighborhood when Kayla first moved. At the time, I hadn't known this was N'Pact's house.

The black SUV from earlier was parked off to the side, blocking my view of the front door. The house was all contemporary modern lines and angles with stone siding and large windows. My memory was a bit fuzzy, but I think it had six bedrooms and six baths, a gym, a recreation room, and a pool. All of the houses blended together a bit.

"We should leave," I muttered as my feet kept moving forward. There was something about this house that was drawing me to it; it was perfect in every way. I stopped at the end of the walkway leading up to the massive front door that was at least four times the size of a normal one.

Movement at the corner of the garage area caught my eye. There must have been a walkway that went down the side that I couldn't see. I squinted as a two-foot-tall beast moved into the light.

Oh, fuck. They had a dog.

"Hi, doggy," I whispered as I looked back at the hedges now blocking my view of the gate. I had no clue if it was secured like my sister's was, but running that way would trap me with nowhere to go. Plus, who knew where that cop car had stopped?

The dog growled and stalked toward me, its teeth glinting in the outside lights. Was this how I died? Being mauled by a vicious Rottweiler while drunk on wine and holding my Squishmallows?

The SUV was about equal distance between me and the dog, but that wasn't an option unless I wanted the entire neighborhood to wake up from the alarm. I stepped off the walkway and onto the grass, hoping there was something I could climb on or hide behind on the other side of the house or in the back. The dog wasn't attacking yet, so that was good, but I had a feeling he would as soon as he was close enough.

Knowing the dog would run as soon as I did, I stepped out of my flip-flops and flung Jane Doe at him, then took off running, hoping the sacrifice would at least slow him down. He barked as I sprinted along the front of the house and then turned down the side of it. There wasn't a gate, thankfully, but the grass gave way to stepping stones with gravel.

I looked back to see the dog nearly to me, and I yeeted poor Princess Leia at him, hitting him right in the face. My guilt only lasted a second as my foot missed a stone and I stumbled into the stucco, my pills falling from my hand.

There was no stopping. I'd come back for them once I got away. Or hell, I'd just get in the car in the morning once I was sober and go back to the compound where I had more and couldn't get myself into trouble.

This trip had been one bad decision after another. It

was unlike me, but I had always kept myself on a tight leash. I had to be the best and couldn't let anyone down. It was like all of that drive had left me once I graduated and didn't match.

The backyard opened up in front of me and I quickly scanned it the best I could. I needed to climb something or...

The pool wasn't exactly an infinity pool but had a thin ledge between it and the glass panel railing. It was my only option because I certainly wasn't going to make it to the outdoor kitchen farther away and climb up onto the counter in enough time.

I was almost to the railing when the dog made its move. It grabbed on to the bottom hem of my pajama shorts with a growl and yanked. The material ripped and pulled down, throwing me off balance. I flailed my arms as I started to fall sideways, my pitiful cry for help loud in the silent backyard.

If I hadn't already alerted N'Pact to my presence by all the noise I was making, the loud splash of falling into the pool and the dog barking sure as hell would.

The water was a shock to my system as I went under. *It might be better to just sink to the bottom and save myself from the embarrassment of being arrested sopping wet with my shorts down.*

Nope. Not down. Now they were off.

My shorts had been pulled far enough down my legs that now that I was in the water, they fought to float back up to the surface, and with all my flailing, came right off my feet. I had never been more relieved to wear underwear.

Needing air, I surfaced in the middle of the pool, causing the dog to go wild. The lights upstairs came on, and I looked around frantically for somewhere to hide. The keys were no longer on my finger, and I hoped I'd dropped them back with my pills and they weren't at the bottom of the pool. Things were a bit of a blur.

I swam as quietly as possible to a round flamingo pool float and went under and into the hole in the middle. I could float it closer to the side, have the neck point toward the house, and maybe they wouldn't see me.

Who was I kidding? I was so busted and was going to end up on the five o'clock morning news being handcuffed and put in the back of an OPS omega transport vehicle. My parents were going to be so disappointed in me.

Biting my lip to stop myself from bursting into tears, I waited, trying to stay calm. The dog wasn't barking anymore, but I could hear his nails clicking on the cement. I didn't know for sure if it was a male dog, but it felt like it.

What sounded like a sliding door came from the house, but also there was the sound of someone running from one side of the yard.

"Alpha, go back inside. I'll check the perimeter." The voice was all business, and I sank lower into the water, only my eyes above the surface. "The perimeter sensors didn't go off, so it might just be a raccoon again."

"Gizmo, come." Someone with a voice that was slightly raspy from sleep called the dog, snapping his fingers. I couldn't tell who it was without revealing myself by peering over the edge.

"They're in the pool under the flamingo." I looked up to see a figure on a balcony upstairs and was certain it was Tate Carter.

"Out. Now," the man who had called the dog barked.

I hadn't had a lot of experience being barked at by an alpha, but I'd witnessed my sister being commanded by our fathers many times. It wasn't a bark like a dog, but its purpose was to control.

This alpha's bark? It washed right over me, only giving me a sliver of motivation to listen to him. Either he was the weakest of the group or there was something wrong with him.

"I think she's naked," the guy who had come running said. "Unless one of you wears pink shorts with unicorns on them.

Suddenly, the flamingo went flying, and I was looking right up at Alvaro Estrada holding a leaf skimmer.

"Hi."

Hi? That was all I could say to the tan Adonis frowning down at me? There were enough lights that I could clearly see his defined abs and the veins popping in his forearms. He must have jumped right out of bed because his dark brown hair was messy, and he was only wearing white briefs.

Good Lord. I'd never seen such a magnificent alpha. Not everyone could pull off tighty whities, but he should really have become an underwear model. I tried not to look too long at the impressive bulge. If he was that big flaccid, how big was he hard? And with a knot? I was starting to feel a bit warm all over.

I subtly inhaled through my nose, trying to catch his scent and was met with the sharp sting of chlorine.

"What the hell are you doing in our pool?" He crossed his arms over his chest and looked over at the other man, who I wasn't familiar with. "You can go, Jonathan."

Jonathan shook his head in amusement and left me with the leader of the pack, who was fishing out my shorts. Tate came out of the house, his sweatpants hanging indecently low. There was no way he was wearing underwear under them.

"Did Jonathan call the police?" Tate stopped and raised an eyebrow. "Oh, Beck is going to have a field day with this." He pulled out his phone and the flash of his camera nearly blinded me.

"Wait. Beck?" I was sobering up, but with how tired I was and the effects of the wine, I was struggling to process what was happening. They were acting so nonchalant, like this was an everyday occurrence.

"No wonder she didn't respond to my bark," Alvaro

muttered, letting my shorts plop onto the cement. "Let's go, Kayla. We'll walk you home."

Now things were making sense. "I'm not Kayla, and I didn't respond to your bark because it could hardly be considered one."

Tate snapped and his pointer finger went up, things making sense to him now too. "The twin... what's your name? Layla? Isla?"

"Kara." I didn't move from where I was, my legs moving slowly under me to keep me afloat. I really did want to sink back under. If I got out of the pool, they were going to see my underwear and my nipples poking through.

"That's right. Kara with a K. How the hell did you get in our backyard and lose your shorts?" Tate sounded very amused by the whole situation and my face heated.

"Your dog chased me." I looked to where the dog was sitting obediently, watching me. "He almost bit me."

"Oh, for fuck's sake. Get out of the pool before I come in and get you. Tate, go get her a towel." Alvaro had his arms crossed and was scowling at me. I guess my observation about his bark didn't give me any brownie points.

With a sigh of defeat, I swam to the steps, my excitement over meeting my favorite band overshadowed by the lump of worry in my throat.

CHAPTER FIVE

Tate

To say I was amused was an understatement. We hadn't had anyone sneak onto our property in a few months, but to find Kayla's twin sister just chilling in our pool? It was the laugh we all needed after being smacked with an assessment tomorrow.

I grabbed a towel out of our outdoor cabinet and turned to head back but stopped in my tracks. She was just coming out of the pool, and she took my breath away. She was tall, probably about four inches shorter than my six feet, and had the longest legs I'd ever seen. They weren't skinny legs either, but strong with solid quads and thighs that would feel like heaven wrapped around my head.

Her black underwear was the hip-hugger type, and yeah, I wanted to hug those hips as I sank my cock into her nice and slow. She crossed her arms over her chest, stopping my perusal of her.

What was I doing? The last thing we needed was to get worked up over an appealing omega. I hadn't even caught her scent yet, and I felt this possessive need to carry her up to my room and make her mine.

"Tate? The towel." Alvaro gave me a knowing look and held out his hand as I walked toward them, shaking it out. Could never be too careful about a spider hiding out.

Bypassing Alvaro's hand, I stepped in between him and Kara and wrapped the towel around her shoulders. The outdoor lighting Alvaro had turned on made her blue eyes glisten like the ocean. Strands of her hair had fallen out of her bun, and my fingers itched to push the curls out of her face.

If I touched her, I wasn't going to be able to stop. There was something about her that just… spoke to my alpha side. It was as if just her mere presence soothed me. This had never happened before, and I didn't know if it was worry over our assessment or if I was losing my mind.

She sucked in a sharp breath through her nose, her eyes shutting. Could she smell me even over the pungent scent of chlorine wafting from the pool and her skin?

"Thank you," she breathed, keeping her eyes shut as my hands hovered over her towel-covered upper arms.

"Tate," Alvaro growled.

"I know, I know." We could look but couldn't touch. But this was way different than when we'd met Kayla and she was unbonded. There hadn't been a bone-deep yearning for her. I backed up so I was next to him and couldn't do anything stupid.

Alvaro was one to talk. He'd been staring at Kara since I'd come outside. "Where's your sister?"

"Sleeping. I just needed to grab something out of the car." She looked past us. "Let me just grab the things I dropped and I'll be on my way. No need to call the cops or OPS."

With her head held high and shoulders back, she walked around us and toward the side of the house. Alvaro and I gave each other a silent look. I could feel the faint hint of desire through our bond, but it was hard to tell these days with it being like a rope held together by a thread.

We followed her silently, Gizmo hot on our heels. She bent over about halfway down the side of the house, not knowing we were watching from the corner.

Alvaro brought his fist to his mouth and bit it, growling softly. He probably thought it would be soft enough that she wouldn't hear, but she wheeled around so fast with a glare that I felt the urge to step back.

"Are you following me?" She adjusted the towel under her armpits and tucked the corner in the top so it would stay in place.

"Did you not just trespass on private property? We've earned the right to follow you." I elbowed Alvaro for being a dick. It was like he couldn't make up his mind if he was mad at her or if he wanted her. He was looking at her like he wanted to devour her, though.

"I'm sure you guys are always having to run off knottyboppers, but I'm not one, I swear. I only have two posters of your pack... and a few shirts." She cringed. "And your limited edition bobbleheads. Nope, not a deranged fan and definitely not a knottybopper. I don't even have the Squishmallows with your faces, so that's proof, right?"

Alvaro snapped out of the lust-filled trance he was in and headed down the path of large stepping stones. "We aren't going to let you walk back by yourself. Do you have any idea how dangerous it is for an unbonded omega to be out wandering around at night and to sneak onto the property of a pack of unbonded alphas?"

My nostrils flared. Not all alphas were dangerous. Despite my reaction to her when she got out of the pool, I would never force myself on her or take advantage of our base needs. I know that was a big concern of many with unbonded alphas, but a few bad eggs didn't make us all rotten.

Which was yet another reason tomorrow was both ridiculous and infuriating. We might all have been a mess, but we weren't a danger to society. We each had our ways of dealing with losing both our omega and our privilege of taking part in Omega Match.

It still stung thinking about how we'd been so close to having everything we'd ever wanted in life, and it had been stripped away from us. All because the omega we matched with freaked out. It *was* our fault for taking her to our performance at a club when she'd barely been with us for a few hours, but she hadn't even attempted to find us. The second we were separated, she went and hid, calling one of her dads who then called OPS and Omega Match.

She probably did us a favor. If it had happened when we had become really famous and had bonded with her already? I shuddered at the thought.

"It's not like I was prancing down the street releasing my perfume with a sign that said *unbonded omega* flashing across my chest." She continued down the path and grabbed a large rounded stuffed toy. "I drove a thousand miles and had no issues with alphas or anyone else bothering me."

My protectiveness flared like she was our omega who needed a stern talking to about being safe. "You drove that far by yourself without a chaperone? That's insane!"

"Perhaps." She shrugged and made it to the front yard, picking up another toy and slipping her feet into discarded flip-flops and wobbling a bit. "It's been great, but I need to get back. I have a gate to fix."

She was putting on a brave front, but there was a slight tremble in her voice. *It wouldn't hurt anyone if I wrapped her in my arms and purred a little, would it?*

"Are you *drunk?*" Alvaro scoffed, crossing his arms over his chest.

She faced us and held up her fingers a centimeter apart. "Maybe a little."

Gizmo suddenly darted from behind us and jumped, knocking Kara down. He wasn't a jumper and definitely wasn't a violent dog unless he was on duty.

Kara squealed and shielded her face as he started licking her arms, trying to get to her face. She giggled and wiggled to get out from under him.

"Giz, no." Alvaro moved forward to pull him off by his collar, but that was unnecessary because Gizmo pounced on one of the round stuffed animals and began to hump it.

Alvaro and I lost it. Gizmo was neutered and he'd never done that before. Seeing the look of horror on Kara's face and Gizmo going at it was just too much after all the events of the night. Cal and Avery were going to be disappointed they missed this.

"Oh my God." Her towel forgotten, Kara snatched the toy as she climbed to her feet. "How dare you defile Jane Doe!"

She cleared her throat, and her voice went up at least two octaves. "This is why all men should be kept on a leash! One second, I'm just minding my own business, and the next, I'm ruined."

Picking up the other one, she held it up to the one she referred to as Jane. "Oh, don't be such a dry nugget. He was just being friendly."

She shook the blue toy, which I now realized was a deer, and I snorted that she'd named it Jane Doe. "How dare you! He had his red rocket all over me."

"What did you drink? I need to get some." I reached down and picked up her towel and pill pack. "Or are you always like this?"

"I'm…" The small smile she'd been wearing vanished, and she shook her head. "I don't know."

Alvaro took the toys from her. "Wrap yourself up and we'll get you back to your sister." His voice had taken on a soft, soothing quality.

"Maybe in a few days, you and your sister can come watch us at rehearsals. We'll talk to Kayla's pack and arrange for security. How does that sound?" I just really didn't want her to cry, and she looked like wherever her head had gone wasn't good.

"I'm making a fool of myself. I'm sorry." She wrapped herself back up, grabbed her pills from Alvaro, and headed back toward the gate.

Alvaro tossed the deer to me and snapped his fingers at Gizmo. "Stay."

Gizmo sat and gave us both puppy dog eyes. We didn't need any more incidents tonight.

"Why do I have to carry the one he was humping?" I held it by its ear and caught up to Kara, who was walking briskly, even if she was a bit unsteady on her feet. "Do you want one of us to carry you?"

"No. How do you open this thing?" She looked around for the button. "This is why I had to break Kayla's gate; I couldn't find it. The Killer Gnomes are probably going to really live up to their name when they get ahold of me."

Kayla's pack was a team of Alphaball players whose team name was the Killer Gnomes. They even had uniforms, gear, and merchandise with gnome characters.

"It blends in." I pressed a button that was the same color as the stone wall and then looked at Alvaro. "Are you going to walk down the street in your chonies? The last thing we need is your bulge all over the front pages of the tabloids."

Alvaro glared at me and stopped walking. "Don't do anything stupid."

"Like almost walk out practically naked?" I held out my hand, and he tossed me what looked like a chicken.

"If you aren't back in five minutes…"

"Yeah, yeah. Go make sure Gizzy isn't humping anything else." I smirked and headed out of the gate with Kara. It was just now fully open, and I could see how it might have appeared to her that Cal left it open—he never waited for it to fully open before darting out on his bike.

I was just about to the end of the driveway when Kara turned around, her eyes wide with fear.

My body instantly tensed. "What is it?"

She didn't say a word as she grabbed my arm and pulled me back. Her touch was like a bolt of electricity that went straight up my arm before turning and heading south.

"Kara." I growled her name, and she made the faintest of whimpers.

Whatever was scaring her was going to die a horrible death.

It wasn't until the gate shut that she let my arm go. "The police are at my sister's."

Well, shit.

CHAPTER SIX

Kara

Was this karma for stealing Ella's car?

My night could not get any worse. First, I'd almost been mauled and drowned by N'Pact's dog, then embarrassed the hell out of myself several times in front of them, and now there were at least two police cars down the street right in front of Kayla's house.

I trembled as I thought of all the things that could have happened. I'd not only left the gate unsecured, but the back door was unlocked. An alpha could have caught one of our scents and wandered onto the property. Or even a crazed fan.

My eyes blurred with tears, and I took a deep breath through my nose only to finally catch Tate's scent. He smelled just like a freshly peeled orange.

I bit my lip to stop from groaning. Oranges not only were my favorite fruit, but with my chocolate scent, we would be a smellgasm together once I got the chlorine smell off me.

"Well, let's go see what's happening." He started back toward the gate that was just now starting to shut.

"No!" I grabbed his arm, and my nipples tingled. I quickly looked down to make sure the towel was hiding them. "We can't. They'll wonder why I'm with an alpha and…"

He looked at my hand on his arm and put his over it. "Let's not panic. I'll stand at the end of the hedge and peek around to make sure you get down there okay. Then you can get my number from Kayla and text me that everything is fine."

"You have my sister's number?" Why did that sit so wrong with me? I knew they knew each other. Did she always text them?

He moved his hand and ran it over his stubbly square jaw. "We all have her number. The Thomas pack trusts us since we didn't steal her away before they bonded with her. Now that she has talked them into staying home alone when they go away on business, it's even more important."

I nodded. It made sense, but I still didn't like it. Sure, she was bonded, and alphas would be turned off by her scent now that it had changed slightly to denote she was taken, but they were still alphas.

Sure, Kara. Keep telling yourself that's the reason.

"I can't go down there with the police there."

His eyes narrowed. "Why?"

I cringed, not wanting to tell him I'd stolen my friend's car and left the compound without OPS permission. "I kinda, sorta lost my mind from not matching."

"Did you kill someone or something?" He was joking, or at least I hoped he was. His blue eyes looked amused, if not a smidge wary.

I'd be wary too if I'd found an omega hiding in my pool and then witnessed her having a conversation with Squishmallows.

"I didn't kill anyone, but no one besides Kayla and her pack knows I'm here. Not even the owner of the car. If I go down there, they are going to see I'm unbonded and call OPS and…"

His amusement left his face and his jaw ticked. "Let's go inside and we'll call Kayla to see what's going on." Tate put a comforting hand in the center of my back and guided me toward the backyard.

I was fine until we got to the side of the house. I started to cry, not only from the embarrassment over falling off the deep end but from the harm I'd put my sister in. "What if someone got in the house and attacked her? I'm such an idiot for leaving her alone like that."

"I'm sure everything is fine." He didn't sound like he

meant it, but I appreciated his effort. He must have thought I was a complete idiot. "Let's get you inside. You're shivering."

It was cool outside, but not cold. Los Angeles had ideal weather, even at night. The temperature wasn't causing me to shiver, the idea of someone hurting my sister was.

He walked me silently to the back door and into the house. Now that some of the chlorine smell had dissipated and I was sniffling, their scents bombarded me all at once. I stopped abruptly and shut my eyes, breathing in deeper.

Besides oranges, there were strawberries, a salty roasted scent that reminded me of pretzels, and fuck me. Was that bacon?

A groan escaped because I was going to combust. One could always hope their pack had complimentary scents to their own, but this? This was heaven.

Tate cleared his throat. "Let me go grab my phone. Have a seat wherever."

I'll take a seat on your knot.

I snapped out of it as he retreated, and I tried my best to stop crying. The wine was starting to wear off and so was the extra bit of courage and relaxation it had given me.

N'Pact's house was just as amazing inside as outside. It was contemporary modern, and the large sliding door we'd walked through was part of a whole wall of floor-to-ceiling windows that looked out over the Los Angeles skyline.

Unlike Kayla's house, this one was open concept with no walls between the kitchen, dining room, and living area. The large dining room table sat between the windows and the kitchen, which had black lower cabinets and gray upper cabinets, and top-of-the-line appliances.

The kitchen island was massive and had five cushioned bar stools. The gray U-shaped couch in the living room was facing away from the kitchen, and it was so big I had to count how many people it could fit. What the heck did they need a nine-seater for?

I walked to it and sat down, putting my pills on the coffee table. The living room was cozy, and the couch faced a large television mounted on the wall. It was the biggest I'd ever seen, at least twice the size of what a regular person would have.

Tate came down the stairs with his phone to his ear, Alvaro right behind him. "Kayla? Hi, this is Tate... from N'Pact. Is everything okay?" He listened for a moment. "She's right here."

He handed his phone to me and sat down as far away from me as possible. I'd have been offended, but having me in their house had to be hard. It was hard enough for me to be here when they smelled so delectable. If their scents weren't distracting me, I'd have been a blubbering mess.

I brought the phone to my ear. "Kayla, I'm so sorry and such an idiot. Did someone break in? I should have never left, but I needed my pills and-"

"Do you have any idea how worried I was when I woke up to Rio yelling through the speaker system that the police were on their way?" She was talking in a low voice like she didn't want someone to hear. "Whatever you did to the gate set off the silent perimeter alarm."

"I didn't know." I sank back into the cushions and put a hand over my eyes. "I had too much wine and couldn't find the button."

She sighed, and for once, I understood how she felt whenever I sighed over her choices. "I covered for you and said I broke it. The police did a sweep of the property and inside the house. I couldn't tell them it was you because you aren't supposed to be here."

"So, what happens now? When are they going to leave so I can come home?"

"The gate company doesn't open until ten and Beck called a private security company to come stand guard. The police are here until they show up. Hold on." Kayla put her hand over the speaker, and I could hear muffled voices. "The cops are going to stay outside the gate until security gets here."

"How am I going to get back in without someone wondering who the hell I am?" I felt something cold on my cheek and jumped.

Alvaro had a cold water bottle in his hand and had touched my cheek with it. "You can sleep here."

I took the water bottle he was offering as he sat a few cushions away from me. "I can't stay here."

Kayla cleared her throat. "Yes, you can. They're harmless. Make them give you a room and lock the door. Put a dresser in front of it if that makes you feel safer."

I stood and walked into their kitchen, out of earshot. "I can't, Kay. Have you smelled them? They smell so good."

"Why are you smelling them? And no, I haven't smelled them. Remember, the only class I aced was Olfactory Management. You did pretty well in it too. What was the first thing we were taught?"

Jesus, was this what I sounded like to her when I was laying into her? It was like we had switched roles. "Never scent unsupervised. Look, I know all of this, but with the wine and being upset at seeing the police cars…"

"How the hell did you even end up at their house?" The police must have been gone because Kayla's voice was back to its normal volume.

"It's a long story, but basically, their dog almost drowned me. Okay, he didn't really, but he pulled down my shorts and I got off balance and fell in." I waited with bated breath for her to respond, but she was silent. "Kayla? Say something."

"You've been perfect for so long, Care Bear, like you put yourself in a box and sealed it tight. And it's like not matching and your carefully laid plans being sidelined caused the seal to break. Except it broke all the way and now, instead of just having a little breathing room, you blew that shit up."

As much as I didn't want to hear the words, I knew she was right. My entire life, I had never wanted to disappoint anyone, especially not after one of our fathers passed away from a heart attack when we were nine. It almost destroyed our family, and I told myself from that point on I would never do anything to hurt or disappoint our parents.

If they knew I'd left the compound and driven to Los Angeles by myself? New tears fell, and I wiped roughly at them.

An arm went around my shoulder, and even though I knew I shouldn't, I turned into Alvaro's chest, seeking his comfort and warmth. He plucked the phone from my grip and took over talking to my sister.

"Does she need to stay here for the night?" Alvaro ran his hand up and down my back and I wished the towel wasn't there so I could feel his touch even better. "She can sleep here in our guest bedroom, and in the morning she can go next door to hang out with our betas... we have an appointment, and she can't be here... no, it's not with knottyboppers... you're welcome."

He hung up the phone and handed it across the island where Tate had moved. I was trying my best not to breathe in Alvaro's scent, but being so close to him and feeling his warm, bare chest against my arms between us, was tough. A little sniff wouldn't hurt, would it?

I breathed in through my nose and the warm salty smell of freshly baked pretzels washed over me. Oh, he smelled good. So, so good.

The fact that he was holding me like he was made him even more appealing. It wasn't appropriate for alphas and omegas to touch if they weren't your pack, but I couldn't bring myself to step away.

Tate cleared his throat, and I turned my head against Alvaro's chest. "We can show you to the guest room." His gaze was locked on me and Alvaro, longing in his eyes.

Alvaro put his hand on the back of my head as if to stop me from lifting my head from his chest. "The guest room has an attached bathroom, so you can shower if you want. In the morning, we'll take you next door until your sister says it's okay for you to go back."

I wanted to know what kind of appointment they had that I couldn't be at their house, but they were a world-famous boyband, and they probably did a lot of things at their house instead of going to certain places. I couldn't imagine how frustrating it would be to be followed everywhere.

Alvaro reluctantly stepped back, his fingers brushing down my jaw. Maybe... I shook my head, dashing away the thought of bringing up the fall match. Me? Matching with my favorite band? Could I handle the life they led?

I'd been around them longer than I'd been around

any other potential pack, and if I'd had this reaction in meet and greets, they would have gone straight to the top of my list.

Alvaro led me across the living room and past the stairs before turning down a long hallway. "We have two guest rooms here on this level, and our rooms are upstairs. The bathroom is stocked with luxury products and plenty of towels. I'll leave you a pair of shorts and a shirt outside the door."

We stopped at a closed door, and he opened it, revealing a large bedroom with a queen-sized bed, dresser, and desk. I wondered who had stayed here or if it was just to have something in the room.

"Thank you." I stepped into the room and turned to face him and Tate, who was now standing next to him holding my Squishmallows. "I'm sorry I-"

"No need to apologize." Alvaro gave me a tight smile. Did that mean he was really pissed about it? That made no sense with the brief cuddle session in the kitchen. "Goodnight, Kara."

Tate waited until Alvaro started to walk down the hall before stepping forward to hand me Jane and Princess. "Don't be so hard on yourself. Accidents happen. I'm glad it was our house and we're able to make sure you're safe. Sweet dreams."

I shut and locked the door as they went back down the hall. If my dads knew I was sleeping in a house with four unbonded alphas, they would have been so disappointed. It didn't matter that they had been nothing but respectful and Kayla trusted them.

I'd let myself spiral out of control, but from this moment on, I vowed to get my act together. The lid was going back on the box, and as I stood there looking at a bed that didn't belong to me, I knew it was for the best.

CHAPTER SEVEN

Kara

Showering in N'Pact's guest bathroom took me way outside my comfort zone. I knew the bedroom and bathroom doors were both locked, but my upbringing made me second guess even being in their house, even though it felt *right*.

The wine was wearing off now, and I didn't have an excuse for what was starting to play out in my head. I imagined what would happen if I had left the doors unlocked, and Alvaro and Tate came into the bathroom.

Warm water pours over me from the two shower heads. The two alphas knock gently on the door before coming in and groaning at the sight of me through the glass shower. I look over at them, biting my lip and nodding my consent. I need them to relieve the building pressure between my legs.

I leaned against the wall, reaching for the handheld shower head and moving the dial until it was at just the right stream. I let it hit my nipples, my breath catching as the sensation went straight to my core.

They strip out of what little clothes they have on and slip inside the shower, their eyes devouring me like hungry wolves. I take them in too as they step under the rainfall shower head one after the other.

I moaned, lowering one hand between my legs and spreading my lips open before lowering the shower head to my clit.

Alvaro reaches down, stroking his thick cock as he steps forward. "I'm going to make you scream, Kara."

"Yes." *I'm panting now, ready for them to claim my body.*

He lowers to the ground in front of me and Tate moves to the side of him, grabbing my leg and holding it up to give Alvaro all the access he needs.

With the first touch of Tate's lips on my nipple, my body trembles. And then Alvaro licks my pussy tantalizingly slow until he reaches my clit.

I needed more, so I moved to the shower seat, thankful the hose of the shower head reached. I put my foot up on it, letting the water fully hit my pussy. I brought my other hand to my nipple, pinching it and closing my eyes. God, it felt so good.

Tate kneads my other breast while he sucks and then switches. One of my hands goes to his head and one to

Alvaro's, holding them in place. My head goes back against the shower wall, my eyes closing as I get closer and closer to the edge.

Tate grabs my chin. "Watch as I stroke my cock, omega."

He lets me go and sits on the shower bench, his hand going to his cock and pumping down the long shaft. God, I want to sit on it and have it fill me.

Alvaro's tongue flicks harder, his hand pumping in sync with his motion. Tate groans, his fist matching our pace. It's too much, and I cry out, my release taking me to a whole new universe of pleasure.

My entire body spasmed as I orgasmed, the water becoming too much for my sensitive clit. I pulled it away and sat down heavily on the shower seat, my toes and fingers tingling as my pleasure ebbed all too quickly.

If only the fantasy had been real...

As I came down from my orgasm, the fog that had been surrounding my brain since the first glass of wine cleared. What was I doing masturbating in a famous boyband's guest bathroom?

I gasped and nearly slipped getting up. *My pills.*

I quickly finished my shower and wrapped a towel around me after drying off. Clothes were on the floor outside the door, and I was disappointed they were freshly washed. There wasn't even the smallest hint of Alvaro or Tate on them. The shirt was a dark gray N'Pact shirt with a photo of them, and the shorts were too big for me but were fine after I pulled the drawstring as far as it would go and rolled the waistband a few times.

My hair was dripping down my back, but I didn't exactly have another shirt to wrap it in. Sometimes I wished I was more like Kayla with my hair. She did not take care of her curls like I did. After I got my pills, I'd take the t-shirt off and wrap my hair in it so I could at least not look like a frizz ball.

The house was dark and quiet as I tiptoed down the hall toward the living room. It was a relief that all pharmacies were required to put medicine for omegas in punch-out packaging because pill bottles could easily be tampered with.

There was a dim light on in the corner of the living room and in the kitchen, giving just enough light to see. I walked to the coffee table and frowned down at it. Where the fuck were my pills?

I was pretty sure I'd put them right next to the controller for the television. I turned around and moved the pillows and then the couch cushions. Besides a few Flamin' Hot Cheetos, coins, and a tissue, there was nothing.

Dropping to my hands and knees, I ran my hand under the couch and glanced under the coffee table. Maybe I had taken them into the kitchen. I had meant to take one.

I started to walk that way, but then stopped dead in my tracks. I hadn't seen Gizmo when I'd first walked into the living room because the couch was in the way.

He was lying on his side on the floor, his tongue hanging out the side of his mouth and his breaths coming hard and fast. And right next to him was a chewed-up sleeve and blister package.

"No..." I breathed out, dropping to my knees in front of him and running my hand down his side. "What did you do?"

He whimpered, and my heart broke into pieces. He'd chewed on the entire thing and most of the pills were missing. Not caring if he bit me, I grabbed his jaw and opened his mouth to look inside.

"Fuck." I couldn't see anything besides lots and lots of saliva. He needed a vet and fast.

I jumped to my feet and ran toward the stairs. This was all my fault, and if the dog died... I couldn't think of that. Dogs swallowed things they weren't supposed to all the time. He'd be okay. Right?

At the top of the stairs in one direction was a completely dark hall, and the other had a faint glow at the end where there was a large open space, like a television was on. There were double doors at the very end of it, which was most likely the primary bedroom.

I ran, bypassing a few doors, not wanting to waste time looking inside. Where there was light, there was life. The hall opened into a living room space with a library and lounge on one side and a television with giant beanbags on the other, one of which was occupied.

"Payne!" The N'Pact member was sleeping, a gaming

controller on his heavily tattooed and muscular stomach.

He stirred but didn't wake up. I said his name again and tapped his foot. He groaned and moved, the controller falling off his stomach, but his eyes stayed closed.

"Wake up!" I leaned closer to him, smacking his knee.

He jolted awake, his eyes widening as he sat up. I didn't have time to explain what I was doing standing right over him in his house before he grabbed me and flung me onto the foam beanbag, pinning me under him.

"Omega," he growled, burying his face in my hair and neck. "You smell so good."

I was frozen, unable to even formulate a thought. The weight of his body on top of mine and the way he was holding my wrists possessively over my head was making my already satisfied pussy think she wasn't so satisfied after all.

"Is this a dream?" His lips brushed against the sensitive skin beneath my ear. "You smell like warm chocolate."

I inhaled sharply. His scent was all alpha, but the bacon undertones made me groan and squirm underneath him. "Wait... I..."

He bit my ear and moved my wrists to hold with one hand. His other trailed down the side of my face to my throat. He wrapped his tattooed fingers around it, putting very little pressure, but just enough that if I had panties on, they would be soaked. Instead, the wetness just pooled between my thighs.

"Payne," I panted. "Gizmo."

I'd never been this close to an alpha before. Sure, Alvaro had hugged me, but I could easily have escaped. But this? My mind and body had gone to a different place, nearly forgetting about why I'd come upstairs in the first place.

Ignoring me, he slid his lips along my jaw and stopped at the corner of my mouth. "This can't be real."

The dog, Kara. Remember the dog.

"Stop! Gizmo is dying." I squirmed, but not trying to get closer to him. I was trying to get away. "We need to go to the vet."

He pulled back, snapping out of the trance he was in. "What? Kayla?" He jumped up, his face looking like he'd just seen something life-altering.

"I'm Kara." I put my hand over my heart. "The dog. He ate my whole pack of suppressants."

He blinked at me several times, confusion on his face before picking his shirt up off the floor. "Where?"

"Downstairs," I choked, wiggling my weight off the beanbag.

He looked down at me and narrowed his eyes. "Why are you in our house? Is Kayla here?"

Before I could answer, he ran down the hall. I managed to get up and go after him, hoping we had time. Payne had only had me pinned for about a minute, but that minute could have cost Gizmo his life.

I could barely see as I made it downstairs just as Payne got to Gizmo. He made a strangled sound as he dropped down beside him, only his head visible over the back of the couch.

"Alvaro!" Payne yelled, and I jumped at the sudden call for the leader of the pack.

He picked Gizmo up, the dog's head hanging limp. He was still panting but had no energy left in his body. I covered my mouth to stop the sounds of my sobs from escaping.

Alvaro flew down the stairs, his eyes widening in fear as soon as he saw the dog. "How did this happen? Shit. Tate!" He ran back up the stairs, yelling for Tate to get his clothes on.

I followed Payne down another staircase and into an entertainment area that I could hardly see through my tears. He headed down another hall, and before he got to the door at the end, it opened, and we all jumped nearly ten feet in the air.

"What the fuck, Avery?" Cal looked from the dog to me and then back to the dog. "What's wrong?"

"Gizzy is sick." Payne tried to move past Cal, but he held up a black helmet to block the way. "Move out of the fucking way."

"Did you take your sleep meds?" Cal lowered his voice, but I still could hear him.

"It doesn't matter."

"It does." Cal backs up into the garage. "I'll drive. Did you wake-"

"We're coming!" Alvaro yelled from down the hall, yanking a shirt over his head. "What happened?"

"Ask her." Payne walked quickly to the back of a smaller SUV.

Cal put his helmet on the ground and entered a code into a metal box hanging by the door. It had several keys hanging on hooks, and he pulled out a pair. He unlocked the doors and then grabbed a pair of flip-flops from a shelf. "I take it you two are going to deal with Kayla?"

"I'm Kara." I wrapped my arms around myself, feeling helpless.

He didn't pay me any mind as he hit a button to open the garage door and rushed to the SUV to help Payne get the dog in the back. I stood back as Tate and Alvaro came out of the house in various states of undress. Tate just had his clothes gathered against his chest, and Alvaro was buttoning his jeans.

Tate went to the shelves and threw a pair of flip-flops at me. "You can stay here or go with us."

I let them hit me and then slid my feet into them. "I'm going."

I ran to the SUV, getting in the back with Payne and the dog. He glared at me but didn't say a word as Cal hopped in the driver's seat, started the car, and started backing out while Alvaro and Tate were still putting on their pants.

"Wait! What about-"

"They can take another car." Cal backed up far

enough so he could turn and drive forward toward the gate which was already opening. "Where's your sister?"

"At her house. It's a long story." I buckled my seat belt as we turned onto the street. I looked out the back window to see if the police were still at Kayla's but didn't see them. "I'm not supposed to be here, and the gate busted so there are security guards until it can be fixed."

"Did they fuck you?" Payne—or did he want to be called Avery?—stroked Gizmo's head.

Cal inhaled sharply and then moaned. "Fuck. Why aren't you on scent blockers?"

My face heated and I shrank against the door. "I am. I didn't fuck anyone." I didn't like how weak I sounded, like a pitiful omega looking for her alphas to soothe her.

Scent blockers weren't perfect, and if an omega was attracted to alphas, the blockers only worked so well. They dulled the scent just enough not to cause alphas to go into a rut, and most places we encountered alphas pumped scent neutralizers through the ventilation systems.

Alcohol also lessened their effectiveness and I'd had plenty of that.

"How the hell did Gizzy get ahold of your suppressants?" Payne was still pissed, but his voice softened a bit.

"I left them on the coffee table. I'd gone out to my car to get them and then ended up in your pool." I looked out the window, not wanting to see either of their reactions. "I had a rough night."

"Not as rough as Giz." Cal turned down a few streets, and a few minutes later, we were in an area that had businesses.

Gizmo was still breathing, and I bit my inner cheek to stop myself from crying again when Cal turned into a parking lot for Hillside Veterinary Hospital. There were only a few cars in the parking lot, which was a relief.

Cal pulled right up to the door and Payne got out with the dog, the weight of him no problem. He went through the sliding door and Cal turned into a parking space. He shut off the car and put his forehead against the steering wheel.

Headlights flashed into the SUV and a sports car parked next to us, Tate and Alvaro jumping out and not even noticing me and Cal still inside.

"I'm so sorry." I wanted to put my hand on his shoulder but sat on my hands instead.

He shook his head and sat up, unhooking his seat belt. "Are you staying out here?"

"Can I? Just for a few minutes?" I needed a minute to breathe and tell myself that everything would be okay.

"Lock the doors when you get out." He handed me the keys over his shoulder and left me sitting in the darkness wondering what else could possibly go wrong.

CHAPTER EIGHT

Avery

The helplessness I felt watching the vet tech rush Gizzy into the back was clawing at my insides. Once again, our negligence was hurting our pack, and I didn't know how much more we could take.

Ever since we'd matched and then had it promptly rejected, things had not been the same between us. On the outside, we looked like a well-adjusted pack who had the world at the tips of our fingers, but we were barely holding on.

We hadn't even spent a full day with the omega before she decided we weren't worth the effort. It was a blow to our pack bond that was ready for an omega, and the added pressure of fame just made it ten times harder.

I sat down in the waiting room, cradling my head in my hands. Gizzy knew better than to eat random shit he found. He was a well-trained dog who could be left beside a steak and not eat it until told to do so.

The sliding doors at the entrance of the hospital opened and clomping feet ran toward the empty front desk. "Where is he?"

My hands dropped to my lap, and I sighed. "They rushed him back."

Alvaro and Tate finally noticed me sitting off to the side. The fear in their eyes probably matched my own. Alvaro looked at the elderly couple sitting on the other side and then came to sit next to me.

Tate rubbed his temples. "How could we let this happen? *Why* did it happen?"

I leaned my head back against the wall and looked at the ceiling, trying to control myself from exploding. "Why was there an omega in our house? An unbonded omega?"

The receptionist that had rushed through the swinging doors with the vet tech came back out, looked at us with wide eyes, and went back to her desk. She wasn't that much older than us and I hoped this didn't end up all over the internet.

Cal came jogging through the doors and went to the front desk.

"Cal." Alvaro sounded as tired as he looked. We all did.

We barely had any time off before we jumped right into rehearsals for our tour. Our record label worked us like we weren't actual people, and as soon as this tour was done, we needed to reassess if this was really what we wanted out of life.

It wasn't what I wanted.

"Here, sweetie. Fill out this paperwork for your dog since we don't have him in our system. As soon as the vet decides what to do, we'll have an estimate for you." The receptionist held out a clipboard to Cal as he turned to walk toward us.

I kept my voice low as Cal fell into the chair next to me. "We have the assessment tomorrow and you decided it would be a good idea to have an omega sleepover? What's the point of having a pack if the rest of us aren't going to be thought of before life-altering decisions are made?"

Most of the time I stayed quiet about what bothered me, but not tonight. Tonight, I was fed up with never having control of my life. We had all the money we'd ever need, but what good was it if we couldn't live life because of the record label and the alpha police?

"She needed a place to stay for the night. We texted you both." Tate was playing mediator yet again. When was he going to get tired of it all and just let us come to blows? "You were pretty much dead to the world, Avery, or we would have woken you up."

The swinging doors opened, and a vet tech walked out. She gave us a half smile, and I felt like my heart was going to rip through my chest and make a run for it.

The tech turned to Alvaro as he stood. "We were able to get Gizmo to vomit but are going to be giving him activated charcoal to absorb anything that wasn't expelled and IV fluids. The receptionist will have an estimate for you in a few minutes. The vet would like to speak to you, so if you four could follow me to an exam room."

My leg bounced with nervousness. "Is he going to be okay?"

"You got him here very quickly, that's a good thing. There are no cases of a dog ingesting heat suppressants, but with these new blister packages instead of the pill bottle, I anticipate we'll see an increase." She turned and walked toward a hallway. "Follow me, please."

The rest of us stood and followed her down a long hallway to a private room with a bench seat and an exam table.

"The vet will be in shortly." The door clicked closed behind her.

The blister packaging was a brand-new thing that had just rolled out a few weeks ago. It was much safer for omegas, and their pills were much less likely to be tampered with. The only problem was now they were easily accessible to pets and children.

As if we all suddenly were thinking of the same thing, we looked at Cal.

"What?" He shrugged off his leather jacket and hung it over his arm.

"Kara... where is she?" Alvaro leaned against the wall next to the door.

"She needed a few minutes." Cal sat down on the bench seat next to Tate. "It's probably better she just stays out in the car. If OPS or the Pack Health shitheads know we're hanging out with an unbonded omega..."

I grabbed the door handle. "Where are the keys? She can't just sit out there unprotected."

"She has them." Cal patted his jacket and pulled out his phone, the conversation finished.

I hated that this was how we were now. We were together, yet we were so far apart. It was completely fucked up that the entire six hours we had everything we ever wanted could fuck us so royally.

Alvaro grabbed my forearms as I started to open the door. "Are you okay to go get her?"

"Just as fine as the rest of you." I wrenched my arm away and walked out of the room.

Finally, I felt like I could breathe a little and paused as the door shut to take a few deep breaths. That was a mistake because all I could smell was scared dog.

There were a few other people in the waiting room now with pets. Eyes landed on me, and I put my head down as I walked to the doors.

We could hardly go anywhere without being recognized, but hopefully, with their focus on their pets, they wouldn't post on social media where we were. The last thing we needed was a two o'clock in the morning mob outside of a vet hospital when our dog was in bad shape.

Did dogs have HIPAA rights? How were we going to explain how he got ahold of heat suppressants?

I made it to the SUV and knocked on the back window. There was a squeal of surprise and then the door opened.

Fuuuuuck me.

There was no way she was on scent blockers because her perfume hit me like a blast of wind from a plane's propeller. I stumbled back a few steps and brought my hand to cover my nose and mouth.

I wanted to breathe her in, to let her pheromones— that smelled a hell of a lot like warm chocolate to me— make my base instincts go crazy. I'd never scented such a tantalizing omega, even all those years ago when we went through profiles and spent days sniffing scent cards.

"Is... is he okay?" She swung her feet out but didn't touch the ground.

No. No, he's not okay. His dick is as hard as stone and his chest is rumbling and aching.

"They made him throw them up. We're waiting on the vet." My voice was barely recognizable with the low growl coming out of my mouth right along with it.

"I don't know why I'm perfuming so bad. I took a blocker not even two hours ago." She crossed her arms in an X and cupped the sides of her neck, which was where two of the scent glands were. "I'm sorry. I was drinking and I'm not thinking straight right now and-"

"You were drinking?" I lowered my hand from my face, shoving it in my pocket to remind me to keep my hands to myself. My skin itched from the need to touch her. Why was she not thinking straight? Did something happen?

She snorted a disbelieving laugh, tears springing to her eyes. "If I hadn't been, none of this would have happened."

"That's why your blockers aren't working well."

"What? They've still worked when we've had drinks before..." She met my eyes and then quickly looked down at the ground.

"Were you around unbonded alphas and drinking before?" My spine straightened, and I dug my nails into the palms of my hands. The idea of her around any unbonded alpha, even at a meet and greet, made my blood boil.

"No, I'm not an idiot." She stood, and if I hadn't been prepared, the scent from her movement would have taken me to my knees. "Have you ever felt so lost that you don't even know who you are anymore or what you're doing?"

That was a little too close to home. I nodded because I couldn't speak, and not just because I was trying not to inhale her scent. She knew what it felt like to have something right within your reach and have it ripped away.

With a shrug of her shoulders, she shut the back door and locked it. "I stole a car to get here from Washington." She held the keys out and I took them. "Cal is an idiot for giving me the keys."

"Cal trusts people too easily." I pocketed them and couldn't take it anymore. I walked toward her, trapping her against the car. "And apparently, so do you."

She shuddered and looked from side to side at my arms blocking her in. "Alpha..." It was barely enough, but hearing that word fall from her plump lips was all it took.

I leaned in the rest of the way, pausing with my lips barely hovering over hers. "Let me kiss you. Just once. I need to taste you and your mouth will have to do."

Her eyes fluttered shut and her head tilted back until it hit the window. "Yes."

There was only one thing on my mind. Her lips. There were no thoughts of consequences or what this would mean. Alphas and omegas just didn't go around kissing, and unless she'd kissed someone before emerging, her lips were mine to take.

But I didn't. Not yet.

I brushed my lips along her chin, up her jaw, and to her ear. She was so intoxicating and made me feel so... alive.

"Has anyone claimed your lips?" I moved one of my hands from the window and ran my thumb over her bottom lip. It was just the right amount of soft.

"No." Her tongue darted out to moisten her lips and touched my thumb. "Kiss me."

There was no resisting that command, and I took her lips in a kiss that had me pressing my entire body against hers. I couldn't stop myself from giving her all of me. My scent. My hands. My stomach. My cock. I wanted her to have it all.

She gasped, and her hands grabbed onto my biceps as I dug my fingers into her curly wet hair. Her taste was more than I could have imagined. I moved my tongue along the seam of her lips, and she opened, letting me in.

Would she spread her legs for me and let me taste the sweetness between them?

I groaned, gently pulling her head to the side by her hair so I could deepen the kiss. It had been so long since I'd kissed a woman, but kissing her was like coming home.

Our tongues tangled, hers fighting with mine and seeking entrance into my mouth. I let her explore and take over the kiss as I moved the back of my hand down her neck, across her shoulder, and down her arm.

My cock was so incredibly hard, and it hadn't even been a minute since I'd claimed her lips as mine. But that wasn't enough.

I growled into her mouth and hooked my arm under her ass, lifting her. She instinctively wrapped her legs around my waist and her arms around my neck, letting me even closer to her body.

There was no way I was going to be able to stop. The heat between her legs was beckoning me, and I rubbed my jeans-covered cock against her.

She gasped, her fingers digging into my hair.

I needed to get her in the car. I needed to-

"Get off of her," Alvaro barked, grabbing me by my shoulder and attempting to pull me away.

I ripped my lips from hers, turning my head and baring my teeth. "Mine." All of the anger and sadness I'd felt over the past three years were poured into that one word.

Alvaro backed up a step, his fists clenching at his sides and his teeth bared. He was pissed, but so was I.

"She's no one's." His chin dropped so I would be forced to look him straight in the eyes. *"Get away from her."*

His bark was more powerful than I'd heard it in a long time, and it sent a tremble through me, forcing me to let her legs fall from around my waist. I tried with all my might to stay close to her, but I was a mess and that was no match for Alvaro's command.

I backed away slowly, my fingers brushing her cheek before Alvaro shoved between us, putting a finger right in the middle of my chest. "Are you fucking crazy?"

I growled, not liking that he was protecting her from me. "It doesn't matter. We were just kissing."

"Just kissing? Just kissing!" He stabbed his finger into me several times. "We're all unbonded and she's not even supposed to be here! You were *kissing* her, Avery. Do you have any clue what could have happened if I hadn't been the one to catch you tongue fucking her mouth?"

Cal and Tate walked out of the vet clinic, paperwork in hand. Their frowns deepened when they saw us. Now I was going to have to listen to all three of them berate me.

I threw my hands up in surrender and backed up. "Fuck it."

"What's going on?" Cal looked past Alvaro. "Why's the omega crying?"

"Avery had his tongue down her throat and was dry humping her against the car." Alvaro didn't take his eyes off me. "You lost control."

"Please don't fight because of me. Just take me home. I'll sleep in my car." Despite her tears, she spoke in a strong, clear voice.

I didn't deserve her. None of us did. Not that we could even entertain the thought of it. Fuck. I was such an idiot for letting my instincts take over.

"You aren't sleeping in your car." Tate went to her and wrapped a comforting arm around her.

I growled.

Alvaro growled.

Kara whimpered.

This was going to escalate to the point of no return. I could feel it in my bones... and in our pack bond. "Is Gizzy going to be okay?"

"He should be. They're going to call us this afternoon." Cal ran his fingers through his blond hair.

I took the keys out of my pocket and threw them to Cal. "I'll walk home." I turned my back on my pack and walked away from them.

No one stopped me.

CHAPTER NINE

Cal

My entire chest hurt as Tate drove the SUV with me and Kara home. I was in no state to drive us after Avery had turned his back on us like that.

Was this it? Was this omega sniffling quietly in the backseat going to push us all over the edge we'd been teetering on for years?

It was hard to watch our bond fall apart. It had been strong since the day we'd met. A brotherhood and love like I'd never experienced in my life. To know it could be gone tomorrow was a slap in the face of how hard we'd worked to get to where we were both as musicians and as a pack.

"Everything is going to be okay." Tate looked over at me as we got closer and closer to home.

I nodded and looked out the passenger window. We hadn't even seen Avery walking along the sidewalk. *Was he coming home? What if he took off and we never saw him again?*

I needed a release, even though I'd just had one.

My pack thought I'd gone out to find a hookup, and sometimes I did, but if they knew where I really went and what I did, they would have worried. Worry was the last thing any of us needed.

"Shouldn't we go look for him? It's a few miles back to your house, and it's so dark." Kara put her hand over the back of the seat and touched my shoulder.

Was she trying to comfort me? If anything, I should have been in the backseat with her, pulling her into my lap and purring away her tears. I didn't know her that well, but I got the gist of why her eyes were sad, even before Avery had taken off.

I put my hand over hers, even though I shouldn't have been touching her. None of us should. "He needs to get his head on straight before he comes home."

"It wasn't all his fault. I wanted it just as much as he did." She sighed and moved her hand, sitting back in the seat.

"Do you have your seatbelt on?" Tate looked in the rearview mirror.

"Yes." I could hear a hint of sass in her voice. "Is yours on, Dad?"

I snorted and looked over at Tate. "Daddy, can we go find some tacos?"

He lifted a brow at me and looked back at the road. "It's two in the morning, Cal. Or are you being inappropriate? Not really the time..."

"It's the best time for any kind of tacos. Just flip a bitch at the light; there's always food trucks outside that one cluster of clubs." I turned in my seat to look at Kara. "Do you like tacos?"

Her stomach growled. "Does anyone not like tacos?"

"You'd be surprised. I once..." I let my voice drift off and cringed. Saying I once briefly dated a girl who hated all kinds of tacos including the dessert ice cream tacos felt wrong. "You know what? Not liking tacos is a major red flag for me."

This was the first time I was getting a good look at her. Even though it was dark, I could make out the blue of her eyes. They were probably even more striking in the light. Her brown hair was curly and fell well past her shoulders.

She wore a band T-shirt, a few sizes too big, but with the way she was sitting, I could see the outline of her breasts. And her legs. The shorts were longer, but her calves were bitable.

What was I doing?

Before I popped a boner, I turned back around in my seat. "I hope the food trucks aren't busy. One of us should probably get out and order."

"Text Alvaro and let him know we're stopping." Tate

made a U-turn and drove back in the direction we'd just come.

I shot a quick text to Alvaro telling him we'd get him his usual. He was super picky about the taco trucks he ate at, but we'd gotten good at figuring out the good and the bad.

"I hate being an omega." She muttered the words quietly, but Tate and I both heard them and gave each other a look. "It's unfair that just because I don't have a pack to 'protect me,' I can't even go to a taco truck and order my own damn tacos."

Tate kept his attention forward but looked thoughtful, like always. "I know that must be frustrating for you. But what happened tonight? I have no doubt that Avery would have been able to stop himself before things got too far, but other alphas might not have."

"I don't regret it." She moved into the middle seat, buckling the seat belt and leaning forward, putting her elbows on the center console and resting her cheeks on her fists.

Tate's hand tightened on the steering wheel. I hadn't taken a breath through my nose since we'd gotten in the SUV, but his reaction made me want to.

"What Tate was trying to say is that alphas are assholes and will take what they want when they see or smell someone they like. And your scent is... desirable." I dug my fingers into my jeans, so badly wanting to scent her. I'd gotten a hint of her earlier and shut my nose right down.

"Why can't alphas take something, then? Omegas have to suffer in solitary confinement because they can't control themselves? Doesn't seem fair, does it?" She sounded angry, and I turned again.

Wow. She was way too close to us.

She glanced at my lips and sat back in her seat quickly. What the fuck was happening? Were we all going to lose our minds over this omega and be in even worse shit with the alpha overlords and the OPS?

Omega Protective Services meant well, but they had been a thorn in our side ever since we matched with Jenna and she called them, crying that we'd abandoned her.

We'd done no such thing. We had no idea how crazy it was going to be after our first single hit. If she would have just waited a few minutes we would have found her.

Jenna hadn't been the first omega on our list of twenty we submitted, but she had been in the top ten. It was weird to think about how it all worked and how detached it was, but at the end of the day, Omega Match worked... most of the time.

It just didn't work for us, and since we were excited about an omega joining our pack and in such a volatile spot emotionally with our career taking off suddenly, it hurt. It hurt more than I think any of us thought it would.

"We're here." Tate's announcement snapped me out of my spiral, and I took a deep breath.

Unfortunately, some air went up my nose, and I groaned. Now I could see how Mr. Celibate snapped.

"Let's just imagine it's a melted chocolate bar left in the car." Tate was struggling just as much as I was. How was she not? Or maybe she was and was just good at keeping her composure.

"Do you want me to get the tacos and give you two a few minutes?" She unhooked her seatbelt as Tate put the SUV in park.

"No!" we both said at the same time.

She laughed, and not to sound cliché and corny as fuck, but it was music to my ears. It was as if all the dark clouds parted and the sun could finally shine through, warming my heart.

I ran a hand over my face. Damn, I was turning into a sap for this woman. It would make for some killer songwriting, though.

"There's a lot of people. Can you handle staying here with her? You're better at not breathing through your nose than I am." Tate held out his hand for money. "You do have your wallet, don't you?"

I unbuckled my seat belt and lifted my ass to grab it from my back pocket. "I paid the vet, didn't I?"

"As soon as I'm able to go back to Kayla's, I'll send you guys some money for the vet bills." Kara's voice cracked, and my fingers froze on the twenties I was about to pull out.

"Kara... accidents happen. The vet even said that the suppressants have an ingredient that is appealing to dogs, and now that they're in the blister packaging, they can smell them once you pop them out." Tate snatched my wallet and opened the door. "What do you want to eat?"

"I'll eat anything. No food allergies." An omega that wasn't picky? She just kept making it harder to ignore how perfect she was.

Crap. Stop it, Callum.

"I'll take my usual." I put my head back against the seat as Tate shut the door.

He jogged the short distance to one of the four food trucks across the street, and I counted down in my head. "Five, four, three, two…"

"Isn't he going to be recognized… oh. Never mind. Wow, that was fast." Kara was leaning between the seats again.

There weren't that many people, but they were already pulling out their phones. Luckily, the food truck he went to was quick at getting orders out.

Out of the four of us, he was the best at dealing with fans in the wild. And honestly, he was the best at dealing with most things. If pretending to be perfectly put together helped him, then so be it.

"Do you ever get tired of it? The fame?" Kara's voice softened, and she touched my arm.

As much as I didn't want her touching me, I also *did* want her to. It brought me a sense of comfort that I hadn't felt in a long time.

"Yes and no. Sometimes the four of us just need a

breather, but pretty much wherever we go, there's always someone who wants a selfie or an autograph. We literally have no days off unless we just stay on our property, and even then..." I sighed and covered her hand with mine.

"Even then, crazed fans find a way onto your property and go for swims in the pool?" She tried to pull away, but I held onto her hand.

"Are you a crazed fan?" I looked over my shoulder at her and then turned in my seat, bringing her hand over my heart. "Or are you an omega looking for your place in the world just as much as we are?"

Her mouth opened and closed a few times like a fish out of water. *What would she do If I leaned forward and kissed her? Would she push me away or would she welcome me like she welcomed Avery?*

She looked at my lips and then down at our hands. "I thought I knew my place for the longest time, but then one thing just..."

"Puts your whole world off kilter?" I removed my hand and instead brought it to her face. "We know that better than anyone."

She closed her eyes and leaned into my touch and, fuck, I wanted to pull her into my lap and fucking purr the hurt away. Her sister had told us all about her and how she hadn't matched with any packs. I found it completely unbelievable that not a single pack would want her.

I wanted her, Avery sure as fuck did, and the other

two just hadn't said it yet, but their eyes did. But the reality was we couldn't have her. It would take an absolute miracle for the Pack Health Organization to give us the all-clear.

With a final stroke of my thumb over her soft skin, I dropped my hand and turned back to face forward. I didn't want to stop touching her, but if I didn't, it would be even harder to see her go.

"Why doesn't your pack have an omega?" She rested her head on my shoulder. Was she trying to torture me? Did she even realize what she was doing to me? To all of us?

She needed to know what she was dealing with before she let herself get too cozy with us. It was in our blood that we were naturally attracted to each other. It was true that not all alphas would find her appealing and vice versa, but if we'd come across her during the matching process, she would have been our number one choice. I just knew deep within me that she was ours.

"We can't have an omega, Kara." My voice cracked like I was twelve again. "We... we matched before, and she rejected us. OPS deemed us unfit."

She didn't move her head off my shoulder, but the feeling in the car shifted. Not many knew about the omega thanks to an iron-clad nondisclosure agreement everyone involved signed.

"But what if-"

"Please, don't. This pack is holding on by a thread and we can't get our hopes up only to have them ripped away again. Especially not with an omega like you." I grabbed onto the door handle. "There's nothing you can do. We are already under watch by the Pack Health Organization."

"It's not fair." She sat back in her seat, making a strangled garbling noise.

"Please don't cry." I didn't like when people cried, omega or not.

"It's all I know how to do anymore." At least I think that's what she said because she had her hands over her face.

"I'm sure that's not true. You're just going through a rough patch." I took off my seatbelt and climbed into the back despite my brain screaming at me that it was a bad idea.

I was working on instinct; there was an omega that needed consoling and I was born to take care of her. It would be fine just this once. I'd caused her pain, after all.

She'd taken her seatbelt off, so I pulled her into my lap. She didn't fight me and wrapped her arms around me, burying her face in the crook of my neck.

"Our stories just don't line up. You're going to find a great pack that will love you and take care of your every need." I rubbed her back and my purr thundered through my chest. "And one day we'll find an omega that can handle the fame and take care of our needs."

She cried harder, and I wished I could lay her down and let my entire body cradle her. Omegas were so precious, and seeing this one hurt so intensely was breaking me up inside.

"It hurts," she choked out, trying to get even closer to me.

"Shhh." I moved her off my lap. "Lie down."

Her face was red and splotchy with tears. She didn't argue, though, lying down as I knelt on the floorboard. She barely fit across the seat, so when I wiggled my way onto the narrow seat, I had to bend my knees and sandwich one of her legs between them.

She was so close that I could feel her breasts pressed against my chest and the tremble of her body. Or maybe it was the tremble of my purr.

She snuggled into me, her body relaxing as she let my purr comfort her. My chest felt like it was going to explode from happiness and longing. What was it about this omega that had me wanting to say fuck it all and run off with her?

We could do it. We had the money and connections to disappear. There were plenty of countries that didn't have Omega Match and let alphas and omegas choose each other just like betas chose each other. Sure, that came with some problems at times, but it had to be better than having your every move watched.

The back door opened, and the smell of tacos wafted in. "What the hell, Cal?"

I lifted my head and shot him a glare. "Nothing is happening. Shut the door before someone gets a picture."

None of the fans had seemed to notice the car he got out of, but I was sure they were watching, if not recording now. It was a good thing Kara was hidden from sight between me and the car seat.

"You can't ride home like that." Tate had only shut the door partially and was blocking the rest of the view with his body.

"I can. Just drive extra carefully." I put my head back down and wiggled in closer to Kara, who wasn't clinging to my shirt quite as hard now.

"Fine." Tate slammed the door, which was surprising, and got in the driver's seat. I couldn't see what he was doing but could hear the plastic of the bags rustling.

"Can you keep it down? Kara needs some rest. She's exhausted." I tucked her hair behind her ear and her eyes were closed. I couldn't tell if she was asleep, but she was relaxed.

"You're ridiculous," Tate muttered, starting the car and pulling out of the parking space.

He turned on some soft music and lowered the volume. So, he did care about her too.

As I continued to purr softly, I knew we had to do something so this omega could be ours. If that meant giving up our career or taking a long break, then it would be worth it.

She was worth it.

And damn it. So were we.

CHAPTER TEN

Kara

Tacos.

That was all that was on my mind as I stirred awake sandwiched between two warm bodies. One second, I'd been having an omega meltdown, and the next...

My eyes opened wide, and I came face to face with Tate, who was still sleeping. How had I ended up in bed with two alphas? That seemed like a very bad idea after what had happened last night... or was that this morning? I never knew what to call it if it was past midnight.

I was still dressed, but that didn't stop me from feeling someone's hard length poking me right in the ass. *Do. Not. Wiggle.*

Sniffing as small an amount of air as possible, I was sure it was Cal with his strawberry scent mingling with Tate's orange one. Had they even enjoyed their tacos last night? Had Avery gotten home all right?

My heart had hurt so bad for the pack. To have a match and then be rejected would be rough on anyone. Omega Match had stiff fines for it which made it less likely to happen, so when it did, there were usually no other options.

But for an omega to reject *them*? They were the perfect gentlemen. What the hell had happened and why was Omega Match not letting them have another omega?

A hand landed on my hip and squeezed. Okay, perfect was a bit of a stretch—no one was perfect—seeing as we were unbonded but starting to act like we were. I'd overstayed my welcome and we were all acting with our instincts.

Which is exactly why I grabbed Cal's hand and moved it to my breast. Just for a minute, I wanted to know what it felt like to have an alpha's hand cup my breast and maybe rub a thumb over my nipple.

Cal sucked in a breath, his chest rumbling with a low growl. "Omega…"

"Alpha." I wiggled against him, and he put his face against my back, his hand doing just what I wanted. "Yes."

This was bad. Bad, bad, bad.

"We can't." He moved his head up so his mouth was

by my ear and I swept my hair out of the way. "Kara, we can't."

His lips glided along my neck, his hand kneading my breast. It felt so good but not enough. I needed more. I wanted his hands and mouth all over me, making me beg for his cock... for his knot.

I rolled my hips, his dick sliding against my crack. He moved a leg between mine, but with him being behind me, and Tate being in the way of him bending his leg further, I was left panting for something to relieve the ache between my legs.

Cal's hand abandoned my breast, and I whimpered, chasing it with my own. He batted my hand away and lifted the hem of my shirt.

This was so hot, much better than I'd imagined in my head.

"Tate will be mad if you wake him up and he finds us like this," he whispered in my ear. "But I think your scent might do that first."

Instead of heading back up my shirt to my breast, he ran his fingers along the elastic of my shorts. Was I going to let this alpha I wasn't even bound to touch me like I wanted?

He grazed his teeth along my neck before sucking on a spot I knew he was marking as his. "Just one little dip in your honey pot won't hurt anyone."

I bit my lip, a smile spreading across my face. "Just once."

He moved his mouth to my t-shirt-covered shoulder

and bit down as his hand slid under the waistband and through my trimmed curls. His entire body was vibrating behind me, but not from a purr. He was straining to stop himself.

His fingers brushed the top of my slit, and I opened my legs for him, slick already making my lips wet for him. My perfume was strong in the air, a thick chocolate that made my mouth water.

Tate's eyes popped open and met mine just as Cal moved his hand to slide a finger up the length of me to my clit. I gasped, rocking my hips when he just let it settle there.

"What..." Tate looked down. "Cal. What the fuck-"

I didn't want this to stop, so I did what I had wanted to do the night before. I grabbed the back of his head and pulled him to me, kissing him.

Yup. I'd lost my omega marbles.

He didn't move at first, making me worry, but then it was like whatever had been holding him back snapped and his tongue pushed into my mouth.

"Fuck." Cal had stopped biting my shoulder, and his mouth was back at my ear. "Reach down and tell me if his cock is as hard as mine."

My mind was already fogging up with desire and need, so I didn't even think about what I was starting with the two of them. I ran my fingers down Tate's well-defined chest, his abs, and brushed my hand over the soft fabric of his boxers that concealed a very hard cock.

"He's hard, isn't he?" Cal moved his finger that was pressed against my clit in small circles. "You're so wet for us. It would be so easy for the two of us to make you ours right now."

I whimpered into Tate's mouth as I pushed his boxers down, freeing his cock. I wanted to be theirs. All they had to do was knot and bite me and then there was nothing anyone could do.

No, Kara. You don't know that.

From what we'd been told all our lives, omegas and alphas never came together without Omega Match. But I was sure it had to happen from time to time. With the way omegas were kept under lock and key, it wasn't likely.

Tate moved his mouth to my neck, scraping his teeth along just as Cal had. All I could think about was one of them burying their knot in me and claiming me with their bites.

No, we couldn't. Not now. It had to be the strongest alpha.

Cal slid his finger down to my entrance and teased it, barely pushing the tip in. I moved against his dick, wishing the fabric between us was gone.

"We should stop," Tate muttered, pulling up my shirt so he could kiss my breast and nipple. "But fuck, I don't want to stop."

He sucked my nipple into his mouth right as Cal plunged his finger fully into me. I moaned in satisfaction, my hips picking up speed, and I wrapped my hand around Tate's length, marveling at how hot and soft the skin was.

Tate released my nipple and looked at me as he moved his hand down, yanked down my shorts, and slid my clit between two fingers. "I want you to come on both of our hands."

I closed my eyes, and my head fell back against Cal's shoulder. Tate's lips were back on me again and Cal added another finger.

"It feels so good," I panted, my entire body humming with want. "More. I need more."

I was trying my best to stroke Tate's cock and rub against Cal, but my body didn't want to cooperate. My fingers and toes felt like they were on fire as my orgasm built in my entire body.

"This is all we can give you, sweetheart. Now come for us, like a good omega." Cal bit my earlobe and that was it.

I was done for and completely lost to these two alphas. My release slammed into me, and I bucked against their hands, my entire body feeling as if someone had set off fireworks. The intense feeling traveled up my limbs and pooled in my core.

"Yes, yes, yes!" I didn't care how loud I was being. It felt so good and so right. "I need a knot! Please, someone fuck me."

"That's it, baby. Come all over our hands. Give us

that slick." Tate had pulled back to look at his hand milking my orgasm from me.

And then their hands disappeared. I opened my mouth to protest, but then Tate grabbed his cock with his slick-covered hand and fell onto his back. His pumps were fast and hard, the cords of muscle in his neck straining.

I moved onto my back and looked between the men. Cal was doing the same as Tate, his eyes squeezed shut as he jacked himself off.

My heartbeat was out of control as my body came down from my orgasm. I wanted to touch them, but they were both in the zone.

"Let me see what you want to spill inside of me." My voice was scratchy in the kind of way that was sexy and seductive. "Spill your seed so your omega can see."

"Fuck, yes!" Cal was the first to go, his hips jacking up off the bed with one last thrust where he wrapped his fist around his barely inflating knot. If it were inside me, it would have fully expanded, locking us in place.

Tate groaned and went over the edge, squeezing his knot even harder than Cal was. I licked my lips, looking back and forth between their cocks.

"Just a quick taste." I leaned toward Tate first because he seemed most likely to bolt if he processed what I was going to do.

The guest room door flew open, hitting the wall behind it so hard that I wouldn't have been surprised if there was a hole. Alvaro stood there, panting, his nostrils flaring.

For a moment, I was scared at the look in his eyes, but then I looked down his shirtless torso to where his cock was straining behind his jeans.

"What have you done?" He stalked forward in a way that had me crossing my legs and squeezing my thighs together.

"Alvaro, we-" Tate sat up, shoving his wet cock back into his boxers.

Alvaro went to the end of the bed, his stare burning down my exposed stomach to my mound. I shivered under his gaze that wasn't so much of a glare as a smolder.

"Spread your legs and let me see what you've done." His command was just shy of an alpha bark, and it made my skin break out in goosebumps.

"Yes, Alpha." I wiggled free of the shorts and took a deep breath of courage. Their scents were thick in the air, mingling with mine in a heady mixture.

I'd never felt more powerful than when I put both feet flat on the bed and spread my legs. My legs trembled and my cheeks heated hearing the growl that came from Alvaro.

I was propped on my forearms and saw the second he lost the constraint he'd been having. He practically pounced onto the bed, making me squeal and Cal and Tate curse.

His head was between my legs and his tongue ran up

and down the length of me before the other two could try to stop him. That was perfectly fine by me.

I fell back onto the pillow as Alvaro growled into my pussy, his stubble rubbing me in all the right places and his tongue lapping up the slick left behind by his pack mates.

Just when my extremities were starting to tingle, Alvaro lifted his head and looked at me with hooded eyes. "You don't come until I-"

The doorbell rang, and he froze.

"What time is it?" Tate grabbed his phone off the nightstand. "Fuck! Shit! Fuck!"

"What's wrong?" I sat up as Alvaro flew off the bed and into the attached bathroom, turning on the sink.

"What are we going to do?" Cal climbed off the bed, not even looking at me. Why wasn't he looking at me?

Alvaro came out of the bathroom, his face dripping water before he brought a towel up to dry it. "Go wash your hands and dicks. Get Avery up. I'll call Jonathan."

"Can someone tell me what the fuck is going on?" My voice cracked, and I reached down to pull up my shorts.

"The Pack Health Organization is here... early." Alvaro threw the towel at me. "Lock the door and shove the towel in the crack. I'll call our betas, Jonathan and Anya, to get you out and spray the room."

Tate grabbed the Squishmallows off the floor and shoved them under the bed. "They might not even look in here."

"Can't risk it." Alvaro went to the door and cringed as he saw the dent in the wall from flinging it open. "It'll be fine."

He didn't sound like it would be fine, and if agents were making a house visit? Things were very much not fine.

What had we done?

I STRIPPED everything off the bed except the comforter, which had been kicked off the end of the bed sometime in the night, and bundled everything up. The sheets and pillowcases were saturated with my perfume, which put me on edge.

I'd missed my suppressant pill the night before too, and the rest of the pills were eaten by Gizmo or had been ruined by slobber. My heart hurt over the thought of the dog suffering. Sure, he'd chased me and pantsed me, but it was all in the name of protecting his owners.

Kayla hopefully had suppressant pills that I could take until I could get back to the compound and get a refill. The last thing I wanted to do was go back, though.

There was a soft knock on the window a few minutes later, and I nearly jumped out of my skin. I peeked out of the curtains as my heart thudded.

I opened the window with a sigh of relief. "Thank you so much for this."

"Let's hurry. They just let the agents inside." Jonathan

looked down the side of the house and then back at me. "Push the tabs around the window screen so it'll pop out."

Jonathan was an intimidating presence and was taller than any of the members of N'Pact. He was over six feet tall, possibly even six and a half feet. His shoulders were wide, and his light brown hair was cut close to his scalp in a buzz cut.

Anya was the opposite of him, and he could probably have easily bench-pressed her. She was shorter than me by a few inches and her blond hair had a pixie cut. She was gorgeous, and a twinge of jealousy ran through me that she had been around my pack.

My pack.

I popped the tabs on the screen and backed up a few steps as Jonathan pulled it off. It was a farfetched dream to think they were my pack.

"Come on. I'll help you out," Jonathan said in a low voice. "Anya will go in after you and clean."

Anya smiled at me, and the hint of jealousy I'd been feeling vanished. These were trusted betas that N'Pact had welcomed into their pack. They were risking their necks helping me escape.

"I already took everything off the bed. The comforter just needs a spritz of de-scenter." I climbed over the windowsill, not even knowing where my shoes were, and Jonathan grabbed me by the waist and put me on one of the large stepping stones.

"Thank you. I shouldn't be long." She reached out

and squeezed my arm before Jonathan hoisted her through the window. "Come back in five minutes."

"Yes, ma'am." They gave each other a quick kiss and then Jonathan turned to me. "So, you're the omega causing all the trouble."

My mouth opened in shock and partially to defend myself when a wide grin spread across his face, making his green eyes twinkle. "You're joking, right?"

"Of course I am. Follow me and stay quiet. We're going around the front since all the curtains are drawn. There are eight agents here and four of them are alphas." He walked along the side of the house, and I followed.

"Oh, shit." My stomach fluttered with nerves. "They're going to smell me."

"It's possible, but alphas can't work as a field agent unless they are bonded, so as long as they don't go in that bedroom..." He looked over his shoulder and raised a knowing eyebrow.

My cheeks felt like they heated a million degrees, and I looked away. "I didn't mean for that to happen..."

"Walk on my right and stay quiet." Jonathan turned around the corner to the front of the house, his pace brisk enough that I had to speed walk and jog a little to keep up.

Two SUVs were in the driveway, and I wondered how they got in through the gate, but then again, they were a government organization, so they probably hacked in.

We made it across the front of the property, past the front entrance, and to the garage area. There was a walkway that disappeared down the side of it and a gate set into the cement wall.

"This is secret agent level," I whispered as we walked through to a garden. "A secret garden."

Jonathan snorted. "This is Anya's pride and joy. When she's not taking care of the pack, she's gardening."

I followed him through the garden to the backyard, which had more of the garden and a pool. "It's nice you live right next door." What I really wanted to say was I was glad they didn't live in the house with the pack.

"It makes things easier." He opened a French door and let me inside. "I'm going to go back for Anya. Make yourself at home and help yourself to a breakfast burrito. We were in the middle of making breakfast for the pack when Alvaro called. Oh, and your car keys are there on the counter. I fished them out of the pool."

He left me, and I looked around their inviting home. It looked a bit smaller than N'Pact's but was just as inviting with an open floor plan and large windows overlooking the back and the city.

I walked around the island and turned on the griddle to heat the tortillas that sat next to the stove. I wanted to make my alphas their breakfast, even if it was just wrapping up a tortilla.

There I went again, calling them my pack. It was a dangerous game my brain was playing. Even if they could do the fall match, that was months away, and a lot could happen between now and then.

The comfort and safety I already felt around them made my heart sing, but it was way too soon to dance. As much as I wanted them, if I'd learned anything over the past month, it was that the only person who could truly protect me was myself.

CHAPTER ELEVEN

Alvaro

Jonathan texted me shortly after the Pack Health Organization agents arrived. He'd been able to get Kara to his and Anya's place without any issues. Luckily, the agents hadn't inspected our house, but even if they had, Anya would have already stripped the bed and sprayed the room with expensive de-scenting spray. That still might not have been enough, though.

Kara's perfume was potent.

All morning, we'd been in our bedrooms with agents, being assessed. They went over everything from our sexual habits, things that showed up in the media, and bodily reactions to stimuli.

That part was the worst. Who wanted to be hooked up to a machine that tracked heart rate, eye dilation, and scent excretion? They showed us videos of everything from alphas and omegas living day-to-day life with each other and alone, to an omega in heat.

Six months ago, my reactions were different; the scenes put me on edge and the heat scene had nearly had me taking my cock out in front of the agents. But this time, I was calm, and when they showed a short clip of an alpha knotting his omega, I was aroused, but more from the idea of knotting Kara.

The final part of the individual assessment was smelling scent cards of ten different omegas. It was the best way they could keep data on whether an alpha was becoming feral. Feral alphas were dangerous to omegas and betas because of their heightened sensitivity to pheromones. All it took was one hit of an appealing omega's perfume, even if lingering on a beta.

Although the agents' faces revealed nothing, I had no reaction to the scents on the cards besides my brain recognizing it was an omega, but not *my* omega. I didn't know how I was going to explain my lack of response when six months ago, I'd moaned and growled over several of them.

I was most worried about how Avery was doing with his assessment. He'd scored the highest on the risk factors last time, and he'd been in a mood since I'd pulled him away from Kara.

Yet I could still taste her in my mouth. I was such a fucking hypocrite.

It was around lunchtime when we finished the individual portion and the agents left for lunch. We had the pack portion next, and if we had any hope of being eligible for Omega Match, we needed to ace it.

I pulled the sandwiches Anya had prepared for us out of the refrigerator and set them on the island where my three pack mates were sitting. I could feel they were all just as worried as I was, which was better than not feeling their emotions at all.

"How did you all do on the individual portion?" I slid their sandwiches to them. If we didn't have Anya, we'd probably have starved or ordered takeout more than we already did.

Tate scrubbed a hand over his tired eyes. "It was weird."

"How so?" I unwrapped my sandwich and hopped up on the counter.

"I wasn't as affected by the stimuli. The agents kept giving each other looks, but I couldn't tell if they were good looks or bad looks." Tate popped open his soda and took a long drink.

Cal, who had been oddly quiet since coming down the stairs and seeing his agents out, had a worry line between his brows. "They asked me flat out if I'd been with an omega recently."

I stopped moving with the sandwich halfway to my mouth. "What?"

"They asked me the same thing." Avery started picking the pickles off his sandwich. "How many times do I have to tell her no pickles? They're gross."

Cal reached over and plucked them off his plate. "If Kara was our omega, she wouldn't forget you hate them."

They all looked to me like I had the solution to the epic shitstorm we'd found ourselves in the middle of. So, I decided to ignore it for now. "What did you tell them?"

"I told them that I hadn't fucked an omega. It wasn't a lie." Cal narrowed his eyes at me. "What did you tell them?"

"They didn't ask me that." Maybe my responses hadn't been extremely different after all, or just not enough.

"They didn't ask me either. You were both rated six and seven on the scale last time. Maybe you dropped so much because of Kara that they are suspicious. I'm sure there is some shady shit that goes on with omegas that aren't in compounds, and we do have a lot of money..." Tate shook his head in disbelief.

The thought of any pack or family doing something like that to an omega made my blood boil. "They can't really think we'd do that."

"Not all countries have Omega Match or compounds for their omegas. What's to stop us from going abroad and finding an omega?" Cal looked down at his sandwich. "Don't tell me you've never thought about it."

"It's illegal," I growled. "And it's not always what's

best for the omegas. Imagine being sixteen and going into your first heat only to have your family sell you to the highest bidder."

"That shit goes on here too. Don't pretend it doesn't. Even if they do end up in Omega Match, they are still sold or arranged bondings are set up." Avery pushed his sandwich away. "Are we going to talk about Kara or not?"

I put my lunch down too, my appetite gone. "If we can't do Omega Match, then we can't have her."

"Why not?" Cal looked at each of us. "If we bonded with her and she wanted the bond, then what could they do?"

Bonding with an omega outside of Omega Match wasn't talked about at all because it didn't happen. In high school, girls were closely monitored by the school and their parents for signs of being an omega. When the transition started, it came fast, and the omegas were taken to a boarding school to finish their high school careers.

Alphas tended to transition around eighteen, and then most of our focus was on establishing a pack. It was the way our minds and bodies worked. Of course I had wanted an omega to rut into when I was a fresh-faced alpha with an aching knot, but one alpha just wasn't enough to meet the physical and emotional needs of an omega.

"If we bonded with her, they still might take her

from us and throw us in prison." I put my plate down and crossed my arms. "And that would kill her."

Avery shoved away from the counter and stood. "And what about what is killing us?"

The room was eerily silent as we all came to our own conclusions of what we should do in our heads. I wanted Kara, but what would it cost us? What would it cost *her*?

"There's no way after what we did this morning that we're going to be able to resist her now," Tate said softly. "If they don't let us do the match, I think we should go for it and deal with the consequences later."

Avery growled. "What did you do this morning?"

Fuck. He didn't know what had happened with Kara yet. Now was not the time to have him flip the fuck out on us.

Tate raised an eyebrow in my direction and Cal was picking at something on the front of his t-shirt. It was my job to protect our pack bond, and I'd done nothing but harm it over and over again.

"Is someone going to answer me?" Avery gripped the edge of the counter, his knuckles turning white where there was skin and not ink.

I cleared my throat. "Tate and Cal fell asleep with her when they got back last night, and this morning I walked in after they had some fun with their hands, and I..."

God, just the thought of it made my dick instantly hard, and my knot pulsed with the need to take her.

Avery looked like he was about to jump across the island and choke me. "You what, Alvaro?"

"He had a tasty omega snack. Well, until the doorbell rang." Cal sighed wistfully. "And there Tate and I were being good alphas and not going that far."

Avery's nostrils flared. "You tasted her?"

"I did." I adjusted my dick in my pants, wondering if I had time to go take care of it before the agents returned.

Avery's eyes closed, his hands still gripping the counter. "What did she taste like?"

"Like hot chocolate on a cold day. Like the last bit of chocolate frosting on the plate. Like... *ours*." I couldn't keep the growl out of my voice. "She needs to be ours."

Avery groaned and lowered his forehead to the counter. "We can't lose her."

I straightened, my eyes pausing on each of them. "We won't. If it's the last thing I do as leader of this pack, I promise you she'll be ours."

Now to figure out how to do it.

THE AGENTS LEFT mid-afternoon after the pack assessment. They observed us while we were hooked up to the same machines as before, solving puzzles, communicating using a back-to-back drawing game, and sharing compliments and complaints about each other and the pack.

There had been a few moments of frustration and

anger, but I could see the want on everyone's face. We *wanted* to work as a pack and get through the hurdles we faced. I just didn't think it was enough to be permitted to do the fall match.

"I need a fucking nap," Cal muttered, going to the refrigerator. The man worked out like an Olympian and ate like a garbage truck. "Oh, hey! You saved our tacos."

"I did." Avery grunted, elbowing him out of the way, grabbing a beer, and heading toward the stairs. "I'm going to game unless we are planning on whisking Kara away to a private island."

He was already retreating into himself, and I didn't want that to happen again. I'd seen some of the happy Avery we once knew peek out during our assessment, but it had already disappeared.

"First off, leftover tacos are going to taste like shit. Just eat the meat. Second, Kara is back at her sister's now and we still have her Squishmallows." I had been wracking my brain for a reason to go talk to Kara without seeming desperate or making her feel uncomfortable.

"The Gnomes aren't going to like the four of us marching up to their place and going inside with their omega there alone." Tate sat on the couch and grabbed the controller. "We should call them first."

My phone buzzed in my back pocket, and I pulled it out. "It's the vet." I'd gotten an update mid-morning that Gizmo was doing much better and once the vet checked him over, he might be able to come home. "Hello?"

"Hello, is this Alvaro Estrada?" I could hear a dog barking in the background.

"Yes, it is."

"Gizmo is all cleared to go home. He is lethargic, but that should clear up by tomorrow. You got him here fast enough that there was no damage from what we can tell. The vet will give you more instructions for his care when someone comes to pick him up."

I sighed in relief, and a heaviness that had been weighing on my shoulders lifted. "Thank you. Someone will be there soon."

"The Gizminator all better?" Cal shut the refrigerator empty-handed. He'd had the damn thing open long enough.

"He's still going to be out of it, but he can come home. Do you two want to go get him? Then you can pick up a snack. I'll go take the Squishmallows to Kara and feel her out." If we all went down there, it would attract way too much attention and piss off Kayla's pack.

Cal's lips pressed together in a tight line. "I'm not a fool, you know."

"Her sister is there. It's not like *I'm* going to do anything." I threw my hands up, wishing I didn't have to be the bad guy all the damn time. "Can you handle going over there right now?"

"Let's go, Cal." Tate stood and stretched, looking over at me. "Maybe take Avery with you."

That was why I loved Tate; no matter how he felt

about the situation, he usually followed my lead. That was how things were supposed to be in an unbroken pack, and although things felt a little stronger today, it probably would never be as good as it was before.

Cal grumbled all the way out to the garage but didn't put up a fight or tell me to fuck off, so that was progress.

I jogged up the stairs and down the hall to the second living room that was currently set up as a gaming room. I nudged Avery's foot hanging off the side of the beanbag because he didn't even look at me. "Hey. Want to go with me to talk to Kara?"

He didn't look away from the game he was playing. "What for? We can't match with her."

I frowned and sat down next to him, causing us to knock heads. "Ow, fuck. Sorry. I don't sit on this thing enough."

"No fucking kidding. You just killed me." He threw the controller to the side and looked over at me, a chunk of his black hair that was normally slicked back falling into his eyes. "Do you really think we're going to get the go-ahead? OPS said last time we asked that our lifestyle was not fit for an omega."

"That's what we should talk to Kara about. We need to know how she feels when she doesn't have fingers or a tongue inside her." I smirked when Avery groaned. "We did well today on our evaluation. That has to count for something."

"You go. I don't feel like it." Avery picked up his

controller and settled back into the beanbag. "Our pack might not survive this again, Alvaro."

My nose started to burn, and I blinked as tears filled my eyes. I didn't often cry, but hearing the pain in Avery's voice ripped at my heart. We were all he had since he'd cut his family out of his life.

"She's ours. If it takes us taking a break from our career or waiting, then that's what we'll do." I put my hand on his arm and he looked at me again. "Our pack isn't going anywhere."

His Adam's apple bobbed, and he nodded. "I still would rather stay here. I won't be able to control myself."

I didn't want to tell him that I was in the same boat, but one of us needed to tell her what we wanted. I just hoped she wanted the same and would be willing to wait for us.

CHAPTER TWELVE

Kara

The side eye I kept getting from my sister as I sat next to her working on a quilt was making me anxious. It didn't help that I couldn't bring myself to shower and wash off their scents.

When Jonathan had gotten a text from Kayla saying it was okay for me to go back, he and Anya had walked me home. They had been incredibly nice the few hours I was at their place. I could see why the pack had them as betas.

"So..." Kayla took a straight pin out of the pin cushion wrapped around her wrist and pinned two pieces of fabric together. "Do you want to talk about it?"

I needed to, but what if she called our parents or OPS? Kayla wasn't a traditional omega, but even she knew when there had to be boundaries, and I'd crossed them all. When it came to my safety, she'd do what she needed to protect me, just like I would for her.

"Do you still have your suppressants?" I slid the rotary cutter down the side of the acrylic ruler. It was therapeutic making quilts, and I could see why my sister was making it a career.

The only career trajectory I had was being an omega.

"I do. Why?" She grabbed the piece of fabric I'd just cut so she could pin it to another. "Where are yours?"

"Consumed by N'Pact's dog." I bit my lip, hoping the dog was all right. I didn't even have any of the guys' phone numbers to text them and make sure. "Can I get their phone numbers?"

Kayla turned in her chair, tucking a leg under her. "Kara. What happened? You smell like them... and not in the 'passing by them' kind of way. In the 'you were *really* close to them' kind of way. Did they..."

"No! God, no." I put the cutter down and sat the same way as her, so we were facing each other. "Their scents... I just... out of all the packs I've met, my soul responds to them."

She raised an eyebrow, her frown turning up a little. "Your pussy is not your soul."

I shook my head. "I know it sounds weird, but I just... I know they're my pack."

"They just had a massive party a week or so ago and the cops were called. They are nice guys and all, but their life right now is nuts." Of all people to be concerned about that, I never expected Kayla.

"They can't have an omega." I fiddled with the hem of my shirt. "But I can't just ignore what I feel."

"Did they knot you?" Kayla reached for my hand, and I let her take it. "Because if they did, we need to report them."

"We didn't do that, but I would let them without question." I pulled my hand away and stood. "I thought you would be more understanding about this."

She followed me out of her sewing room, which was right next to her nesting room. I held my breath as I passed the closed door. It did nothing to stop the scents inside from seeping into the hall.

"I do understand, but I don't know them *that* well. Why can't they have an omega? And why are you suddenly just... being impulsive and ignoring everything we've been taught and told?" She wasn't wrong in her assessment of current Kara.

I got to the bottom of the stairs and turned toward her, making her stop a few steps from the bottom. "Because what we've been taught and told are lies."

"So, it's not true that when unbonded alphas are around an unbonded omega they will try to claim you as theirs?" She put her hands on her hips, and if it wasn't for her straightened hair, I would think I was looking at old me in the mirror.

"This isn't that! Weren't *you* around them unbonded? Did they try to claim you?" I crossed my arms over my chest. I hated arguing with my sister, but I needed her to understand. Otherwise, I would be alone in this.

"They knew I was claimed. I just don't want you to get hurt or be disappointed. You barely know them. How can you be their omega if they can't do Omega Match?"

"I don't know, but I know them better than if I'd met them at a meet and greet. I've spent hours with them instead of minutes. I've experienced how they'll take care of me." My stomach twisted into a knot, and I let my hands fall to my sides, my shoulders slumping. "I know I need to protect myself, but just thinking about them and smelling them on me..."

"Then go take a shower and change out of those clothes. I'll get you my heat suppressants before you send yourself into heat. That's the last thing you need, and if you are attracted to alphas and they're nearby... I really don't want you going into heat here. My pack will be home tomorrow night." Kayla scrunched her nose, and I couldn't blame her.

With both of us being omegas, it was surprising enough that we were as close as we were. Even more surprising was that she hadn't flipped out over me staying with her.

"I thought they would be gone for longer." The whole reason I'd come was because I knew they'd be out of town on a business trip.

"With the gate thing and our bond being so new, they're freaking out." She shook her head in annoyance. "I needed to see what it was like being bonded and being away from them. None of us are ready to let any betas close to us, so this is how it has to be."

She shuddered, and I put a comforting hand on her arm. She'd been through a hell of a lot in the past month, and I was surprised her pack had let her stay by herself, even if she was locked inside.

I'd go with N'Pact wherever they went. I was certain of that.

AFTER A SHOWER AND A LENGTHY NAP, I felt like I could finally think clearly. There had to be a workaround for Omega Match, or at least a way for me to convince them to let the pack take part.

I didn't know what the assessment they were doing entailed, but they hadn't been at all feral toward me. Yes, there had been moments where none of us could hold back, but that was a natural reaction when anyone was attracted to someone, not just alphas and omegas.

Mid-afternoon, Kayla and I put on a movie and had just dug into a bowl of popcorn when the front gate buzzed. We looked at each other before we both jumped up at the same time and ran to the intercom that showed video.

"It's Alvaro… and he has Jane and Princess." My thighs squeezed together as my core did a happy little dance that it should not have been doing. "Let him through."

"We don't even know why he's here. He could be holding them hostage." Kayla pressed a button with a speaker on it. "We didn't order anything. Go away."

I pulled her away and pushed the button. "She's joking. She's going to let you through. Hold on."

I thought Kayla was going to fight me on it and I threw my arms around her as she pushed a button and the gate opened. I was a little bummed it was just one of them, but one was better than none.

"I'm not leaving you alone with him." Kayla went to the door and opened it. "I feel like we've done a twin swap and now I'm the perfect one and you're the one that's getting mayonnaise all over your sweater."

"Maybe we've both always been the ones to get mayonnaise on our sweaters, but I'm better at hiding it."

Since the day I hadn't matched, exhaustion had taken hold of me. It wasn't easy trying to do everything right all the time day in and day out.

That had been my life.

Alvaro came up the stairs from the driveway and I barely suppressed a squeal of joy as I skipped outside like a kid on Christmas morning discovering Santa had visited. He grinned, dimples appearing in his cheeks where I hadn't seen them before, at least not in person.

I could feel the burn of Kayla's eyes as I threw my arms around Alvaro's neck and kissed him. His chest rumbled in a barely audible growl, and he dropped my Squishmallows to wrap his arms around me.

His lips were so soft and moved against mine with a skill and need that made my knees weak. I didn't know if his intention was to come over and tempt me, but he was, and if my sister wasn't shooting daggers at my back, I would have stripped naked right then and there.

Kayla coughed loudly, and Alvaro and I broke the kiss but didn't move away from each other. "Time to go before any bones are jumped or knots are formed." She walked to us and picked up my Squishmallows.

I put my forehead against Alvaro's chest and readied my Squishmallow voice. "Oh, no. Kayla has turned into such a mom! Jane, remember that one time she ran down the hall in the dorms in her bra and panties, dildo raised shaking in the air and yelled she was queen of the schlong?"

Kayla groaned and Alvaro's chest shook with laughter. I smiled, loving the sound of his laugh. It was deep but had a musical quality to it.

"I sure do, Princess! And there was that time in Advanced Pack Management she did a presentation applying the theories to managing a sanitation facility instead."

"All right, all right. That's enough or I'm taking Princess and Jane to my quilting room." Kayla whacked me on the back with one. "Don't make me regret leaving you alone. Here."

I lifted my head and turned around, only to be hit in the face with one. "Hey!"

She dropped them both and ran into the house, shutting the door behind her. At least my sister hadn't completely lost her carefree attitude.

I bent down, picked up the stuffed animals, and heard a growl from behind me as I stood up.

"Don't do that," Alvaro said through clenched teeth. "You just presented your ass to me."

My cheeks flushed, but I wasn't about to apologize. "You're here alone. Where's everyone else?" There was a planter box off to the side of the door and I went to it, sitting down on the edge.

Alvaro peeked out between his fingers and then joined me. "Cal and Tate went to pick up Gizmo. He's going to be fine but will be lethargic for a few days. We got him to them in enough time, thanks to you."

I hugged the squishes in my lap and folded over to rest my cheek on them while looking at him. "Thanks to me he was in that predicament to begin with."

He reached over and cupped my face, putting me at ease. "He's going to be okay. That's all that matters."

I shut my eyes, and he moved his thumb back and forth across my cheek. "Where's Avery?"

He grunted, and I looked to find him staring off into space, his frown making a small sliver of doubt creep in. Did Avery decide I wasn't worth the trouble? Did they all? Was that why only the leader of the pack was here to break the news?

"When we formed our pack during college, Avery was in a rough place. It's his story to tell, but the rest of us helped him heal and we started talking about the future and having an omega and a family." He looked over at me. "That was ripped away from him and it opened a lot of old wounds for him. If last night was any indication, he does want you, just like we all do, but letting that hope take hold and it not happening will break him completely."

A tear fell and he wiped it away. "You want me?"

He sighed and put his forearms on his legs, staring at his hands. "We do, but we don't know if they will let us do the fall match. We did better on our assessment, but they won't tell us our results until later today."

"We won't use Omega Match. We can just bond and-"

"I'm not going to risk that, Kara. We don't even know what they'll do. They could take you from us or throw us in prison." He stabbed his fingers into his disheveled hair.

"They wouldn't break a bond."

"If it's newly formed, they'd do it. We'd all be in the hospital for a bit, but... no. We aren't going to risk it. I understand completely if you don't want to wait for us, but you deserve more than a rushed bond because we-"

I dropped to my knees and took his face in my

hands, barely able to see through my tears. "I'll wait for you as long as you need me to."

His hands covered mine and our foreheads pressed together. "You barely know us. We'd understand completely."

"I know you better than I would meeting some pack for five minutes of a meet and greet. I feel safe with you… like I've found my home." It was so hard to explain how it felt. For some alphas and omegas, it took longer, but some got lucky and knew right away. "Unless your pack isn't sure."

"We're sure." He sat up and pulled me into his lap, burying his face in my neck. "We're so sure and it hurts that we can't have you right now."

I thought not matching was the worst feeling in the world, but the ache in my chest knowing I couldn't stay with them was so much worse. "There has to be a way…"

"I will try everything in my power to see if there is. We have our tour coming up in a few weeks. At the very least, we have to do that. A lot of people's jobs depend on that tour…" Alvaro's voice shook, and he sounded so lost and conflicted. "Maybe taking time off and extending our contract to make up that time would be enough to satisfy the record label and OPS."

His lips brushed along my neck, and he ran his hands over my body as if he was memorizing my curves. He was saying goodbye, but I wasn't ready to let him go.

"Stay, just for a little while longer," I whispered, my own hands moving along his neck and back.

The longer I was around him or any of them, the harder this was going to be. I knew that. Every single part of me yearned for them and what could be, what would be.

One day.

CHAPTER THIRTEEN

Kara

For three long and torturous months, Alvaro, Tate, Avery, and Cal consumed my every thought from the moment I woke up to the moment I went to bed.

Then there were the dreams.

I often woke up panting with slick coating my thighs. The dreams left me so hot and bothered I masturbated every morning and sometimes in the middle of the night. My brain was in a haze of want, and despite letting my heat come full blast over the summer, I felt like I was always on the cusp of another, even on my suppressants.

After my conversation with Alvaro, I'd left to return

to the compound the next day, since Kayla's pack would be coming back. She hadn't wanted me to drive, but I couldn't just leave Ella's car in Los Angeles, and I needed the time to think.

I'd called Ella on my drive and confessed to my crime, leaving out that I'd found a pack. She was disappointed but didn't seem angry. In fact, the day I was set to return, she used her dean of students pull to get me back into the compound without much fanfare.

The Estrada pack had done well on their assessment, but because of the sudden change in their results, the Pack Health Organization wanted to assess them again in the new year before recommending that Omega Protective Services allow them to participate in Omega Match again.

I didn't think I could make it until spring without them.

My phone buzzed with a message as I sat in my office at the academy, waiting for an omega to show up to discuss her failing a test. I was filling in for a bonded omega who was out on maternity leave, and I had to admit, I loved teaching, and it kept my mind occupied throughout the day.

> Tate: We have a surprise for you.

> Me: It's not a pallet of Squishmallows, is it? Jane and Princess were not happy with the sudden influx of cuddlers on the bed.

> Cal: It wasn't a pallet... it was a very large box.

> Me: It came on a pallet, and they removed it with a forklift. I had to tell everyone I accidentally ordered one pallet instead of just one, and then when they offered to take them off my hands, I told them no and looked like I was a crazy Squishmallow lady.

> Alvaro: You are a crazy Squishmallow lady, though.

> Me: I'll remember that.

> Alvaro: I look forward to it.

> Avery: Can we not start down this path... we have a show tonight and our dancing sucks when we have boners.

> Me: Spoilsport. I can't wait to see you guys perform tonight.

I bit my lip and swiveled around to look out the window. If I thought about how close I was going to be to them, I would burst into tears like I had every time I had over the past week.

We talked nearly every day by text messages and occasionally on the phone and video chat. We'd discovered quickly that hearing and seeing each other was not the best idea. It made us all irritable, and with them being in the public eye, that was the last thing we needed.

> Avery: One of us has to be the voice of reason.

> Alvaro: Says the alpha who has pictures of her plastered all over his bunk, including a large one on the ceiling.

> Tate: We all have pictures of her...

> Me: Go on. This is great for my ego.

> Cal: Avery's is stalker level, though. Sometimes I'll lie in there and...

> Avery: Don't finish that sentence. Time to sage my bunk to get out the spunk.

> Me: Sounds like your next hit single. Spunk In The Bunk.

> Alvaro: Gross. We are being called for sound check. Want to know the surprise or actually be surprised?

> Cal: Tate just had to open his big mouth, didn't he? I vote for a surprise.

> Me: I like your surprises, so I don't think you should tell me. Just knowing there's a surprise will help me make it through the rest of today.

There was a knock at my door, and I quickly

swiveled around and put my phone screen down on my desk. "Come in."

It wasn't long ago I was a student, so it felt a bit weird speaking to other omegas that I once passed in the halls or sat next to in the dining room as an authority figure.

Blair Connor walked in, not even looking the slightest bit concerned about why I had scheduled a meeting with her. The academy had only been in session a few weeks and she was already failing Advanced Pack Conflict Resolution. From what I saw in her file, this had been an issue since she started at Elite Omega Academy and now she was in her final year.

"Have a seat." I pulled up her test results on my laptop and moved it so we could both look at it. "How are you doing this afternoon?"

With a heavy sigh, she flopped down in a chair across from me and dropped her bag dramatically on the seat next to her. "Can we make this quick?"

In a way, she reminded me of how Kayla used to be, but a little more extreme. "Well, that's up to you. I wanted to go over the test questions with you and make sure you understand the material. This year is a very import-"

"Important year, blah blah blah." She scooted the chair, so her knees were against the front of the desk and put her elbows on the top. She tucked her pink hair behind her ears and rested her fists on her cheeks. "Let's just go over the questions."

I clicked on the first one to bring up her response. The first unit had been short, and I'd given the same short answer test the regular instructor did. Out of the hundred omegas I had in my five classes, Blair had scored the lowest.

"Do you have your notes with you?" I wanted to try to figure out why she had the lowest percentage in all of her classes over the years, even if they were just general education. She was barely passing, and there had to be a way to improve her scores.

She huffed and grabbed her bag, pulling out a spiral notebook and opening it to a page full of intricately drawn squiggles. "Before you try to lecture me on how to take notes, I know how, and I don't need them."

"I think with just a little note taking, it will help with studying for exams. With the match at the end of the school year, you'll want to have your grades be as high as possible to appeal to packs." I was trying to put things as gently as possible. Packs might be enamored with her at first, but once they saw her poor academic record, they might change their minds.

She sat back in the chair, crossing her arms over her chest. "How did all of your perfect little grades work out for you? It's not worth the time or effort."

Ouch.

I sat up straighter and decided not to respond to her jab. If I'd learned anything in my life, it was that those that hurt others usually were hurting themselves. It wasn't an excuse, but reacting would give her satisfaction.

"We are given one chance to choose how to spend our time and efforts. I know you can do better than answering a question about conflict resolution with 'kick them in the balls and lock them out of the nest.' You have to at least have them please you first." I had to admit, I did laugh when I read her answers on the test.

The tiniest of smiles peeked through but fell as quickly as it appeared. "What would you do if all of your choices were taken away from you?"

"Aren't they already?" Even I wasn't brainwashed enough to see that omegas were left with very few choices besides the list of packs they got to put on their match applications.

"You have the choice of packs. You might not have matched, but you chose the packs, and they chose you. When you finally do have a pack, you'll get to choose if you work, your heat schedule, if you want children." She looked past me and out the window. "I don't get those choices."

"Are you in trouble, Blair?" I asked softly.

She shrugged, and the shield was back over her emotions. "There are few things I can control, but while I'm here, I can control the color of my hair, how I dress, and the grades I get. None of it will matter when spring match rolls around and decisions have already been made for you."

"Are you trying to say that someone is going to

decide what pack you match with for you?" My heart beat a little faster. It was illegal to tamper with match results or force a match decision against an omega's will.

"My whole life has been decided for me, Kara." She stood, grabbing her notebook and shoving it into her bag. "Just... let me have my time to rebel before I'm forced back into my cage."

"You can go to OPS. They'll-"

"Fuck." She put both her hands on the desk and leaned forward, causing me to lean back. Her cheeks were tinged pink, and her brown eyes were wide. "You can't say a word. It's not just about me. Promise me, please."

"Are you going to be in danger, though?" I couldn't promise anything when she looked like she either was about ready to burst into tears or wring my neck.

"No more danger than anyone doing Omega Match." She stood up and put the strap of her bag over her shoulder. "I shouldn't have vented to you. I'm sorry."

"I just want to make sure you're safe." I opened the top drawer of the desk and pulled out an OPS card, sliding it across to her. "Just in case you need it."

She took it and shoved it in the side pouch of her bag. "Thank you. And don't worry about my grades, seriously. Your teaching is great, I just... want to give my dads the middle finger."

Families could be complicated, especially ones with packs. My parents were a pack of six alphas, and I didn't know how my omega mom handled them. They were overprotective but not too overbearing. Kayla and I had been lucky.

"Anytime you need to talk, I'm here," I added as she walked to the door and opened it. "Are you going to the N'Pact concert?"

She looked back over her shoulder, her smile a little shocking since she was upset just a second ago. "Wouldn't miss it for the world."

CHAPERONING fifty omegas to a boyband concert was almost as crazy as me stealing Ella's car and driving to Los Angeles. Omegas in their senior year had a lot of activities they got to do, including attending events nearby.

Now that I was on the other end of the outing, I didn't know how the academy could handle the stress. There were at least ten bodyguards in our group, with more being provided by the stadium.

I was well acquainted with the stadium since it was where my sister met her pack back in the spring. She hadn't known they'd be her pack at the time, and the memory of her telling the head of her pack they had shrimp dicks brought a smile to my face.

For the concert, we had two connecting luxury suites which comfortably fit all of us and the staff needed to protect the unbonded omegas. My job was just to make sure no one did anything stupid, which was funny considering everything I'd done in the past several months.

Ella came and sat next to me at the back of the rows of seats. "Finally, I get to relax. Let me tell you... I've had a week from hell finding my replacement."

"Don't remind me you're leaving me all alone." I was a little surprised Ella hadn't come back from visiting her parents until school started. She was from a small town where there were no unbonded alphas, so she'd been allowed by OPS to stay there unaccompanied.

Plus, she was Ella Monroe. She wasn't the youngest dean of students in the entire omega academy system for nothing.

"You handled all that and did a kick-ass job arranging for us to attend this." I clasped my hands in my lap, my stomach twisting at seeing my alphas in person, even if it was from far away.

"You've been quiet since we got on the bus." She put her hand on my arm. "Are you feeling all right? You're a little flushed."

"I'm just trying to control my excitement." I flashed her a smile, even though I felt like crying.

They were going to be so close, yet I wasn't going to have the chance to feel their warmth, inhale their scents, or have them wrap me in their arms.

Ella leaned in closer so only I could hear. "We haven't announced it yet, but N'Pact is going to come up here for a meet and greet after the show. Not sure if they're doing fall or spring match."

I think my heart stopped.

I didn't have a chance to even respond or ask any questions because the entire stadium erupted in screams and cheers and the lights lowered.

Ella stood, along with the rest of the omegas in our box, but my legs wouldn't work.

Was this their surprise? I wanted to see them so badly, but around all the other omegas? What if they thought someone else smelled more appealing? It was unlikely they would be able to pick out individual scents with all of us on blockers and de-scenter pumping through the vents, but what if?

The first beats of their song dropped, and I finally sucked in a breath. I hadn't even realized I'd not been breathing. I needed to see them. Just one glance and then I'd need to go sit in the suite. My heart couldn't handle watching them perform and knowing they were going to be around so many unbonded omegas.

I rose, and it was like everyone else disappeared. There they were, running onto the stage, the lights focusing only on them as their backup band began playing their first song.

A shiver went down my spine as Cal sang his first note. But the shiver didn't stop. It wrapped around my stomach and settled in my core, quickly turning into an ache.

My eyes widened, and I quickly scooted past Ella and went into the suite. I heard her say my name, but she didn't follow, needing to stay and help supervise.

I burst into the bathroom that connected the two suites and, luckily, found it empty.

"No, no, no." I went to the sink and looked in the mirror. My pupils were dilated more than I'd ever seen them, even when I went off suppressants to have a full-blown heat.

My eyes had started feeling sensitive right after my meeting with Blair, but I had just thought I was tired. I wasn't due for a heat for another month, and it wouldn't hit so suddenly.

I gasped as cramps nearly made me fall to my knees and a gush of slick coated my panties. I whimpered, turning on the cold water and splashing my face.

This couldn't be happening. Not to me. Not right now in a stadium with who knew how many unbonded alphas.

Breakthrough heats happened, but not like this. This already hurt more than when I'd had my full-blown one.

I turned off the water and waddled to the paper towel dispenser. Slick was already seeping through my panties. Luckily, I'd worn dark jeans. My scent was thick in the air, and I knew this was going to be a disaster.

The door opened and Blair walked in. "What in the fuck?" She shut the door quickly and flipped the lock before running across the bathroom to lock the other one. "Why the hell did you come if you were about to start your heat?"

I dried my face and gave her a helpless look as I

waddled to the largest stall, locking myself in. "I wasn't. Thank you for locking the doors."

"What's your plan here? Is there protocol for something like this? Jesus, girl. You're releasing perfume like you are trying to summon every alpha in a ten-mile radius." She went into the stall next to me. "Please tell me you aren't about to finger yourself in there."

I choked on a laugh and a sob as I wiped the slick from between my legs and from on my panties. "No. I'm cleaning myself up. I think… seeing them set me off."

Blair flushed the toilet and exited her stall. "Seeing who?"

I folded up toilet paper and placed it in my underwear before pulling them up. "Uh… a pack I met."

She watched me in the mirror as I came out of the stall and joined her at the sinks. "Well, if they cause that big a reaction… match with them, girl."

I wished I could tell her all about N'Pact, but that would have put our plan to match in the spring in danger. "I need help getting out of here. Can you help me?"

My mind was already starting to think of nothing but being knotted by the four men currently singing and dancing their hearts out on stage. I didn't care that I was a homing beacon for alphas. I needed them. My body needed them.

"What do you mean? Like escape? That is the dumbest thing I've ever heard. Do you want to send all the alphas here into a rut?" She dried her hands and then handed me dry paper towels. "Let me get Dean Monroe."

"No! Just... there can't be that many unbonded alphas here. It's a boyband concert. I'll go out the emergency exit by the elevator we came up." We'd come in up a service elevator down the hall and there was a stairwell right next to it that led down to the ground level. "The buses are right outside."

She sighed. "And if the bus drivers aren't there?"

"They will be. Our buses can't be left unattended. Now, are you going to help me or not?" I gave her a pleading look. "I'm helping you by keeping my mouth shut about what you told me."

I wasn't proud of the low blow, but I was really starting to hurt, and if I didn't get out of there right away, I was going to need to be carried.

She put her hands on her hips. "You're really going to stand there starting your heat and blackmail me?"

"Not blackmail," I gritted out, doubling over as a cramp took hold. "Omega helping an omega."

"This is so stupid. You need security to-"

I lunged for her as she turned to go to the door, grabbing her arm. "Please, Blair. I don't want anyone to know."

Ella wasn't stupid. She knew N'Pact lived down the street from my sister, and although I hadn't said a word about it, she would connect the dots that they were who brought on my sudden heat. I couldn't have her questioning why.

"Your scent is so strong." She crinkled her nose. "I can probably create a big enough distraction that you can be out the door before they notice the room suddenly smells like burnt chocolate."

I didn't think I smelled like that, but I was a bad judge of my own scent at that moment. My vision was starting to swim, and my legs were shaking so badly that I hoped I didn't collapse in the hallway.

"Let's do it."

CHAPTER FOURTEEN

Kara

As I held onto the railing in the stairwell with white-knuckle force, I started to question my sanity. This was even stupider than when I decided to go for a thousand-mile joyride, or when I darted through N'Pact's open gate. Those were risky decisions, but this? This was a pure lack of common sense.

My brain didn't care, though, now that my base instincts had set it. My goal was to get away from the people, the scents, the *noise*. The noise of the concert was so grating on my nerves that I wanted to curl up in a corner of the stairwell and cry.

Almost there.

The last few months I'd been working out since returning to the compound, but my lungs did not appreciate descending stairs while trying not to fall down them. I should have just risked taking the service elevator.

I was finally on the last flight of stairs and nearly cried in relief. Things would be better outside with the breeze and the cool air. It was more difficult to smell a perfuming omega in wide open spaces with a nice breeze blowing around the scent molecules.

The first thing I was going to do when this heat was finished was file a complaint about the heat suppressants and perfume blockers. They weren't a hundred percent effective, but everyone acted like they were.

I reached the bottom and sat down on the steps to catch my breath. The door said an alarm would sound if it was opened. Shit. Fuck. Shit.

I felt my phone vibrating in my purse and pulled it out. Kayla was calling, and I answered with a sob. "Kayla... I'm scared."

"My twin radar was going off," she said softly. "What's wrong? I told you it would be a bad idea to go to that concert."

There was male laughter in the background, and that made me cry harder. "I know, and they're doing a meet and greet after with all the omegas. I saw them and my entire body went haywire, and now I'm starting a heat and it's bad. So bad, and I'm trying to escape to the bus and the door says the alarm will sound." I sucked in air after finishing my ramble.

"Holy knot on a cracker... you're alone? Kara, that's so dangerous!" The room she was in went silent. "You need to get yourself to that bus, even if that means setting the alarm off."

"But-"

"Kara Marie, get your ass up right now." Her voice was so stern it shocked my sobs into silence. "Is there a door that doesn't set off the alarm?"

I hiccupped. "Yes."

"Go peek out of it and tell me what you see." I grabbed onto the railing and pulled myself up on shaky legs to go to the door. It opened with a small squeak and looked out into the hallway. "It's clear. We came in this way but went up the service elevator."

"Okay, so is there a door or something you entered through? Did that have an alarm?" She was making so much sense. I was so grateful that she knew my mind wasn't all there and I needed to be told what to do.

"No, I don't think so. It was where they unload the food." I tried sniffing through the cracked open door, but my nose was stuffy from crying. "I can't smell if there are any alphas."

"It won't matter. You're going to open that door and walk as quickly as possible to the door you entered through. Right now."

I wiped my eyes with the back of my hand and crept out into the hallway, looking in both directions and not knowing which one to go in. "I'm not sure which way."

"Pick a way, and if you don't find the exit in a minute, then go back the other way."

I shook my head at how ridiculous it was that I couldn't think of something that simple. The brain fog hadn't been this bad when I'd last had my heat. "Don't hang up, okay?"

"I won't. Just focus on getting out of the building." Her voice shook ever so slightly, and my tears were back again.

My first choice of direction was correct, and I kept my head down as I passed by betas working to move pallets on forklifts. I could see the green exit sign and picked up my pace, shoving the door open as soon as I got to it.

I breathed in the fresh air and sagged against the wall next to the door. There was a small walkway that opened up into the parking lot, but I didn't know if the buses had moved and if I'd have to hunt for them. I just needed a moment to regroup.

"Kara? Are you outside? Don't stop now. Alphas can be anywhere, and you just left a scent trail, right?"

She was right. I had to keep moving because even if I encountered one alpha, I didn't have the strength to fight him off if he was unbonded.

"I need them, Kayla." I panted as I stumbled the short distance to the end of the walkway so I could look out into the parking lot. "The buses are too far."

I could see the two vehicles on the other side of an area of cars. My legs were barely working now and the pain between my legs and in my lower abdomen was so intense little black dots swam at the edge of my vision.

"My pack can call the stadium and see if someone can come out and find you or-"

"No!" The last thing I wanted was for a search party to come after me and find me a blubbering mess on the ground. "Just give me a second and..."

My thoughts left me as I spotted someone with a black hoodie covering their hair, a dog pulling them along. Sweet baby alpha, it was Anya.

"Kara? What is it? Are you okay?"

"It's... Anya!" I yelled Anya's name and my sister squealed. "Kayla, it's Anya with Gizmo! She can take me to their bus. They have a tour bus. I can wait there for them to take care of me."

"That's a bad idea for so many reasons." Kayla sighed. "Is she coming to help you?"

Anya was headed toward me, practically running to keep up with Gizmo. They had been near a patch of grass between the lot I was in and the next lot over.

"Yes. Thank you, Kayla. I love you." I didn't know what I would do without my sister. She had more than made up for the countless times I'd saved her ass over the years.

"I love you too. Please be careful. Don't let them bite you." I disconnected the call before she could say more.

My decision was already made. I needed my pack,

and maybe we weren't official yet, but that was the least of my worries.

"Kara, what the hell are you... oh, shit." Anya had her phone out of her pocket and to her ear before I could even express how grateful I was to see her.

"Wait." I lowered to my knees, unable to stand anymore. "They're performing."

Gizmo reached me first, sniffing the air and then butting his head against my chest. I wrapped my arms around him, letting him support some of my weight. He knew me, and my heart felt so full it could have burst. Instead, my eyes did, and I sobbed into his fur.

"Jon? We have a situation. I just found Kara in the parking lot in heat. What should I do?" She was quiet, and I could hear Jonathan's deep voice giving her instructions. "And we're certain that's what they would want? Like, one hundred percent?"

What would they want? Me? How could she even ask that when she'd been on a tour bus with them for the past several months? Didn't she know? She was a part of the damn pack.

"I know, but they've been doing really well, and this..." She looked down at me and bit her lip. "They're not going to let her go after this. This could cost them everything."

That was the last thing I wanted, and I used the brick wall beside me to push to my feet. "I'll just go."

My legs weighed at least five hundred pounds each

as I started dragging them toward the buses. One foot in front of the other, that was how I'd make it.

"Kara!" Anya caught up to me—not that she had far to go to do so—and wrapped her arm around my shoulders. "Let's go to the tour bus."

I was comforted by her touch, even though her half of the conversation left me with a bitter taste in my mouth. "I'll ruin everything."

She let me go briefly to take the phone out from between her shoulder and ear. "They were a mess when you went through your heat without them. We almost had to cancel a few shows. Pack Health has been doing regular check-ins with them, and luckily, they hadn't dropped in then."

I let her steer me toward the grassy area and the other parking lot. "They didn't tell me that."

"Of course they didn't. They didn't want to worry you. They at least have each other to get through it all. Jonathan will tell them what's going on after the meet and greet, and they can decide what they want to do. He thinks if they back out of the meet and greet it will get back to Pack Health and they'll start asking questions as to why."

We walked in silence the short walk to the other lot, where semi-trucks, buses, and a few cars were parked. She lifted her hand and waved to a security guard who was patrolling by an exit.

I finally found the energy to form a complete thought as we walked between two buses and stopped outside the door of one. "This is bad, Anya. Really bad. They set off my heat the second I saw them on that stage."

"I can't say I'm surprised." She took a key out of her pocket and opened the door.

Their scents hit me so hard I stumbled forward, nearly taking Anya to the ground as I crawled up the stairs and into the bus. Gizmo barked, running in behind me and jumping onto the couch that was behind the driver's seat.

I rolled onto my side, curling my knees up to my chest as another cramp tore through me. It felt like my entire lower body was being ripped in half. I needed relief before I passed out from the pain.

"Let's get you to the back room. They have it set up as another living area, but I'll move some of that shit out here and get their bunk mattresses in there." Anya grabbed me under my arm and helped me stand. "Try not to breathe in their scents until we get you all situated. It's not an ideal nesting situation, but it will have to do for now. How long do your heats usually last? Did you not have any preheat warning signs?"

"Too many questions." She was making my head hurt.

There hadn't been any signs besides being tired and feeling a little warm all day. I thought it was just because it had been a long week. If it had been more than a day, I would have picked up on the signs.

The tour bus was bigger than I expected, even

though I'd seen video and pictures of it. The pack, Anya, Jonathan, and Gizmo stayed on this bus while the backup band and other tour staff stayed on the other buses. Then there were seventy-five semi-trucks with all of the staging, costumes, and whatever else there was. It was excessive, but their stadium concerts were sold-out events with tens of thousands of people.

We passed through a living room area and into a small kitchen area that had necessities but wasn't meant to be used as a full-service kitchen. There was dim night-time lighting on, which was a relief because I couldn't handle any more lights.

We next came to the bathroom before Anya pushed open a pocket door to a bunk area with eight bunks. I whimpered, unable to completely block out the scents coming from them. If they decided they didn't want to be with me during my heat, I didn't know what I was going to do. I'd probably need to go to the hospital.

Anya slid open another door and flipped a switch which turned on tiny ceiling lights that looked like twinkling stars. I liked that and knew the room would be suitable for a nest. It wouldn't be perfect, but beggars couldn't be choosers.

I fell onto the couch, grabbing a pillow and inhaling the scents on it. My jeans were soaked through, and I rubbed my thighs together, needing relief.

"If you can wait until I get you set up in here..." Anya turned on a small fan and pointed it at me. "That couch folds out into a bed too, but I don't know if it's strong enough for whatever you might get up to."

"Hopefully, I'll be getting up to something," I muttered into the pillow.

She put her hand on my forehead, checking to see how hot I was. "I'm sorry if I hurt your feelings, but Jon and I care deeply for them. We just don't want them to hurt anymore, and they've been doing everything they can to push being in the fall match."

I looked up at her, surprised. "They are?" My excitement was in my voice, even if it was strained. "Do you think it's a possibility?"

"I think it is. After the tour ends, there's a two-month break before they head back to the studio. The match is right at the end of their break, so they've been talking to management about starting the recording right after the tour and shifting their time off. Well, if the powers that be let them do it."

"None of this is fair." I sat up and took off my purse. "I'm friends with the dean of students. I might be able to convince her not to report that I'm missing."

"But what about everyone else?" She dragged one of the two gaming chair rockers toward the door. There was a recliner as well, but I didn't think that would fit out the door without some help to maneuver it.

"She can say I got a ride back to the compound." I pulled a hair tie out of the front pocket of my purse and could barely lift my arms. "Can you put my hair up for me?"

"Let me get all of this extra furniture out first." She pulled the chair out of the room, and I grabbed another pillow and shoved it between my legs.

It was going to be a long few hours until the concert was over.

CHAPTER FIFTEEN

Tate

There was no greater high than finishing a concert knowing your girl was watching. It had gone so perfectly, and I could feel the excitement radiating off Alvaro and Cal as we made our way off the stage and walked toward the locker room which was acting as our dressing room.

Avery had even had a great show but was still mostly a closed book with his emotions, not letting our bond penetrate his walls most of the time. He was doing better overall but had moments where he got into his own head and couldn't get out.

One of our assistants opened the locker room door, and I entered first. Most of the stadiums we performed at had luxurious locker rooms, and this one was no different. There were areas for each athlete to store their gear, a large seating area with couches facing a screen, and lounge areas.

"Fuck, yes!" Cal threw the empty water bottle he'd guzzled across the large room as he entered after me. "The energy of that crowd was fucking spectacular!"

I collapsed onto the leather couch and snatched a water bottle off the side table. "I think we all know why we performed so well tonight."

"I could feel her watching us. It was incredible." Cal was always hyper as fuck after shows, but he was practically vibrating with unspent energy.

"Great show, guys!" Jonathan came into the room after Alvaro and shut the door behind him, the noise in the hallway dulling. "Let's get a move on. We have the meet and greet, and you four are swimming in your own pheromones."

"We literally just got off stage. Give us a few, man." Avery opened the mini fridge brought in for us and pulled out a protein shake. "It takes us five minutes to shower and change."

It was true. We had the quick showers down to an art. We usually had a little more time to unwind, but with fifty omegas and Kara waiting for us, the schedule was tight.

God, I couldn't wait to see her. I hoped she wouldn't be upset with our surprise. We had planned on telling her so she could be prepared, but that plan fell apart quickly.

Alvaro glanced my way, sensing my sudden uncertainty. "Don't." He went to the mini-fridge and grabbed two energy drinks, tossing one my way. "It's going to be great. She probably already knows and has a little bit of time to prepare."

Avery stared into the small opening of his protein drink. "I think I'm going to have to skip the meet and greet."

Jonathan made a noise of disagreement. "I think you all need to stay together. What if agents show up and wonder why you're avoiding the omegas?"

There was something off with Jonathan, but I couldn't quite figure out what. There was a hesitation to his usually sure voice. "The agents just visited us a few days ago. They wouldn't come again so soon."

"This will be your first time around this many omegas in a long time. A lot is riding on this. You've all said so yourselves. This will prove that you're ready to do the fall match instead of the spring one." Jonathan clenched his jaw like he was holding something back from us.

Alvaro took a sip of his drink, his eyes narrowing on Jonathan. "What's wrong?"

"Nothing's wrong, Alpha. Just tired and want to get this meet and greet over with." He crossed his arms as he leaned against the door. "They're expecting us in fifteen minutes."

Cal, who had been skipping around the room, fell onto the couch next to me. "Are you worried about how we're going to be around Kara?"

Jonathan grunted and pulled out his phone. "It's complicated. Don't worry about it right now. Worry about showering and getting dressed so we can get going."

"Where's Anya?" Alvaro walked toward Jonathan, and he straightened, clicking his phone off and shoving it in his back pocket.

"She's on the bus. Didn't feel good." Jonathan flinched as Alvaro grabbed him by the front of his shirt. "Alpha..."

The room fell silent except for the noise out in the hall and the whir of the air conditioner. He wasn't telling us something. Although none of us had a connection like we had with each other, Alvaro could pick up on negative emotions from him from time to time if he focused.

Jonathan and Anya were in our pack but were more like an extension of it and not smack dab in the central bond. They couldn't pick up any emotions from us.

Alvaro didn't say anything to Jonathan because he didn't need to; his dominating presence was enough. Jonathan's eyes dropped to the ground, and he remained silent, which caused Alvaro to growl.

"Let's not do this right now, guys. We can discuss this later." I had no idea when because as soon as we were done with the omegas, we would be heading toward our next city on our tour, and Jonathan was the driver.

Alvaro let Jonathan go with a small shove. "Get your shit together, or you can go to the bus with Anya."

"Yes, Alpha," he muttered, smoothing out his black shirt. There was no need for Jonathan to worry so much. Since we had Kara in our lives now, our reaction to unbonded omegas was practically nonexistent.

I pushed to my feet and went to the locker area where my after-concert clothes and shower bag were laid out. During our first tour, we sometimes didn't have the luxury of showering, but now that we were pulling stadiums full of people, the locker room showers were an added benefit.

The four of us went to the showers, leaving Jonathan in the main part of the locker room. I wasn't that big a fan of communal showers after performing my ass off, but for some reason, even upgraded locker rooms stuck to no privacy.

Cal threw his stuff on a bench and stripped out of his clothes. "Have you ever wondered what the sports teams get up to in here?"

"They shower. It's an efficient way to make sure they're quick." Alvaro was the first to finish undressing and went to one of the nearest shower heads in the center. The shower was shaped like a half donut. "They have the good shampoo and soap."

Avery grunted and went to a spot along the wall.

"They probably spend thousands on it but can't afford to build at minimum half walls in here."

"Don't complain, Payney boy. You know you like checking out my ass." Cal went a few spots over from him and turned on the shower. "Fuck, that's hot."

"Cal," Alvaro warned, knowing that when Cal started taunting Avery that it would be a long night. He'd been doing well with giving Avery space lately, but with the high of the show and of seeing Kara, he was like a dog who had the zoomies.

"Sorry, sorry." Cal stepped back under his shower head as I joined Alvaro at the center of the room. "Maybe I should jack off before we go up to see Kara."

"I'm about to sew his lips shut, Tate. I swear." Alvaro rubbed shampoo in his hair.

"Please don't touch your dick in front of me," Avery growled.

"What if we got up to the suites and she was alone. That would be amazing. I'd grab her around the waist and pull her to me." Cal clearly didn't care that we were all together or that we had such a short time to shower. "She'd whimper just before I kissed her. What would you be doing, Avery?"

"Kicking your ass."

I chuckled, and Alvaro rested his forearm against the wall, putting his forehead on it as he let the water run over him. We masturbated all the time in our bunks on the bus, and back before Kara, we occasionally shared women, but this was different.

We weren't just detached, watching porn or getting off with some randoms for the night, we were all thinking about the same woman we'd kissed and wanted as our omega. A woman we'd all share for the rest of our lives.

"I'd move in behind her while you kissed her and pull her hair to the side. God, she smells so good I just want to bite her, but instead, I kiss her neck." Alvaro grabbed hold of his cock, his hand stroking it as he hardened. "It's never enough. I need to taste her like I did that day."

We all knew which day he was referring to. At least, Cal and I did. The memory of her slick on my fingers and her scent filling the room made me groan and brace my hand against the wall.

"If she was here... in this shower..." Avery panted, clearly giving into Cal's plan of all of us getting relief so that we had a lower probability of going too alpha over Kara. "I'd lift her and pin her right against the wall. Her legs would wrap around me, and I'd sink into that hot, tight pussy."

"Fuck." The pressure was already building, and I wrapped my hand around my shaft, putting my thumb right on the top so it would rub my crown with each pump. "I'd bend her over one of the benches and eat her out from behind while she sucked Alvaro's cock."

"She'd swallow my cock until I was right on the edge." Alvaro stopped speaking to catch his breath. "Then I'd sit down on the bench so she could ride me. She feels so fucking good. When she comes, I bet she squeezes our cocks so good and takes our knots like the good little omega she is."

We were all getting close. I could feel the satisfaction coming through our bond as we all took ourselves closer and closer to climax.

"And she'd beg us to bite her. 'Please alphas. Bite me. Make me yours.' Ah, fuckkkkk!" Cal cried out, setting the rest of us off.

The pressure released in a burst of pleasure that left me gasping for breath as my cum shot out of me and onto the tile wall. I squeezed my knot, heightening my pleasure and nearly causing me to thrust into the wall.

I released my dick after every drop spilled and leaned my forehead against the cool tile. "Let's not tell anyone about this."

Cal's laugh echoed through the shower. "That was hot. You know, we should do this more often instead of going at it alone in our bunks. Maybe it would improve our bond even more."

I snorted a laugh and pushed off the wall, standing back fully under the spray of water to finish showering.

If it helped get us Kara, I'd do anything.

S*he's not here.*

That was the first and only thought I had as we entered the suite and a metric shit ton of scents hit me. The de-scenter helped to an extent, but with so many omegas in a semi-confined space, it could only work so well, and I didn't detect even a hint of chocolate mixed in.

We all seemed to realize she wasn't in the room at the same time because we shot each other worried glances. I could feel it through our bond, and even though Avery's walls were up, his eyes said a lot.

There were a few squeals, and then the omegas descended on us. Our security team positioned themselves in front of us to keep them back.

"Ladies!" One of the older omegas stood on a chair and clapped her hands. "If you want them to stay, you will have to get in a civilized line. No touching them!"

I didn't know who she was, but the omegas quickly arranged themselves in a line. It was easier to see them all, but I still couldn't see Kara anywhere.

Alvaro stepped back and whispered in Jonathan's ear, and he disappeared out the door. I raised a questioning brow as he stepped back into place beside me.

He leaned in so I could hear him over the excitement in the room. "He's checking the other room. Ten minutes in this room, ten in the other." He smiled and greeted the first omega, who was holding out a Sharpie and a... bra.

Jesus.

I wanted to ask where Kara was, but then people would wonder how we knew her. We had a plausible reason, but any unwanted attention to what had transpired between us already wouldn't bode well for us.

Ten minutes felt like ten years, and then we were moved out into the hall and into another room. Jonathan was already inside, and he shook his head as we filed in. The girls in this room were a lot calmer. The woman from the chair was already here and situating them for us.

She was very calm and collected for an unbonded omega. I think I heard someone mention she was the dean, which was a feat in itself for an omega.

The first omega came to me after Alvaro signed a picture for her. "I wish all of you were here. Payne is my favorite."

"Huh?" I quickly signed my name and handed her the picture and pen back.

"Payne. He's not here." The omega looked ready to cry.

I looked to my left at Cal and saw no Payne on the other side of him or behind him. I quickly scanned the room. He was right behind me when we'd left the other room.

Shit.

CHAPTER SIXTEEN

Avery

The faintest hint of chocolate hit my nose as we exited the first suite of omegas, but it wasn't in the direction we were going. When we got to the door of the second suite, her scent was nowhere and I stopped, pretending to tie my shoe next to the door.

Where was she?

As soon as everyone was through the door, I stood and went back in the other direction. Something was off about the scent. It was unequivocally hers but more potent than I remembered. Like the chocolate had been melted.

I looked back over my shoulder before heading down the hallway, her scent getting stronger. Everyone had been so focused on the omegas they hadn't even noticed I'd ducked away. I wouldn't be alone in the hallway for long, so I quickened my pace.

Her scent was coming from the stairwell, and my stomach clenched in an odd way. It wasn't fear, but it wasn't pleasant either.

I opened the door and nearly fell to my knees from her scent but quickly shut the door behind me before breathing in deeply. Since I emerged as an alpha, I'd only smelled an omega in heat once and there was no mistaking it.

Their scents were not only amplified but had something that was like a beacon. It was an instinct that made my cock immediately stiffen.

Adjusting myself in my pants, I ran down the stairs, pulling my phone out and fumbling to unlock it. I pulled up the group text between me, the guys, and Kara.

> Me: Kara, where are you?

I got to the bottom of the stairwell and went back into the stadium, nearly running into an employee pushing an empty cart. Her scent was faint again, probably from it not being a confined space and the de-scenter that mixed with the air. Her scent was still there, though.

> Me: Where the fuck are you? You're in heat. I can smell it.

I wasn't surprised Cal, Tate, and Alvaro weren't responding yet. I'd only been gone for maybe two minutes tops.

> Kara: I'm on your bus... Anya found me.

A growl left me, causing a few workers to look in my direction. Jonathan knew. No wonder the fucker had been acting weird. Why would he keep this from us? Betas weren't affected by an omega's heat in the same way as we were.

"It's Payne! Payne! Hi!" One of the women dropped the box she was moving and headed for me. Now was not the time for fan interactions.

I ran toward the exit sign, which was right past the women, ignoring a few other shocked and excited cries from employees as I burst out into the night.

Her scent was completely gone now, thank fuck. The last thing we needed was for other alphas to smell her and try to take her from us.

I ran for the bus, my energy suddenly restored and my mind on one thing: get to my omega.

Anya was outside with Gizmo, blocking the door as I rounded the front of the bus. She was texting away on her phone and looked up as I skidded to a stop across the pavement.

"*Move*," I barked. She was keeping me from my omega when she needed me.

Anya cringed and stepped to the side, unable to

shake off the command. "Jonathan said to try to stop you."

"I'm going to rip Jonathan's throat out the next time I see him." I yanked open the door and Kara's scent walloped me again. It was just as potent as in the stairwell, but worse now because I knew she was somewhere on the bus, waiting. "The stairwell by the service elevator needs to be sprayed. Other alphas probably already scented her."

I pressed the button to automatically shut the door and headed for the back of the bus. The coffee table and two of the gaming chairs were cluttering the living room area, and despite being annoyed we hadn't been told about Kara, I was grateful Anya had been there for her.

"Kara?" I called as I opened the first sliding door into the bunk area.

I kicked off my shoes while unbuttoning and unzipping my pants. The need to be inside her hurt as I went to the next door. I hadn't even bothered to ask her in the text if she wanted us for her heat, but she was here.

She's here.

I slid the door open and groaned, grabbing my cock and pulling it free of my boxers. It was already rock hard, and my knot ached to be inside her slick pussy. Her perfume was concentrated in a way that made me dizzy.

She wasn't visible under the mound of blankets and pillows, but I knew right where she was as she moved under them. "Avery." Her whimper cut through me like a knife.

I kicked my pants and boxers off as I ripped my shirt over my head. "I'm here, sweet girl."

The room was rearranged with the couch off to the side so all the other space could be covered with our bunk mattresses. The space was a decent enough size that the four of us easily lounged around here when we had time.

One of the gaming rockers was pushed into the corner, and my eyes zeroed in on the streak of wetness on the seat. Had she sat there while she pleasured herself?

"Kara." I fell to my knees and crawled to the mound of blankets pushed up against the bottom part of the couch. "How are you in heat? What were you thinking running off by yourself?"

"You came on stage and it just... hit me." Her voice was muffled, and I grabbed a handful of blankets and pulled them away.

Omegas were usually hot during their heats, so it baffled me why she was buried under so many. How had Anya let her do this?

She finally appeared, naked and curled into a ball, her back to me. I had to clench my fists to stop myself from throwing myself on top of her. It would have been so easy to just slide right in, I knew she was slick just from her scent.

Her back was flushed and dotted with beads of

sweat, and as the cool air in the room hit her skin, her entire body broke out in goosebumps. She shuddered hard and whimpered again.

"Were you trying to suffocate yourself?" I lay down behind her and she straightened out against me, her ass brushing against my cock. "I'm here now. What do you need?"

"It was the only thing that helped. It hurts so bad." Her voice cracked, and she shuddered again. "Please, Alpha. Touch me."

I slid my hand down her hot skin to the apex of her thighs. My hand wasn't even between her legs yet and there was slick everywhere.

She opened her legs for me, and I groaned as I slid my fingers over her slit before plunging one into her heat. Her skin was feverish, and her cunt felt like an oven. It was going to feel so amazing around my cock.

"I'm going to kill Jonathan for not telling us you were in heat." I buried my face against her neck, which was free of her hair thanks to the double braids down the back of her head.

"No. Told them not to tell you." She wrapped her hand around my wrist as I moved my finger in and out. "More. I need more than just your fingers."

"If I sink into this pretty little pussy, I'm not going to be able to hold back and you're a-"

She cut me off from saying virgin with a wiggle of her ass against my dick. "I've fucked myself with plenty of dildos. I can handle whatever you're going to give me."

I pulled my finger out and moved it to her clit, teasing it in circles. It was taking every ounce of my strength not to plow into her, and maybe a few months ago if this had happened, I would have, but now I wanted this to be good for her.

"If you want my dick and my knot, I want to see you." I nipped at her neck and then pulled away, moving onto my knees. "Show me what's mine."

With a huff of frustration, she rolled onto her stomach and got on her hands and knees. "Where are the others?"

"They'll be here." Was I being a selfish asshole by taking her first? Yes, but I needed this. I needed her.

She stood on her knees, her hands falling limply at her sides, and turned toward me. "Kiss me."

My breath caught in my throat seeing her naked in front of me. Her breasts were the perfect handfuls, her rosy nipples hard and waiting for attention. The small patch of hair on her mound glistening with slick made my mouth water.

With a growl, I lunged for her, taking her lips with mine. I hadn't stopped thinking about our kiss outside the vet hospital and how close I'd been to losing my mind over the taste of her.

Her tongue ran across my lips, and I opened for her as my hands ran down her back to her ass. I dug my fingers in, eliciting a moan and a shiver from her. My cock was throbbing with an intensity I'd never experienced, and fuck...

I needed to take her.

I broke our kiss and lifted her onto the couch before standing and looking down at her. Her blue eyes were dark with her blown-out pupils and her lips were reddened from our kiss.

"Show me what's mine, Omega." I grabbed the base of my cock, just below my knot, and squeezed, hoping I didn't blow my load at the sight before me.

She leaned back, brought her legs up, and grabbed the back of her thighs. "Please."

I licked my lips, wanting to sink back to my knees and bury my face in her glistening folds. I wanted my face covered in her and her mouth screaming my name. But that wasn't what she needed right then, and there'd be time for that later. She was ready, and I'd made her wait long enough.

I leaned over her and guided my cock right into her. She cried out as I seated myself fully. The position let me get as deep as possible and my knot pulsed, nearly ready to lock us together.

"Is it okay? You still want this?" I kissed her forehead and then both of her cheeks. She let go of her thighs and her legs fell open further.

"Fuck me, Alpha."

She didn't have to tell me again. I pulled out and thrust back in, my resolve to go slow snapping in two at her command to fuck her.

"You're so perfect." I kissed her quickly, my thrusts too strong to keep lip contact for long.

"Yes, yes, yes!" Her eyes closed and she held onto my forearms, her nails digging into my skin.

Nothing had prepared me for how it would feel taking care of my omega during her heat or how good it would feel after not being with a woman for so long. It felt like our bodies were made for each other, fitting perfectly like two puzzle pieces.

I had been blocking out my pack mates, but just this once, I let down my walls completely so they could feel the pleasure and happiness I was experiencing for the first time in a long time. They should have been with me, experiencing this too.

Their worry flooded our bond, nearly overpowering my own emotions. But my heart was full, and the feelings I felt cut through. It wasn't that they could feel what I did, but it was more of a sixth sense, an internal knowing.

Mixed emotions came back at me; desire, excitement, and anger.

I had no regrets about coming to the bus knowing Kara was in heat. Alvaro had every right as head of the pack to rip me off her as soon as they got here.

I wrapped my arms around Kara, still impaled on my cock, and lifted her off the couch to lay her on the floor. My body ached to be closer to her and my chest rumbled in a satisfied purr as I settled between her legs, now able to take her tempting nipples in my mouth.

Her fingers grabbed onto my hair, and I sucked her nipple while lightly pinching the other. She moaned and pulled my head closer to her. My thrusts were deep, and after every few, her walls squeezed around me.

"Knot me, Avery, please!" She arched her back and locked her legs around me, spurring me on. "I need it! I need you!"

"So good. So, so good." I pushed in all the way, my knot filling and locking me to her. With a few more pumps, I would be done for.

"Yes!" Kara's body shook as her release built.

The door slid open, and my pack's scents flooded the room. Kara clenched so hard around me that I saw stars, the last grind of my hips sending me over the edge. Her nails dug into my back, and I reached between us, rubbing her clit.

"Come, sweet girl. Let them hear you scream." I wanted to kiss her but also didn't want to silence her.

"Avery!" She screamed as I spilled inside her, my body giving hers what it wanted.

The pressure around me was something a hand or a toy could never give. Only an omega could bring me as much pleasure and satisfaction.

She trembled as the last tremors of her orgasm rolled through her, and then relaxed completely underneath me, a satisfied smile on her face. This was what I'd yearned for, an omega of my own.

I gently lowered my body onto hers, wrapping her in my arms and rolling us until she was resting on top of me. She sighed and rested her head on my shoulder, her lips brushing my neck.

"You did so good, Kara," I whispered, trailing my fingers down her back. "Perfect."

I started to purr again, and Kara melted into me. It was an odd sensation, a slight tickle and warmth spreading throughout my body.

Alvaro cleared his throat, and I looked over at the door where he was standing... alone. Where had Cal and Tate gone?

It had been a while since I'd used our bond with each other, and I felt around for them. They were blocking me, which was deserved. I'd blocked them for so long and then hit them all with a whammy.

Alvaro wasn't blocking me, though, and my purr stuttered to a halt.

"When your knot deflates, we'll leave to a safe place where no one can hear or smell us." Just as he turned to leave, the bus rumbled to life. "And we'll talk."

He shut the door and blocked our bond. I closed my eyes and blew out a breath. I'd fucked up, I knew that, but blocking me when I'd just let them in? It made me want to close myself in my bunk.

"Shit. I didn't mean to piss them off." Now, instead of enjoying this moment with Kara, I'd be in my head, worrying.

"Why are they mad at you?" Kara traced the lines of the tattoos on my chest. "You were just doing what I wanted you to. What I needed."

"They've always worried about me, and I probably shouldn't have come to you alone." Any number of things could have happened. I could have hurt her, and they knew that. "I'm the reason we haven't been approved to have an omega."

Her fingers stopped for just a second before continuing their exploration. "That can't be true. You were in complete control."

"Barely. If I was in complete control, the second I knew you were in heat and where you were, I would have made sure they knew too. In terms of pack hierarchy, I'm the lowest." Now that my mind was a little less distracted, I was mad at myself for letting my instincts overtake my mind. "Alvaro should have had you first."

Her hand stilled over my heart. "I'm not an object, Avery. If I didn't want you, I would have told you no. I know the lead alpha usually has a say, but…"

"But you're in heat and… oh, God." I needed out of her before I did even more damage and she left us. "I took advantage of you."

She hissed in a breath as I tried unsuccessfully to move my dick from where it was nestled inside her. "Avery, calm down. It's okay. You didn't take advantage of me. If anything, I took advantage of you by coming to your bus in heat when we aren't even matched."

I lifted her chin so I could see her face. "Never say that. Do you understand? I came here because I wanted to." I shut my eyes, the fear of losing her and my pack taking root again.

There had been moments in the past few months when I started to believe everything was going to be okay. I let myself have hope, and now with this, what if they kicked me out of the pack?

Her fingers brushed over my eyelids. "You aren't going to lose me, Avery."

I hoped for all of our sakes she was right.

CHAPTER SEVENTEEN

Kara

Maybe it had been a bad idea coming to their bus.

Now that my mind was a little clearer, I could already see the pack was having issues. It was ridiculous if they were mad at Avery for following his instincts, but it probably ran deeper than that.

We didn't know what would happen if we were caught together without being matched. It couldn't be good, though.

My phone buzzed in my purse, and I wiggled my hand under the pile of blankets to find it, Avery still knotted inside of me. He'd been quiet for the past ten minutes, and I'd nearly fallen asleep.

I didn't even need to look at the screen to know it was Ella calling.

"Hi, Ella. I was just about to call you." I tried to sound normal and not like a whiney omega during heat.

"Kara," she yelled in a hushed whisper. "Where are you? Please tell me you did not run off again."

I flinched, and Avery stroked my cheek. "I can't tell you where I am, but I'm safe. Could you, um... just say I got a ride back to the compound because I wasn't feeling well if anyone asks?"

"I'm asking!" I could hear giggles and talking in the background. "We're headed out to the buses right now and you aren't here!"

Avery's knot was starting to deflate, and I wanted to whimper at how empty I already felt. I was going to need another knot pretty quickly.

"Please, Ella. You know I wouldn't put myself in harm's way." That wasn't necessarily true anymore. I was going through some kind of phase where I just didn't care about the consequences. Twenty-two years of near perfection did that to a girl.

"Who are you with?"

Avery's chest rumbled in a purr, his body reacting to my unease over the conversation with Ella. I put my finger to my lips, and he gave me a look like he couldn't help it.

"If I tell you who I'm with, will you cover for me? I'm not sure how long I'll be gone." I bit my lip and rested my cheek on Avery's chest.

"Is that purring?" If Ella wasn't in a room with others, I was sure she'd be shrieking. "Are you in heat?"

"Yes, and before you freak out, I came to them. I know them and we're going to match." I just didn't know exactly when that was going to happen.

"If OPS finds out..." She sighed heavily and the noise in the background stopped. "It's not you that will deal with the consequences, it's them."

Avery's knot was completely deflated, and I lifted off him, wincing from both the wetness and the slight tinge of pain from being without him inside me.

"Well, if I bond with them, then there's not much they can do." I grabbed a small towel from a stack of towels Anya had supplied and held it between my thighs as I stood on wobbly legs.

"They can still take you away from them. I've seen it happen and it isn't pretty. If you're going to do this, promise me you won't bond with them until you go through all the correct channels to have them be your pack... whoever they are."

I dropped my towel in the plastic storage container that was acting as a hamper. "I can't promise anything."

"Check in daily or...." She didn't say it, but I knew she was threatening to call OPS. I would have done the same if I was in her position.

"I will. Thank you. I have to go." I hung up before she could ask me any more questions and set my phone on the shelf under the mounted television. "That's one hurdle crossed."

I turned to find Avery still lying on the floor, watching me. His dick was already hard again, and I licked my lips, wanting to sink back down and never come up for air.

"I should go face the music." He sat up to my disappointment and ran his fingers through his disheveled dark hair. "I'm sorry for being a weak alpha. You deserve better."

I put my hands on my hips, vaguely aware of how I must have looked doing it naked. "Avery Payne, you knock that bullshit off right now. I want to scratch that wench's eyes out for making any of you think you aren't good alphas. You have been nothing but kind and respectful to me. But not just to me, to my sister too."

His face went from being scrunched in tension to relaxed. I'd tell him how amazing he was every day for the rest of our lives if I needed to.

There was a knock at the door before it opened, Alvaro peeking in. He opened the door fully and his eyes heated as he took me in. "The bus is taking off. Get settled so you don't fall."

He left the door open and walked out of sight. I swallowed a whimper because I had the ridiculous thought that they didn't want me here. They hadn't stayed when they first got on the bus, and even though I could only have one knot in me at a time, they could have stayed and helped me in other ways.

"Hey, come here." Avery grabbed two pillows from the pile next to the couch and put them against the wall.

I grabbed another towel for him to clean himself up before lowering next to him, just as Alvaro, Cal, and Tate came into the room and shut the door.

The tension was thick, and I curled into Avery's side, grabbing a blanket and pulling it over my exposed body.

My makeshift nest was putting me slightly on edge, and now that the bus was moving, it made the feelings of unease grow. I had barely been able to lift my arms, let alone get my nest ready. I'd had such grand ideas for my first heat with my pack, and this wasn't it.

Fuck.

The tears came on fast, and I couldn't stop them. I put the blanket over my head and wrapped my arms around Avery, trying to stop the flood of feelings overtaking my brain.

Their scents wrapped around me before their touches did. Someone had moved to my other side, their hand rubbing my back, another was somehow stroking my head, and someone grabbed my ankle.

My body tingled all over, and I sighed contentedly into Avery's skin. This was what I needed; them working together as a pack.

Someone pulled the blanket down just enough for my head to be free. Alvaro and Tate were on my other side in rather uncomfortable-looking positions, and Cal was at my feet.

I drew my legs up to my chest and he crawled in closer, setting his cheek on my knee. His blond hair was a mess, and his hazel eyes were tired. They were all tired.

"Hi." He was just close enough that he could brush his lips across my temple. "What do you need?"

I shut my eyes as they all continued to brush gentle touches over me. I wanted to rip the blanket off and have them touch my naked body, but we needed to talk before this went further.

"I need for you to be a pack." I lifted my head from where it was resting against Avery's shoulder. "And I need you to be honest if this is what you want. I don't think things are going to be easy for us, but this is what I want."

Cal looked at Avery with a sneer. "Being a pack isn't running off to risk everything because you can't control your dick."

Avery tensed, and I squeezed his thigh. "And what would you have done, Callum?"

He frowned at me. "I would have gotten the head of our pack."

"You were in a room full of people. By the time I realized what I was doing, it was too late to go back." Avery ran a hand down his face. "I know what I did wasn't what packs normally do, but I... I don't regret it. I can't regret it. Kara doesn't deserve to have an alpha feel regret over easing her pain."

"You were damn near feral a few months ago. It was poor judgment. You could have hurt her. You could have attracted unwanted attention." Alvaro hadn't stopped smoothing his hand down my braids since someone had moved the blanket off my head. It was comforting but was also making my skin prickle with awareness.

"And all four of us running for the bus wouldn't have?" Avery was starting to tense again.

Tate had been quiet, a thoughtful expression on his face. He was the calm in the middle of the storm. "You rubbed it in our faces. For three years, you locked us out."

The conversation was so uncomfortable for everyone that I could sense it, despite not having a bond connection with them. It was hard not to whimper in distress.

"That wasn't my intention when I did it. I wanted you to know how happy I was... even if it only lasted a few minutes." Avery moved like he was going to get up, and I grabbed his arm. "I need some space."

"It's always 'I need space' or 'let me suffer in silence.' What about us, Avery? Did you forget that we were hurting just as much as you?" Cal jumped to his feet, his nostrils flaring as he breathed hard. "We needed you and you locked us out!"

Avery pulled his arm free and got to his feet, causing Alvaro to also stand. I wrapped my arms around my legs and tried not to freak out. My body was already starting to tremble, and if this argument got any worse, I was going to go full-out weepy omega.

It sucked having no control over my emotions sometimes.

The three alphas swayed as the bus moved, and now I had something new to worry about: them falling over and hurting themselves. Tate scooted next to me and pulled me into his lap, wrapping another blanket around me.

"Cal, why don't you go to your bunk until you cool off." Alvaro was ready to jump between them if fists flew.

Cal threw his hands up in surrender. "We're supposed to be taking care of our omega."

"I *was* taking care of her." Avery's fists were balled at his sides. "You're acting like a petulant child."

"Sure, Avery. I'm the one acting like a child. Excuse me for being upset that one of my best friends hasn't acted like much of a friend in years." Cal's face was red and his eyes glossy.

I cleared my throat, hoping the lump that had taken up residence there wouldn't make my voice shake. "Please, stop fighting and sit back down. You're going to fall and-"

The three of them stumbled on unsteady legs as the bus accelerated. Alvaro sat down heavily on the gaming chair I may have forgotten to clean after sitting there for a while, Avery hit the back wall, and Cal went flailing into Avery. He lost his balance completely and fell to his knees, coming face to face with Avery's dick.

The look of horror on Cal's face made me giggle, but then he breathed in harshly. A growl came from him and then his tongue darted out and licked Avery from knot to tip.

My mouth fell open and my legs threatened to do the same.

"What the actual fuck are you doing?" Avery was frozen against the wall, but he hadn't made any movement to stop Cal from doing it again.

Cal's head turned toward me with such speed that it was like he was possessed and about to spew pea soup. He licked his lips and then he crawled to me so fast I didn't have time to scramble out of Tate's lap before he yanked the blankets off me.

My eyes went wide and my stomach fluttered with anticipation. His eyes were wild, and his growl was low and dominant. This was what they had feared Avery would do, but I wasn't scared. I was getting slick with need.

"Cal!" Alvaro struggled to get up as the bus made us all lean to one side. "Stop right now."

"Need you." Cal tried to grab me around the waist, but Avery was there, tugging him back by the shoulder. "Let me go, asshole!"

"Calm the fuck down." Avery tried to pull him up by the arm, but Cal wouldn't budge. "You can't be with her like this."

"It's okay, he just-"

"No, Kara." Alvaro finally rolled off the chair onto his hands and knees before standing. Those gaming chairs were awfully complicated to get up from unless you were nimble.

Cal went for Avery's dick again, but this time, it wasn't to lick it. He was trying to punch it.

Alvaro growled. *"Cal, get up."* His bark was lethal, and a jolt of excitement went down my spine.

Cal growled right back but got to his feet. Alvaro and Avery grabbed him by the arms and forced him out of the room.

"This is all my fault. You guys weren't ready for me to be in heat. Not like this. Not when the stakes are so high." I tried getting out of Tate's lap, but he held onto my waist even tighter.

I was butt-ass naked in an alpha's lap and already horny again. This wasn't going to end any other way than with orgasms and hopefully another knot.

"Not your fault. Cal is a very emotional person, and he tries to hide it so much that sometimes the lid explodes off." Tate ran a finger across my collarbone and my skin heated more than it already was. "Are you okay?"

"Yes. I just don't want to cause fighting." I lay my head on his shoulder as his finger trailed down between my breasts. "What do you think you're doing?"

"Showing a lot of self-restraint right now." He ghosted his fingers over my stomach and then put his hand on my thigh, his thumb barely brushing the skin next to my slit. "Are you hurting?"

It was cute he was trying to ask me if he could have me in a roundabout way. "Touch me, Tate."

He groaned, his mouth going for the closest nipple and his hand pushing my thighs apart. I was sideways on his lap, which wasn't the best position, but his other hand was clamped around my waist, preventing me from moving.

My hand ran over his short hair, the sensation making me shiver. He ran his finger up and down my slit, teasing me and spreading my slick along my lips. It was driving me crazy, and I moved my leg to give him better access and an invitation.

He sucked hard on my nipple before releasing it with a pop, his other hand finally releasing my waist. I thought he was going to show some attention to the other nipple, but instead, he grabbed the two French braids Anya had done and pulled my head back and to the side, baring my neck to him.

"You are so damn beautiful." He licked a line from my ear down and then sucked the sensitive skin at the same time he ran his finger through my folds up to my clit. "Mmm... you just got even slicker for me, baby. Do you like that?"

He pulled his finger away and barely touched my slit as he ran it back down to just below my entrance. It was both maddening and felt so good at the same time.

"Feels good," I breathed as he sucked my neck again and stroked two fingers up to my clit. "Don't stop."

"Wasn't planning on it." He gently circled his two

fingers with my clit between them, and heat and wetness flooded my core. "That's a good girl. Get nice and wet for me."

He repeated the same thing with his fingers and used my braids to move my head so he could kiss me. Only, he didn't kiss me. He ran his tongue over the seam of my lips just like he was doing to my pussy.

I whimpered, rolling my hips to urge him to stop teasing me. I could hear how wet I was, but he continued taunting me and making my poor omega body suffer through his ministrations.

After what felt like decades, he plunged two fingers into me, taking my lips in a full kiss to capture my cry of pleasure. He was way too skilled at driving me crazy.

He hooked his fingers and hit the sensitive spot inside me that had my orgasm crashing into me so quickly and suddenly that I didn't know what was happening. One second the sweet pinch of need was overtaking my every thought, the next I was coming like I never had before, the pressure of it making me feel like I was peeing.

Only I wasn't.

My scent filled the space around us, and my legs and stomach trembled as the wetness just kept coming. I didn't know whether to be embarrassed or turned on even more that he'd made me squirt.

He broke our kiss, his fingers leaving me empty and wanting something else to fill me. "You're drenched." He cupped my sex, rubbing his palm right over my clit and sending lightning bolts of pleasure through me. "This is all mine. Every last drop is going to be on my tongue or my cock."

I nodded because I'd forgotten how to speak.

He lifted me out of his lap and then set me on the couch. Kneeling between my legs, he started at my knee and licked a line up to my thighs.

"Tate..."

I was surprised no one had interrupted us yet, but when I looked, the door had been closed at some point between dragging Cal out and now. I should check on him...

"Eyes on me," he barked. "When we're together, I don't want you thinking of them."

My mouth opened, but once again, he left me speechless. His lips turned up into the cockiest grin I'd ever seen.

He lowered his face to my cunt, running his tongue from my entrance to my clit. He groaned as he licked and sucked.

"I'm going to come." I arched my back and tried to find something to grab onto on the leather cushions. "Tate! Oh, yes. Right there." I was sure if there was a pussy fingering and eating contest, he would win first place.

But I needed him inside me. I wanted his cock filling me and his knot locking us together.

He lifted his head, his face covered in my juices.

Fuck, that was hot. "Do you think you're ready for my cock?"

"Yes." I cupped my breasts, running my thumbs over my nipples. "Please, Alpha. Give me your knot."

He stood and began undressing. I wanted him so bad I was starting to hurt for him. I moved one of my hands down and he paused undoing his pants.

I barely had my hand between my legs when he grabbed me, flipped me, pushed my chest onto the couch, and positioned himself behind me.

"I didn't say you could touch what was mine." He unzipped his pants. "Don't move."

"Okay." I was shaking from anticipation, and I spread my knees wider and wiggled my butt to tease him.

"Fuck me," he muttered, the sound of his clothes falling to the floor building my anticipation even more.

I'd never imagined it would be like this. Yes, I knew there would be lots and lots of sex during my heat, but the foreplay was unexpected. His restraint not to take me as soon as the others left the room was impressive.

But everyone had their limits, and Tate's was me reaching between my legs again.

I'd made a few circles around my clit when the head of his cock pressed against my entrance, and when I pushed back, he sheathed himself in one powerful thrust.

We both made strangled noises. I didn't know what his was for, but mine was to stop myself from screaming.

The stretch was so good, and he hit me so deep that if he were any bigger, he would have been too big. His cock was made for me.

He took hold of my hips as he slid in and out, his pace infuriatingly slow and torturous. "Can you hear how wet you are?"

My face burned, and I nodded, my head resting on my arm.

"Let me hear you say it." He wrapped his hand around my braids near my scalp and pulled.

I pushed myself up the rest of the way, his chest against my back. "I hear it."

"What do you hear?" He let my hair go and kissed along my shoulder as he moved his hand to my clit.

I whimpered, my brain turning to mush. "I hear... your cock sliding in and out of me."

"It's my new favorite sound." He picked up his pace, and I couldn't stop the sounds that came from my mouth.

He groaned and sighed in my ear as the spring was compressed more and more until it finally released, sending me straight into the atmosphere.

"Going to knot." He gasped as his knot expanded and filled me, along with his cum.

I saw stars and started to fall forward, but he locked an arm around me to hold me in place as the pleasure settled in my core.

Somehow, we moved to a spooning position on a

mattress, and I yawned, wrapping my arms around Tate's arms as he held me.

"That was... how? How was that so good?" What would sex with him be like when he wasn't trying to be gentle? I could tell he was holding himself back.

"Have to be at my best for my omega." He kissed my shoulder. "It's late and you should get some sleep. Your heat just started and it's going to be a long few days. I'll clean you up when my knot deflates."

"With your tongue?"

He chuckled and nipped my ear. "Not tonight. Sleep."

There were so many things on my mind about how this was going to work with them having tour obligations and what was going to happen with Cal and Avery, but I fell asleep faster than I had in a long time.

I was finally with my pack, and if I had any say, I'd never leave their sides.

CHAPTER EIGHTEEN

Cal

I didn't know what was wrong with me. One second, I was ready to punch Avery in the gut, the next I was licking his dick because Kara's scent overwhelmed me when he'd been right there in front of me.

Fuck. I licked his dick.

Then I'd snapped, because holy mother of all things knotty, she tasted amazing, and it hadn't even been from the source.

Just the thought of licking her slick cunt made me growl and start to try to get up from the couch where I was sandwiched between Avery and Alvaro.

I bared my teeth but sat back, crossing my arms over

my chest so I didn't attack them. I'd already fought enough, and them together was enough to stop my slightly feral ass from running down the length of the bus and taking what was mine.

"Tate is alone with her. He could be hurting her." Just as the words left my lips, we heard a faint cry of pleasure through the two closed doors, and I tried to jump up again.

Alvaro grabbed a handful of my hair and forced me to look at him. He was more pissed off than I'd ever seen him. *"Do not move from this couch."*

I hated that Alvaro's alpha bark had become effective again. On one hand, that meant our bond was healing, but on the other, it meant he could boss us around.

Gizmo got up from his dog bed and trotted over to me, putting his head on my knee. He always knew when I needed comfort, and I stroked his head.

Anya, who was sitting at the kitchen table at her laptop, took her noise-canceling headphones off. "I found a cabin rental about two and a half hours south. It's right on our path to the next concert venue which is another half hour away. Lots of acreage for privacy. We can get the keys at eleven. Want me to book it?"

"We don't have much of a choice since we don't know how long her heat is going to last. We'll need to book a car or SUV too." Alvaro pulled out his phone and swiped it open to our schedule. "Let's see if we can cancel or reschedule the two appearances we have for tomorrow—or I guess it's now today—we can just say we're sick. We won't know if we need to cancel the concert the next night until that morning."

"Is that what we're going to tell management?" Avery released my arm that he was holding now that I wasn't about to move. I mean, I still wanted to, but my bond was keeping my ass parked.

"I'll email them, but they might want to speak to you. That will have to wait until we are somewhere... umm... quieter." Anya put her headphones back on right as another sex sound came from the back.

"Jonathan, did you get all that?" Alvaro leaned forward so he could see into the very front of the bus.

"Got it. Anya just sent the address to me, and I'll find a place we can safely park for the rest of the night."

Thank fuck we had betas we could trust because I didn't know how we'd survive otherwise. They took care of so much for us on a daily basis, and now they were helping to take care of our omega too.

"Anya?" I waited for her to pull a headphone off from one ear. "Can you message me the address we're staying at?" I pulled my phone out of my pocket and groaned at all the messages. "Someone leaked my number again."

"Stop giving it to knottyboppers." Avery nudged me with his elbow. "You shouldn't be doing that anymore anyway."

I rolled my eyes and deleted all the text messages from chicks wanting in my pants. "I haven't since we met Kara. Someone must be pissed I haven't texted them back."

"I'll get you a new phone number in the morning. Why do you want the address? You just had to be dragged from the back room and this is the third time in six months I've had to change your number." She looked at the all-mighty Alvaro, waiting for him to decide.

"Oh, for fuck's sake. I'm going to order some shit for Kara's nest." I needed to do something to keep my mind occupied or I was going to lick Avery's dick again. "Can you go wash your cock?"

He'd pulled on sweatpants, but I could still smell her on him. I wanted to smell her on me, and I didn't understand how Alvaro could remain so calm not being back there with Kara.

"I don't think it's a good idea to have anything delivered to the cabin." Alvaro was texting on his phone and didn't look up. "And I agree with Cal. Go wash your damn dick."

"Can we not talk about dicks in front of my girl?" Jonathan snorted a laugh. "There is probably a Nest & Knot store in Portland. Place an order, and once we have a vehicle, Anya and I can go pick it up."

Avery muttered to himself but got up. "Don't place an order without seeing what Kara wants. It's her nest, not yours."

He was right, but I wasn't about to agree with him. "It's our nest. We're going to use it just as much as she is."

Avery didn't move but swayed a bit from the movement of the bus. "You would have done the same thing, Cal."

I didn't look up at him because I couldn't. There was nothing worse than seeing pain in his eyes. "Let's just forget about it."

Alvaro sighed and then yawned. "I think this has been hard on all of us and emotions are running high. We should talk this out, but let's wait until tomorrow."

Avery walked to the bunk area without another word, and I pulled up Nest & Knot's website and got to work adding everything an omega could want to my cart.

Sleep is a funny thing. I was epically exhausted but found myself staring at the ceiling of my bunk, wide awake.

Her scent was everywhere, like it had permeated every surface. My cock had a bit of relief when I'd jacked off to the thought of her taste and her moans of pleasure, but I was stiff as a board again.

It didn't help that I was on one of the spare mattresses that wasn't broken in and didn't have my scent.

I pulled my curtain aside and looked into the hallway. The dim lights along the baseboards were on and the gentle hum of the bus's ventilation was the only sound.

Our tour bus had eight bunks with four on one side and four on the other. Under each set of two were drawers with storage, and we used the two remaining bunks to keep things as well. Back when we didn't have an omega, we had a bed in the back room, but this tour, we'd swapped it out at the last minute for a lounge.

I hung my legs over the side, hoping Alvaro, who slept below me, wasn't awake as I used the edge of his bunk to get down. His curtain was wide open, and he definitely was not in there sleeping.

Avery's curtain was closed, and above him, Tate's hand hung out the side. Had I missed something?

After my little lapse in judgment and shopping spree, we'd gone back to the nest to find Kara and Tate sleeping soundly, Tate still buried inside her.

Lucky bastard.

I tiptoed to the door and slid it open a crack. My mouth instantly watered and my body vibrated with a need to fling the door open and stake my claim.

Alvaro had Kara positioned over his face, eating her like she was his last meal. Something was shoved in her mouth, making the noises coming from her dull.

Her eyes met mine and widened before her head tilted back and her whole body shook. Her hands cupped her tits, and she rocked harder on Alvaro's face.

I slipped into the room, shutting the door behind me. I leaned against it and pulled my cock out, not willing to face Alvaro's alpha wrath by interrupting.

Kara's eyes were back on me again and she braced

one of her hands on Alvaro's stomach, leaning forward far enough to wrap her hand around him.

Did she have...? Oh, fuck. She had Alvaro's white undies shoved in her mouth. I could just imagine her blue eyes looking at him in shock as he shoved them in there, or had she put them there herself?

I stroked up and down my shaft, giving just enough pressure to keep me wanting more. Kara watched me carefully and matched my strokes, right down to how I twisted my hand slightly at the crown.

Alvaro had to know I was in the room, unless his nose was so full of her scent that he didn't pick up on it. What I wouldn't give to lick and suck at her sweet cunt like he was.

Her eyes squeezed shut and her hand worked harder, her tits swaying as she rocked faster and faster. Alvaro growled into her pussy and her hand fell away from him, her back rounding as she came all over his face.

I growled, my need so strong I was going to come if I didn't stop touching myself.

And then Alvaro raised his hand and crooked a finger in my direction, beckoning me to join the party. He didn't have to tell me twice.

He helped Kara off him, his face so wet I knew she was nice and ready for me. Or for both of us.

"Turn around and sit on my cock." Alvaro gave her ass a soft slap, and she whimpered.

She was wobbly on her knees and reached up to take the gag out of her mouth.

"Leave them in." I stalked toward them, pushing down my boxers at the same time. "Tell me, Omega, have you ever had two cocks fill you?"

I stopped in front of her and tipped her chin up. She nodded, her eyes bright and her nostrils flared as she breathed heavily through her nose.

That was not the answer I expected. "Two fake cocks?"

She nodded again and whimpered through the fabric shoved in her mouth. Thank fuck she'd been referring to dildos because otherwise, I'd have lost my shit.

My thumb ran across her bottom lip, and she made a noise that I couldn't decipher. "Are you nice and wet to take two real cocks? The only cocks you'll ever have in your body again, do you hear me?"

"She's drenched." Alvaro sat up since she hadn't moved yet and ran his hand between her legs. She shut her eyes and her head lolled to the side. "She's ready to take both of us and she's such a perfect omega preparing for anything her alphas want to offer."

"I'm not convinced she can handle two cocks. Let me check to see for myself." I dropped to my knees and trailed my hand from her chin down between her legs. She was trembling ever so slightly, her perfume so strong I could taste it on my tongue.

I groaned as two of my fingers ran through her slick folds to her entrance and plunged inside. She braced her hands on my shoulders as I added a third.

"What do you think? Think she can handle both of

our big cocks?" Alvaro's hand joined mine, sliding in a finger. "God, I love how her pussy sucks us right back in."

"She can handle it." I kissed along her jaw to her neck. Alvaro was still sitting but was using his other hand to knead her ass.

Another one of his fingers joined mine. She was stretching so nicely. She didn't have to use her words to tell us she could handle it; her body was doing that for her. It was made for us, just like we were made for her.

"I'm knotting her." Alvaro didn't even have to tell me that was what was going to happen.

Her chest was heaving, and I stroked the side of her breast. "Sit on his cock, Kara."

She reached up and took her gag out before I could stop her. "Kiss me."

As soon as our lips touched, her walls clenched around our six fingers. I felt it all the way to my cock, and my knot tingled in anticipation.

I broke the kiss and slid my fingers from her, bringing them to my mouth. She hit my tongue and I damn near nutted. "Fuck, you taste so good. No wonder Alvaro wanted you parked right on his face."

"Right now, I want her parked on my dick." He lay back down and sucked his own fingers clean.

She bit her lip and smiled. "You can both knot. Cal can just keep his outside of me."

Oh, she was naughty. Pun definitely intended.

"Let's make sure you can handle both of us first."

Alvaro spanked her ass and she yelped, her hand quickly covering her mouth.

I helped her turn around and straddle Alvaro, so she was facing him. She grabbed him at the base and slowly sank onto him, moaning. I'd never heard a more beautiful sound.

She put her hands on his chest and raised and lowered her body, taking him deeper and deeper. I put my hand in the center of her back and pushed her forward. The position opened her for me to be able to slide in alongside Alvaro.

Had I ever done this before? Not in the same hole and not with Alvaro. He rarely partook in group activities, and if he did, he watched or wanted us to watch without interacting.

But Kara was ours. We'd been waiting forever for an omega to call ours and now she was here, trusting us to get her through her heat.

I moved back a bit and watched the connection between them. "You're making his dick so slick. It's fucking beautiful."

Alvaro snorted. "Thank you."

I smacked his thigh. "I wasn't talking about your dick, although…"

Kara started to giggle, but then I slid a finger in beside Alvaro. I quickly added a second, reassuring myself that this was possible.

"Are you ready, baby?" I straddled Alvaro's thighs and replaced my fingers with the tip of my cock. She was so slick that I didn't need to worry if there was enough lubrication for this to work.

She went still. "Yessssss," she hissed as I slowly pushed in.

"That's a good omega, taking both of your alphas," Alvaro reassured her. "So tight. That's it, sweetheart. Let him in."

My neck muscles strained, holding back from going crazy and fucking her brains out. I'd never felt anything like it, and the added sensation of Alvaro's cock wasn't helping.

By some miracle, I stilled once I was most of the way inside her. An omega's body was so incredible. They had to take care of themselves when they went through heats before they had packs. It was a bit twisted the government made us match to help each other's carnal urges.

"I'm ready, just... go slow." Kara's voice was strained.

Alvaro brushed a stray curl behind her ear. "Are you sure? You tell us to stop if-"

She rocked forward and then back with a whimper. She was ready, and I wasn't one to make a pretty omega like her wait any longer.

I pulled out so just the tip was in and then pushed back in torturously slowly. Alvaro's cock brought a whole new sensation to the underside of my cock, and my eyes nearly rolled back in my head.

"Yes, Cal. It feels so good." Kara lowered to her forearms and kissed Alvaro.

My body was on fire as I thrust into her, Alvaro occasionally contributing by lifting Kara's hips to slide her up and down his cock. Once we were perfectly in sync, I picked up my pace.

"Fuck, yes!" His fingers dug into her hips, our bodies creating the perfect harmony of sound with our noises of pleasure.

"Please. Oh, God. I need more. More, more, more!" She screamed the last *more* as I reached between her and Alvaro and pinched her clit.

"That's it, baby. Come all over our cocks. Give us every ounce of slick you have." I could feel her walls starting to squeeze, and her limbs shook as she held herself over Alvaro.

"I'm going to-" She screamed in pleasure as my cum shot out of me, my knot inflating just a little before I pulled it far enough out not to get stuck.

"So fucking good!" Alvaro punctuated each word by thrusting his hips up.

He exploded inside of Kara, his knot inflating faster than mine ever had. Liquid heat surrounded my cock, and the pressure... the pressure made my vision narrow as the edges blackened.

Kara's body was still twitching as my orgasm ebbed, leaving my entire body feeling heavy and tingly.

I stopped my assault on her clit and kissed the center of her back. "Are you okay?"

"Yes." She collapsed the rest of the way onto Alvaro, and he wrapped his arms around her.

Well, this is awkward.

I was stuck on my knees behind her, partially impaling her and unable to slip my dick out without hurting both of us. The tip of my dick was sandwiched between Alvaro's knot and her walls.

"Can we maybe... go to our sides? My knees are starting to hurt. Or I can try to pull out." I winced, hoping that wasn't the option she chose.

"Let's roll to the left, on the count of three." Alvaro counted and then, by some miracle, we pressed our bodies together to stay connected.

"You did so well taking both of us." I stroked Kara's arm and then her hip. "And Alvaro did so well sharing you with me."

She sighed contentedly and rested her hands on Alvaro's chest. "More sharing, less arguing."

Alvaro lifted his head so he could see me. "You good?"

I reached for our bond and let him in. It was still taking a conscious effort to do it when, for so long, we'd all held our emotions close.

He did the same, and our combined happiness made me grin. It had been a long time since I'd felt that myself, let alone from one of my pack mates.

She was everything to our pack, and I felt cautiously optimistic she was going to be ours forever.

CHAPTER NINETEEN

Alvaro

We were all exhausted after having a concert and several hours of heat sextivities. I'd never slept so hard in my life until whimpers woke me sometime mid-morning for another round.

Cal and I had fallen asleep with Kara snuggled between us, and I was surprised Tate and Avery hadn't returned. They had been mad when I suggested they go sleep in the bunks and let me take care of her for a while.

But now? Now I wished I hadn't sent them away because I could have used a few more hours of sleep.

After taking care of our girl, she drifted off back to

sleep and I got up, feeling a bit dizzy and unsteady on my feet. We all needed food and hot showers.

I peeked out of the curtains to see we were parked at a rest stop. It wasn't ideal, but we were parked away from the trucks at least. Jonathan probably hadn't slept at all knowing him.

Never could I have imagined this was what would happen. Kara wasn't due to have another heat for at least a month, but just seeing us had set her off. That both boosted my already overinflated ego and worried me.

Cal yawned and sat up. "What's wrong?" he whispered.

"Nothing. I'll find some food and see how long it will be until we can check in at the cabin." I walked over to a bag by the door where Anya had left us water bottles and tossed Cal one before grabbing one for myself.

This wasn't how her first heat with us was supposed to be. We had the perfect spot in our house, nestled away in an alcove that was supposed to be a seating area of the main bedroom. The room had gone untouched for years, but after Kara went back to her compound, we gutted it and redid it as a surprise we'd hopefully soon be able to show her.

A nest in the back of our tour bus or in some strange cabin in the woods brought a growl to my chest and I sucked down almost the entire bottle of water to stifle it. If my mom, who was an omega, knew about this, she would have thrown a chancla right at my head.

Kara deserved better than this. Life with a band was

not the life for an omega, and maybe everyone had been right in not letting us participate in the match again.

I slid the door open to the bunk area and gently shut it behind me. Avery was still sleeping, a soft snore coming from where his scent was. Tate was awake, talking softly on his phone.

The right thing to do would be to let him know of my presence, but instead, I listened, because who the fuck would he be talking to?

"I'm not just throwing it all away... no, all I said was that we might need to cancel the show tomorrow night... we're tired... the fans will just have to understand that we are human beings... we have never canceled a show before... that's not fair... you'd really do that to your own son?... Oh, so I'm only your son when it's convenient for you... I'm not being stubborn, you're being an asshole... fine."

I squeezed the bridge of my nose. Tate's father, Marcus Carter, was vice president of ABO Entertainment... our record label. At first, it had been amazing having someone to guide us, but now that we were older and more hardened by the industry, we realized we were idiots for listening to him.

We were worth a lot of money to the record label, and they had not been happy when we'd put our foot down about shuffling our schedule so we could hopefully participate in Omega Match and have time with Kara.

"I know you're there," Tate muttered. "Is Kara okay?"

"She just fell back asleep." I grabbed a pair of shorts out of a drawer and pulled them on. There was no point in putting on anything else. Odds were we'd all be naked again soon.

"My dad called because Anya canceled our two appearances for today. He wanted to know what the real reason was." He opened his curtain and rolled out of his bunk.

I handed him a pair of shorts. "I don't know how much more of this record label shit I can take."

"Same. Suddenly, the money isn't really worth it anymore, you know? But the fans..." Tate pulled on the shorts and looked over at Avery's bunk. "He's wanted out for a while."

"Deep down, I think we all have." The realization hurt my heart because I fucking loved performing, but I was tired, and my pack was too.

"What we need is a new legal team to work this out for us." Tate slid his phone into his pocket and went to the door leading to the front of the bus.

"We can worry about that after the tour. Only a few performances left, and then we can finally breathe and come up with a better plan. Fall match is not that far." That was if we got the go-ahead to participate.

The front of the bus was quiet besides the low hum of the generator giving it the power to run lights and the air conditioner.

I followed Tate, and we found Anya sleeping on the couch and Jonathan nowhere to be found. Since Gizmo wasn't in his bed, my guess was he took him out to go to the bathroom.

"We need to find some food," I whispered.

Anya made a sleepy groaning sound. "In the fridge."

"Thank you," I whispered. "Tate, I'm going to go talk to Jonathan. Take the food back to the nest."

He cringed. "I wouldn't go as far as calling it a nest."

"Shh." Anya rolled over and pulled the blanket over her head.

I patted her head through the blanket as I passed her, smiling to myself. She and Jonathan deserved a nice long vacation after this tour and helping take care of Kara. If we didn't have them, we would never have kept her a secret as long as we had.

I slipped on one of the pairs of flip-flops we kept by the door for Gizmo bathroom emergencies and stepped out into the cool morning, regretting not putting on a shirt. My nipples instantly hardened, and not in the good, turned-on kind of way.

I crossed my arms over my chest and spotted Jonathan on the grass with Gizmo. Bringing a dog on tour was a lot of work, and while the guys and I did help a lot with him, our schedule was so crazy some days that we barely even saw our four-legged friend.

There weren't very many regular vehicles at the rest stop, but I still didn't want to be seen wandering around without my shirt, so I waited by the side of the bus.

Gizmo spotted me before Jonathan did and let out a happy yip, his butt wiggling with his little stub of a tail. I didn't like that he'd had his tail docked, but it was already done when we got him. It made me feel a little better about it that it was done so someone couldn't grab his tail while he fought them off.

I still couldn't believe he'd gone after Kara and instead of hurting her had made her fall in the pool. The memory made me grin, and the security video footage of it would be fun to show to our kids someday.

"A grin when it's this cold?" Jonathan smiled as he let Gizmo go a few feet away.

I squatted down and let Gizmo attack me with kisses. "I was just thinking about how we met Kara."

"Ah, how is she?" He shoved his hands in his pockets and leaned against the side of the bus. "It sounds like things are going well. I did come out here a few times to make sure people who walked by couldn't hear."

Instead of feeling embarrassed, I felt damn smug about how well we were taking care of Kara sexually. I just wished we could take care of her need to nest better.

"She's doing okay. She hasn't said it, but I can tell being on the bus is putting her on edge. She's been covering herself with way too many blankets." I grabbed Gizmo's leash and stood. "What time is it?"

"Half past ten. I was just bringing Gizzy out before I head to the cabin. Once we get you guys set up there, we'll go get the SUV we rented and pick up the stuff Cal ordered, plus anything else you guys need."

My stomach growled. "Food. Anya has been keeping a list of all the things we find out Kara loves."

"She already put in a grocery order for pickup." He put his hand on my shoulder. "You're doing everything right, Alpha, and soon she'll be with our pack permanently."

I knew he was right, but that didn't stop the small sliver of doubt from slipping through.

THIRTY MINUTES LATER, we arrived at the cabin, which was nestled in the trees away from the road and any other houses. It was small, only two bedrooms and two baths, but it was cozy and enough space for the five of us short-term. Anya and Jonathan would be staying with Gizmo on the bus to give us privacy.

After moving everything we needed from the bus to the house, I wrapped Kara in a blanket and carried her to the main bedroom. We'd pushed the furniture to one side of the room and brought all the bunk mattresses in until the ones Cal ordered specially for nesting arrived.

"Al..." Kara muttered, holding onto my shirt as I lowered her onto the makeshift bed. "Don't go."

I didn't care for the name Al, but I would let her call me Alvie if she wanted. I had to have something that belonged to me, and my family's nickname for me was one of those things. But I guess she was family now.

"You can call me Alvie." I lay down on my back and wrapped my arm around her as she situated herself by laying her head on my shoulder and throwing a leg over mine.

"But you said in an interview that you don't like that." She yawned and started petting my shirt. "So soft."

"I only let special people call me Alvie, not people I don't know." I kissed the top of her head. "Are you hungry? We saved you a sandwich, but if you don't want that, Jon and Anya will be back soon with more food."

"I'm hot... and horny." She moved against my leg and her scent blossomed to life. "But I feel really gross."

"There's a really nice clawfoot tub looking out over the trees. I can run you a bath and bring you your sandwich." I sat up, bringing her with me.

"Where is everyone else?" She finally seemed to be waking up and looked around the bedroom with a cringe. "It's too bright in here and..." She sucked in a breath.

I purred, pulling her into my lap and against my chest. "I'm sorry this isn't what you expected for your first heat with us."

She looked at me and took my face between her hands. "It's been perfect considering the situation. You're four amazing alphas, and don't let anyone else make you think otherwise."

Shit. Why was I feeling emotional all of a sudden?

"Life on a tour bus is not for an omega. We should cancel the rest of the tour and-"

She kissed me, and I swallowed my words. I should have been comforting my omega, not letting her comfort me and reassure me I was good enough. It was hard not doubting myself and the pack after everything.

I pulled away. "I'm sorry. You don't deserve to have us keep bringing up the past."

She brushed her thumb across my bottom lip, her bright blue eyes drowning me in their depths. "The past shapes who we are. We experienced disappointment and sadness when we had prepared for happiness with a match."

"We never touched her." I felt the need to reassure her because we never talked in great detail about anything other than being separated from her the first night.

"Even if you had... it doesn't matter now. If she showed up here today and told your pack she now wanted you as hers, would you kick me to the curb and let her into your hearts instead?"

I reeled back, shocked she'd even ask me that. "No fucking way. We had no attachment to her other than the idea of her as an omega."

"And if Omega Match told me today that not matching was a mistake and there was still a pack from my list that wanted me..."

I growled at the thought of her leaving us for another pack. "I'll kill them with my bare hands before I let them take you from us."

She put her hand on my chest, over my heart. "I'm glad we're both on the same page. Nothing will keep us apart. Not Omega Match, OPS, the Pack Health agents. No one."

Her expression was fierce, and my cock instantly sprang to life because, fuck, that was sexy. She gave me a knowing smirk and then wiggled out of my lap.

"You are asking for it." I adjusted myself in my shorts as I got up.

"I'm always asking for it, Alvie." She dropped her blanket. "I'm ready for lunch in the tub."

I rubbed the corners of my mouth. On one hand, she needed food and a relaxing bath, on the other, she was practically begging to choke on my cock.

"That ass is mine as soon as you're done." I couldn't help but give her a love tap as she turned to head to the bathroom.

"Hey!" She shielded herself with her hands. "What if I did that to your dick?"

"He'd probably enjoy it." I hooked my arm around her neck and pulled her to me, kissing her forehead, her cheeks, and the tip of her nose. "Thank you."

She scrunched her nose. "For what?"

"For trespassing, not running away, being patient." I brushed my lips over hers with each reason.

"Did you ever think when you found me dripping wet in your pool that we'd be here?" She sighed as I kissed down her neck to where I planned on marking her.

"I knew as soon as I scented you." I pulled back. "If I

don't start the bath, I'm going to end up bending you over the counter and taking you again."

She made a humming noise like she would be okay with that, but I needed to keep my sights set on making sure her basic needs were met.

We had a lifetime of me bending her over things ahead of us.

CHAPTER TWENTY

Kara

A bath and food were just what I needed to feel somewhat like myself again. My body still ached, but not nearly as bad as before I got in the bath.

Even though I was on suppressants and had just gone through a full-blown heat the last time, this one felt similar. The only difference was that it didn't hurt nearly as much because I had four alphas making sure I was taken care of.

After soaking in the cool bath for a while and eating the sandwich and chips Alvaro brought me, I quickly showered and emerged from the bathroom wrapped in a towel. There was really no point in putting on clothes when I was likely to strip them off again soon enough.

The bedroom wasn't bad, but it wasn't good either. It had been a struggle the night before not to lose my omega sanity over being in the back of a bus for the first wave of my heat. I thought it would be fine, but every time the bus had moved or whatever came on to power things, I'd feel twitchy. Not to mention there was absolutely no privacy, even from my alphas.

Now, I was in some stranger's space, and not only was the bedroom large, but it had windows up high with no blinds. I didn't like feeling needy and picky, but something about feeling like your insides are being ripped in half from not having sexual relief and a knot just brought out the codependent side.

My nose burned with the urge to cry. I hated being so vulnerable and being away from a safe space where I was comfortable. But I'd chosen this and chosen them. There was no turning back now.

There was a shirt and shorts on the bed for me, but I ignored them, tucking the towel tighter around me. I was in search of a brush or a comb. I had a whole regimen for my hair but was just going to put it back in braids again.

"Hey, sweetheart." Tate jumped off the couch, nearly knocking the Sprite out of Cal's hand as a timer went off on his phone. "Feeling better?"

I thought he was going to come wrap me in his arms, but instead, he went into the open kitchen and opened the oven to pull out a sheet of chocolate chip cookies. At least, that was what they smelled like.

"Yeah." I scrunched my nose at the television showing a college football game. "Why do sports have to be on every day all the time?"

Would they rather be watching football than in my nest with me? The thing was, I knew my brain was being ridiculous, but I couldn't stop the sudden feeling of loneliness.

Cal wiped the side of his hand where some drink had spilled on his sweatpants. They had all showered. I could smell the soap mixing with their scents, and I didn't like it one bit. "Do you want me to put it on something else? There's every channel known to man on here."

I shook my head and rubbed the back of my calf with my opposite foot. "I just..."

And then I burst into tears.

Cal was to me first and picked me up, sitting back down on the couch. "What's wrong? Alvaro said he left you clothes. We put the ones you were wearing in the washer."

"I don't want clothes." I buried my face in his chest.

Tate tucked a large blanket that looked like it belonged on a king-sized bed over me and Cal. "Is it because we aren't in the nest? We just thought you might like some time to yourself. Let me go get Avery and Alvaro."

"It's not a nest." I pulled the blanket over my head. "I'm sorry."

"Jonathan and Anya are getting a rental car and are going to pick up some stuff I ordered and groceries." Cal brushed my wet hair over my shoulder and began stroking up and down my back. "We can maybe pay off a flight crew and fly back to our house."

"But your tour. You can't cancel the rest of it." The thought of being on an airplane while in heat gave me heart palpitations. "I just need a good cry."

I shut my eyes and focused on my breathing, which only made things worse because I didn't smell like them anymore.

Cal pulled the blanket over both of our heads. "We're going to make you the best temporary nest you've ever seen, okay? And then we'll move it all to the bus when we leave here in a few days."

I nodded and wrapped my arm that had been trapped between us around his waist. He was cooler than I was, and I untucked the towel and pulled it open the best I could so our skin could touch. The blanket wasn't too thick, so it wasn't hot under it and there was just enough light peeking under the edges to see his face.

While still caressing my back, he ran his other hand up and down my thigh. "Is this okay? Do you need a knot? An orgasm?"

I smiled through my tears. "This is perfect. I wish I wasn't so emotional; I hate that the first time in months that we get to see each other in person, I'm a blubbering mess of an omega."

"How else should you be? Heats are crazy from what we know about them. Your body goes through a lot and so does your mind." He kissed the crown of my head. "Was there not a blow dryer in the bathroom?"

"I need a brush or comb before I braid it. I have nothing here with me." I was going to fall asleep again if he kept cuddling me like he was.

"Want a cookie? Fresh baked... right from the package they came in." Tate lifted the blanket down by my feet and poked his head under. "This is cozy."

Cal grunted as Tate shoved the plate of cookies at him to take, and he lifted my legs to sit down. "No one invited you into our cavern of solitude."

Tate snatched the plate back. "Then you can't have any of my cookies."

"They're everyone's." Cal took one and brought it to my lips.

I bit into it and groaned as the chocolate chips hit my tongue. It was so good, even if it came from a pre-made container. Cal watched me with heated eyes as I finished the cookie and then licked the bit of chocolate from one of his fingers.

"I think they're all hers." Tate's voice had deepened, and he held another cookie to my lips.

I giggled and took another bite. Being fed wasn't on the list of things I thought I'd like. It was sensual to have them feeding me and watching my lips as I ate.

"More?" Cal reached for another cookie.

"No, I'll save some for everyone else. Where are Alvaro and Avery?" I wanted them all with me on the couch, absorbing their scents back onto my clean skin.

"They went for a walk to see if anything is around here that doesn't show on the map. Just to be on the safe side." Tate picked up a cookie and took a bite, shutting his eyes and moaning. "Not homemade, but fucking hits the spot."

"I think our girl's pussy needs a little break. Stop that moaning bullshit." Cal took a cookie and shoved the whole thing in his mouth. "Hawwwt!" He opened his mouth and fanned at it.

"That's why you don't shove the whole damn thing in your mouth." Tate smirked. "I heard you say you need to do your hair. I can braid it for you. I used to help my auntie braid my cousins' hair."

A shiver ran through me, and my nipples pebbled. Oh, yes. I liked the idea of him doing my hair. My perfume blossomed under the blanket and both alphas' chests rumbled with growls of pleasure.

Cal swallowed hard and coughed while trying to talk. "I want to learn how."

"I'll go get a brush and comb." Tate set the cookie plate on my lap and disappeared out of our cocoon.

"Feeling a little better now?" Cal swiped his finger over one of the melted chocolate chips on the top of the cookie and then smeared it on my nipple. "Because I sure am."

"Callum…"

He lowered his lips and sucked the hard point, swirling his tongue. He released it with a pop and already had more chocolate on his finger, which he smeared on my bottom lip.

"What happened to giving my nether region a break?" I couldn't stop my legs from opening, my scent growing even stronger under the blanket.

"I love hearing my name come from your sweet lips." He licked along where he'd placed the chocolate, gathering it on his tongue before sliding it between my lips and into my mouth.

I moaned, tilting my head and deepening the kiss. Did my body need a break? Maybe. Was that going to stop me from sitting on his cock that was pressing against my hip? Probably not.

Things had been calm between my legs until they started feeding me, and then the chocolate on my nipple? I was done for.

I broke the kiss and moved the plate to the side table, managing to keep the blanket over us. Cal readjusted it, pulling it farther over our heads so it would stay put.

"What are you doing, Omega?" He walked his fingers up my leg and stopped before getting to the apex. "Do you want me to take you to the bedroom? Jonathan and Anya could be back at any time."

"Don't care." I got out of his lap, staying hunched under the blanket, and then straddled him.

His hard length pressed against my wet center, and I

kissed him as I moved against it. He'd started this and I intended to finish it. I could sense Tate was back in the room, but he didn't say a word or try to join us. I appreciated that because they had been acting like Cal was going to lose his mind.

"Kara." His head fell back against the cushion as I slid up and down, his sweatpants and the pressure from inside them hitting me just right. "Let's do this without my pants."

"Feels good..." I kissed down his neck and sucked his skin where I intended to leave my mark. "I want to ride you, Callum."

"Fuuuuck." He groaned, his hips lifting to meet my movement. "Lift up for a second, baby."

I did, and he pulled down his sweatpants just enough for his cock to spring free. Sitting back on his thighs, I wrapped my hand around him. "Are you going to knot me, Alpha?"

His head went back to the cushion, and he groaned as I started to stroke him. "Yesss. Fuck, Kara. Get on my cock already."

"Impatient." I teasingly circled his crown with my finger before running it under his shaft. "Maybe I want to play a little."

I didn't really, not with how wet I was between my thighs and the ache slowly building in my core. I needed his knot, but I also wanted to see him yearn for me and possibly beg for it.

"You can play with your mouth." He reached forward

with both hands and pinched my nipples.

I shivered in pleasure and cupped his balls, stroking my thumb along the seam. They were velvety soft, and I could have touched them all day. "Maybe Tate can bring us some melted chocolate chips and I can drizzle it all over you and lick it up."

"Karrrraaa," he half growled, half moaned. It was the sexiest sound, and I found myself grinning. "I'd bend you over the coffee table and let you have it, but I really want you to ride me."

"Oh, yeah?" I used my other hand to wrap around his shaft and began stroking him firmly. "You want me to come all over you?"

I heard Tate sit on the other side of the couch and was keenly aware he was going to listen to us. There was something super arousing about him not being able to see us.

"Yes, and watch these delicious tits bounce." He pinched my nipples again and then grabbed my hips, yanking me forward. I broke contact with his balls and cock and braced my hands against his chest. "You're a little tease, aren't you?"

"Maybe." I circled my finger around his nipple. "Your cock jerks every time I do. You like it."

He grabbed a handful of my pretty damp hair and brought our lips together in a hungry kiss. I whimpered and wrapped an arm around his neck to give me some leverage to lift my body.

He held onto the base of his cock as I slowly sank

onto him. Our tongues tangled in a dance as I began sliding up and down his cock.

On the other side of the couch, I could hear Tate's breathing get louder and assumed he was stroking himself. I loved not knowing what he was doing and that he was listening to us.

Cal scooted his butt toward the edge of the couch. and I grabbed onto the back. My breaths were coming faster and faster as I thrust my hips, my clit hitting just right against him to send jolts of pleasure through my limbs.

"You feel so good wrapped around me." Cal's eyes were half shut and he dug his fingers into my ass cheeks, helping me move on top of him. "Fuck, you ride me so perfectly."

My brain was starting to short circuit, and little moans left me each time I slid my clit against him. And when he slid down just a smidge lower and took one of my nipples in his mouth, I clenched around him.

"Oh, God, Cal. You feel so good." I was losing control, my knees burning as I chased my orgasm. I was right at the edge, every cell in my body trembling and on alert for the explosion that was about to come.

Cal released my nipple. "That's it, baby. Ride my cock like a good little omega. Fuck, yes." His hand smacked my ass, the sting and heat of it sending me plummeting straight over the edge.

I cried out, my body stiffening and my movements out of control. "Cal! Yes!"

He grabbed ahold of my hips and sank lower on the couch, his hips jacking up to thrust into me. It was not enough and too much all at the same time.

"I'm... oh, fuck!" He exploded, his hot cum spilling inside me, and then the tight squeeze and pinch of his knot filled me.

Tate groaned from the end of the sofa.

My stomach muscles contracted, and a full body clench roared through me before releasing. I was gripping the back cushion so tightly my knuckles hurt.

Cal wrapped an arm around my waist and shimmied up the couch. He wasn't hanging off, but his butt had been pretty close to the edge. I rested against him, both of our chests heaving.

Tate was quiet, but I hadn't heard him leave and could somehow still feel that he was there. Had he come all over his hand and stomach? I wanted to peek out from under the blanket, but my limbs were heavy, and I couldn't quite move yet.

"Stretch out your legs." Cal scooted back down the couch, taking me with him. It was a bit awkward unfolding my legs after they had been bent like they had, but I managed to.

"Fuck. I can't move." Cal chuckled, only his upper back and shoulder on the couch. "Little help here, Tate."

Tate grunted and sounded like he stood up before the blanket was pulled away. Tate stared down at us, his cock hanging limp and his stomach and hand still covered in his release.

"Give me a second." He grabbed the back of his shorts and did a half-run-half-waddle to the kitchen.

I giggled and Cal groaned, his neck and face straining. "Are you okay?"

"Legs. Cramping. Going to fall." He sucked air in through his teeth and I braced myself for the jolt, but then Tate was back, helping Cal to lie on the couch. "Please tell me that's water that just touched my back."

Tate looked at his hand and then grinned. "I must have missed some between my fingers, sorry." He didn't sound very sorry to me.

I laughed, burying my face in the crook of Cal's neck as Tate re-covered us with the blanket.

It oddly was comforting to have it completely covering us, and given the circumstances, it was perfect... for now.

CHAPTER TWENTY-ONE

Tate

My morning had started on a bad note with a phone call from my dad, but after baking cookies and an orgasm, I was feeling much more like myself.

As the son of four parents in the music industry, I always felt like I had eyes on me. Two of my dads and my mom worked on the music production side of things, while my third dad had climbed the corporate ladder to become a top executive.

Had our band had help producing our first single and releasing it? Yes. Did my dad remind me of that every chance he got? Absolutely.

Most artists in the industry had some kind of

connection to get their foot in the door, and if they didn't, they made those connections by going viral or catching a music executive's eye. I was certain we would have made it regardless of the help we had, and it sucked that my own damn father liked to throw it in my face whenever the band made a decision he didn't agree with.

Like canceling two morning show appearances.

After Cal's knot released Kara, they both cleaned up and Kara sat on the floor between my legs so I could do her hair. She seemed to be feeling better, and having her hair done would help even more.

Her hair was wavy when damp, and I combed through it, careful to hold the hair at the scalp to work out any tangles. Her curls were beautiful, but with her being in heat, it was better to just pull her hair back.

"I could get used to this." Kara sighed as I massaged her scalp after I was done detangling her hair.

"He gives good shoulder massages too." Cal had his eyes glued on the game; our alma mater was down by three in the fourth quarter.

"If this singing career doesn't work out, you could be a masseuse... or a hairstylist." Her head lolled to the side as I grabbed onto her shoulders, digging my thumbs in.

"I only know how to do braids because growing up I spent a lot of time at my aunt's house and was the only boy. Plus, I assumed because I came from a pack, I'd emerge as an alpha and I wanted to learn for my omega."

I grabbed my comb and parted her hair down the middle.

"You're so full of shit," Cal muttered.

I grabbed a throw pillow and smacked him with it. "See if I ever massage your shoulders again."

"You two fight like brothers." Kara snorted. "Kayla and I didn't fight a ton, but when we did, it was horrible. We were complete opposites growing up. She was always busy doing something with our dads, and I was shut in my room reading or doing homework."

Her voice held a note of sadness, and I smoothed one of my hands over her head in comfort. "What's wrong?"

"Just been doing a lot of thinking about what I sacrificed to be the best and if it was worth it. One of my dads died unexpectedly when we were nine, and it broke our parents for a while, especially our mom. I didn't want them to worry about me, so I always worked my ass off to not disappoint them."

Cal muted the TV and turned toward us, bending his leg on the couch. "It's tiring trying to be perfect all the time. I used to freak out anytime I even had a point taken off a paper or exam. I didn't really let that go until I met the guys in the dorms."

"So, you're saying they're a bad influence?" Kara teased.

"Exactly. Everyone thinks I'm the wild child of the group, but Alvaro is the one that got me drunk for the first time the night before a very important final. I studied drunk." Cal looked over at me. "And Tate over there, don't get me started."

"I'm an angel. You're just making up lies." I grinned as I began French braiding one side of Kara's hair. Her hair was thick and soft, and I wanted to run my fingers through it some more.

"Tate was the master of pranks. He doesn't do them much anymore, but occasionally he'll pull a real zinger on us." Cal let out a wistful sigh. "One time, he put a fake snake in Avery's dorm room. I've never heard a man scream so loud."

"I feel like I missed out on so much fun being at the Omega Academy... well, besides when my sister did something crazy." Kara reached up and patted one side of her head as I finished. "That's nice. I'll have to give you a nice tip later."

"I'll hold you to that." I leaned forward and kissed her fingers. "You can be however you want with us."

"Thank you." She sniffled, and Cal practically flew from his spot onto the floor next to her.

The back door of the cabin opened, and Alvaro and Avery walked in with Gizmo. Avery was singing something, and Alvaro was humming along with him. It wasn't anything I'd heard before and my ears perked up.

All of our heads turned in their direction as they walked into the kitchen, and both grabbed a cookie. Anya always kept our bus fridge stocked with pre-made dough because nothing hit the spot like a freshly baked cookie.

Alvaro's humming stopped. "We should get this down before we forget."

"On it." Avery took a bite of his cookie and groaned, looking over at me, Cal, and Kara. "Don't you three look cozy playing beauty shop. It smells like sex in here too. Is that a new service you're offering? Free orgasms with a hairdo?"

It was nice to see Avery happy and having an air of excitement surrounding him. He was optimistic about the future for the first time in a long time, just like the rest of us.

Gizmo trotted across the living room and let out a grunt as he folded dramatically in his dog bed and put his head on his paws. He'd been really good about staying away from Kara. The last thing we needed was for him to try to hump her leg.

"Avery, if you aren't careful, we won't be able to call you Payne anymore," I joked.

He walked into the living room and stood in front of us, blocking the TV. "Why not? It's my last name."

"He can still be a pain in the ass if he's not in mental anguish." Cal was still on the floor and stroking Kara's arm. "You're in the way."

"Maybe the pain is in my ass from dealing with you." Avery didn't move out of the way and crossed his arms over his chest. "I have nail polish on the bus. When Jonathan and Anya get back, I can paint your nails."

"I'd like that." She looked up at him, and although I

couldn't see her face, I could hear the adoration in her voice.

"I'm going to go write this song down." Avery leaned down and kissed her before heading toward the spare bedroom where we were keeping our overnight bags and electronics so we didn't have to go out to the bus.

Alvaro sat down on the couch and reached over to give the braid I just finished a light tug. "We walked a wide perimeter around the cabin and there are no other people within a half-mile radius."

Cal looked up at me. "We have four days after our show tomorrow until the next one in the Bay Area. We can leave the night before the show and get there by the time we have soundcheck. Do you think your dad will flip his lid?"

"Probably." I sat back on the couch and ran a hand over my face. "We'll have to cancel a few more appearances too."

"Management isn't happy we separated from the other buses. I told them we are grown-ass men and to stop acting like our mothers. They didn't like that." Alvaro chuckled to himself. "They think we're off getting drunk and hosting orgies or something."

"Well…" Kara giggled. "One part of that isn't too far from the truth."

"It's the last two weeks of the tour. They just need to get over it. We're tired." Cal got up off the floor with a groan and flopped down between me and Alvaro. "My ass is asleep. Come up here, Kara. We need your ass in tip-top shape and not sore from the floor."

She stood, adjusting the shirt of Alvaro's she was wearing with nothing underneath it. She was more relaxed than I'd seen her since her heat started, and it filled me with pride that we were taking good care of her. At least, I hoped we were.

"Come here." Alvaro reached for her and grabbed her wrist, pulling her onto his lap. "I like seeing you in my shirt."

Her long legs stretched out over Cal, and she wiggled her toes. I couldn't resist running my finger up the bottom of one to see her reaction.

She snatched her foot away with a laugh. "Don't you dare."

"You really shouldn't have let him see your weakness." Cal ran his hand up and down her calf. "He's N'Pact's resident tickler."

A thoughtful expression passed over Kara's face. "I have a question that you guys never answer when you're asked… and I've been curious."

Alvaro groaned. "I know exactly what you're going to ask."

"You can't blame me. Anytime someone asks what the N is for on N'Pact, you guys get these sheepish little grins and I'm dying to know why. I promise I won't tell a soul." She batted her eyelashes and put her hands together in a plea. "Pretty please?"

"We're the only four that know its meaning. It's

highly classified and confidential," I warned, serious as all get out.

"We can do a blood oath or pinky promise if that makes you feel better." The hopefulness in her eyes was enough to make us all putty in her hands.

"Tell her," Avery said, walking out of the bedroom in just his boxers, his iPad in hand. He sat down in a chair and started writing on the screen like a man possessed.

Alvaro touched Kara's cheek so she'd look at him. "Swear on all of our knots you won't even tell Kayla this."

She gasped and put her hand to her neck as if she were clutching her pearls. "Not your knots!"

"Swear it. It's the only way." I wrapped my hand around her foot. "You breathe a word of it and no more knots for you."

She raised her hand. "I swear on all four of your knots that I will not tell anyone."

We let the silence go on for longer than was necessary before I nodded for Alvaro to go ahead.

"When we were coming up with name possibilities, we started playing with our names, like many bands before us have. The only two words we could come up with that would have a letter for each of us was beta and pact. There was no way we were using beta, and since Avery's last name is cool, it made sense to use his last name for it."

Kara nodded because this was common knowledge. "Yes... but the N. And why not an M?"

The number of times we'd been asked both of those questions was laughable. I squeezed her foot, drawing her attention to me. "Someone, who shall remain nameless, is bad at spelling and thought the word had an N at first. But it did sound better."

"That's it? That's honestly kind of lame." She was asking for her foot to be tickled again.

Avery stopped and looked up from his iPad. "I mentioned we could find another meaning for it. Something only we knew. This was right after we started singing together, so although we'd seen each other around, we hadn't formed a pack yet."

Cal chuckled. "Alvaro was like… *well, we discovered each other naked.*"

"And since we had been drinking, we settled on using an N to represent how we met and the apostrophe we like to think is a dick." Alvaro grinned. "It's stupid, but we were eighteen and nineteen years old."

Kara blinked several times, her lips turning up into a smile. "What do you mean you met naked?"

"One night, we were all showering, and Tate started singing. Then we just all joined in, and it was so effortless and amazing that we decided to start a group. We were acapella at first and then started songwriting and recording with Tate's parents." Cal sighed. "All those good grades didn't even matter in the end."

Kara patted his hand that was resting on her thigh. "They matter. They shaped who you are."

Avery put the iPad on the table next to the chair. "What's the plan here? With us as a pack? With Kara?"

Kara's smile fell, and I could see her brain going through different scenarios, mostly ones of worry. "I thought... I thought you wanted me."

"No! I mean. Shit. Fuck." He stood and came over to the couch, lowering to his knees in front of it. "I meant now that you're with us, what's our plan? I'm going to have a real hard time letting you go."

"Jesus, man." Cal reached forward and flicked his ear. "Don't stress out our omega like that."

"Children, let's not start a fight." Alvaro flicked Cal's ear. "Once we get Kara through her heat, we'll just have to hope they let us do the fall match. If not..."

"If not, I can move to the Los Angeles compound and hopefully find ways to sneak out." Kara sat up straighter. "Or I can tell them that unless they want me to come forward about the probable tampering of my matches and everyone else's, they need to match us."

"Blackmail?" Alvaro snorted. "That's just going to create even more problems."

She deflated like a balloon poked with a needle. "Omega Match needs to change."

We all agreed, but not even what happened with Kara's sister was enough to cause any crazy changes. It wasn't like any of us had any ideas about how it should be done. The most important thing was that omegas were protected, and Omega Protective Services and Omega Match did a good job of that.

"No one knows you weren't at the meet and greet besides that girl you said helped you escape and your friend. You could write a letter to Omega Match telling them that you really hope we're in the fall match. They know who you are, don't they?" I didn't think there were any other options, and if worst came to worst, we'd have to deal with it when the time came.

"I can do that." She leaned her head against Alvaro's shoulder and yawned. "I need a nap."

The front door unlocked, and Anya stuck her head in, jumping slightly when she saw us all on the couch. "Am I interrupting? I come bearing gifts." Anya's timing was impeccable.

The wariness in Kara's eyes faded and she jumped up, nearly kneeing Avery in the nose and flashing her bare ass at us. "Let's go, boys. It's time to build my nest."

I had a feeling it was going to take a long time to set it up if the looks in all of our eyes were any indication.

CHAPTER TWENTY-TWO

Kara

My nest was perfect, and I hadn't realized how much it was affecting my emotions and mood until I was safely snuggled inside.

It took up most of the main bedroom, even with all of the furniture shoved to one side and was just big enough for the five of us. The nesting pads were top-of-the-line with a microfiber texture that could easily be cleaned off. They also folded up so they could be moved with ease.

There was also a tent that had dark, heavy drapery to make the nest feel like it was in a smaller space. Not all omegas liked being in a small room when they needed comfort, and I was one of them. I preferred there to be some openness around the outside.

Inside, there were soft pillows and blankets and even a few Squishmallows. Outside one of the flaps, we put the mini fridge from the bus and filled it with drinks and quick snacks.

The corners of the tent had hooks for battery-powered lanterns to give us as much or as little light as we needed.

The best part of it was I had my four alphas with me, ready to take care of me in any way I needed. And boy were they needed later that evening when my heat hit me hard. It was like my body knew I was perfectly safe and comfortable and decided to go crazy on me.

It lasted so long that we finally passed out sometime around three in the morning, my body satisfied. I didn't know if that would be the worst of it, but I hoped so because they had a concert I'd convinced them not to cancel.

A soft knock on the bedroom door woke me, and I yawned as I sat up. Alvaro, who was on the edge by the exit flap, rolled off the nesting bed and out of the tent.

I was feeling refreshed and there was a pleasant ache between my legs. It had been a lot of sex, but that was what my body was built for, and the amount of slick definitely helped the situation.

I heard Alvaro open the bedroom door, and Anya whispered to him. He sighed, and the door shut softly before he crawled back into the nest.

I sat up and stretched, the other three alphas still fast asleep on either side of me. "What's wrong?"

"Nothing is wrong. It's noon and we need to get ready to go..." He turned on one of the lanterns in the corner, bathing us in dim light. "Unless you don't want us to. Still time to change your mind."

Avery grumbled in his sleep and rolled to his side, burying his face against my hip. They were all so exhausted from the whirlwind of sex. I could hardly even remember some of it. I'd gone into a sex haze.

"I don't want you guys to cancel your show. I feel great right now." I leaned forward and grabbed the squirrel Squishmallow I'd named Nico from the foot of the bed, hugging it to my chest. "The worst that could happen is it flares back up again, and I have to use a toy."

Alvaro looked over at the toys on the side of the bed. Cal had purchased several sex toys for us to play with and for me when they weren't around. We'd only used them a little the night before and they would help if the pain started again.

"I'm only going to agree to this if you promise to call us or Jonathan if it starts up bad again." He reached over Cal and touched my cheek. "Everything inside me is screaming not to leave."

I leaned into his hand and shut my eyes. Deep down, I didn't want them to go, but it would only be about ten or eleven hours, and if they didn't go, people would start to ask questions.

"We have four days of no interruptions after it." We'd

have to spend some of the time on the bus, but Anya had already found us somewhere to stay on the way there that was secluded just like this place was.

The heats I'd had so far in my life had lasted anywhere from three days to a week and a half. Some had heats that lasted for longer than two weeks. It depended on the environment and if the body was getting what it needed. The whole purpose of us having heats was to become pregnant, and since I was on birth control and around alphas, I expected mine to last longer.

Tate yawned and sat up. He was on the other side of Avery and had been the one to suggest Cal and Avery be the ones next to me since they were the ones that would have the hardest time leaving me today. Tate and Alvaro would too, but they hadn't been almost feral before meeting me.

"Time to leave?" Tate opened the flap on his side and grabbed three water bottles from the mini fridge, handing me and Alvaro one each. "It will be interesting to see how we perform tonight."

"You guys had better put on a good show. Pretend I'm there cheering you on." I took a long drink of cold water and my nipples pebbled.

Alvaro's eyes went right to them. "If we pretend you're there cheering us on, we're going to be dancing around with hard-ons the whole time."

"I don't think my dick can get hard anymore." Tate looked down at it. "Oh, never mind."

"You two are ridiculous." I laughed as I crawled on my knees to the opening. "Let's shower. Cal and Avery are pretty much dead to the-"

"Shower?" Cal muttered, his eyes peeling open and finding me across the tent.

"Mm." Avery rolled over and hugged Nico. "Soapy boobies. Me likies."

I was pretty sure I was in love with these four men.

AFTER THE PACK left with Jonathan driving the bus, Anya and I did some cleaning and put together a lasagna to bake for a late-night dinner after the concert.

Growing up, my mom and dads didn't have betas, so being around two that were in a pack was different for me. A lot of packs did not bond betas to them, but I liked the idea of having an even bigger family.

Anya and I just finished cleaning the kitchen when Gizmo nudged at the back door. She'd just taken him out a few hours ago, but when a dog's got to go, they've got to go.

"You want to come outside with us? It's nice out and you can wear my sunglasses." Anya held them out to me and slid her feet into her shoes. "Fresh air is good for you."

I put the glasses on the top of my head and looked down at the leggings of hers I'd borrowed and the oversized t-shirt of Avery's I was wearing. "I want to, but..."

"No one is going to see you. We're just going behind the cabin, not to a park." She laughed and opened the back door, letting Gizmo outside.

She was right. I slid my feet into a spare pair of flip-flops since I'd had on heels at the concert and followed her out the back door. The sun was starting to set, and I wondered what my alphas were doing. Were they wondering what I was up to?

We'd texted throughout the afternoon when they could, but now they were preparing for their concert and doing pre-performance interviews and meet and greets. I hadn't asked how Cal and Avery were doing, but they'd struggled to leave me.

"You've been pretty quiet this afternoon." Anya looped her arm through mine as we walked into the cleared area of the backyard where Gizmo was taking care of his business.

One of the big plusses of having betas bonded to my alphas was, when they weren't around, their friendship eased my anxiety. I had certainly been a little wary of Anya and Jonathan at first, but after all they'd done for me, I trusted them.

"I've just been thinking a lot. I really want for this to work out, but there's that fear, you know?" I hated that the doubt kept creeping in, but it would until I was bonded to them. "It's all been a bit of a blur, honestly."

"All things considered, I think you're handling everything well. Other omegas would have been a mess over everything, but you... you just roll with the punches."

She led me around the perimeter of the open space. It was nice to be outside and getting some non-sex-related movement in.

"Oh, I've been struggling. I'm just good at hiding it." I shrugged and kicked a rock, losing my flip-flop in the process. "The nesting stuff helped a lot."

Anya steadied me so I was standing on one leg and then jogged the short distance to it. "I'm glad. I wasn't so sure about Cal wanting to buy a bunch of stuff, but he clearly knows better than I do. He probably got straight As in all of his omega relations classes they had to take." She snorted and dropped the shoe back in front of me.

"Thanks." I slid my foot back in. "Where'd Gizmo go?"

She turned around and scanned the yard. "Damn dog. Probably wandered out into the front. He's so used to patrolling the perimeter. Come on."

I followed her, and Gizmo's bark came from the front of the cabin.

"Stay here." Anya glanced back at me over her shoulder. "Or go in the house."

She jogged the rest of the way to the cabin and around the side of it. I walked as quickly as I could to the side of the cabin, staying out of sight of the front. I strained my ears to try to hear, but my heart was pounding too hard, and Gizmo had stopped barking.

I crept along the wall, plastering myself to it, and inched closer and closer to the front. There were voices, both male and female. I stopped just before the corner. I couldn't see what was going on, but I could hear it.

"Where is she?" a female voice asked, deadly calm.

"Where's who?" Anya's voice trembled slightly, but not enough that strangers would have noticed.

"The omega. We know they're keeping one here."

My blood ran cold, and I felt a little lightheaded. How did they find out? The only other people that knew I was here were Kayla and Ella. Kayla would never do that to me, but Ella was the dean of students and we'd only just recently become good friends.

Had she called it in to Omega Protective Services?

"I don't know what you're talking about. I'm just here enjoying the quiet."

"You're employed by Pack Estrada, are you not? Anya Hughes? Beta? Your credit card has a rather large Nest & Knot purchase on it."

"A friend is celebrating her bonding and I got her some things. Hey! I didn't give you permission to go in the house!" Anya's voice had raised enough that if I were inside, I would have heard her. "This is illegal! Where's your search warrant?"

I was pretty sure she knew that OPS did not need a search warrant if they suspected an omega was being abused.

My stomach rolled with nausea, and I peeked out around the side of the house to see an OPS SUV, a Pack Health Organization vehicle, and two sheriff's cars.

I was fucked.

Anya stood helplessly in the front walkway, Gizmo by her side. He spotted me, nudged Anya's hand, and started to walk toward me.

"Gizmo, come here." Anya grabbed his collar, and our eyes met.

She was scared shitless, just like me, her eyes wider than usual and brimming with tears. "Hide," she mouthed.

Hide where? I looked at the trees and decided that was my best bet. I was not dressed for running and hiding but didn't have much choice. They were going to know I had been at the cabin and that I was in heat. The whole place was covered in our scents.

I moved as fast as possible in my flip-flops, trying not to make too much noise. The trees weren't that close together, but some of their trunks were wide enough that I could hide behind them.

Feet and then loud panting came from behind me, and I darted behind a tree just as Gizmo bounded up to me. Shit.

"Go back," I whisper-yelled at him, pushing his head in the direction of the cabin. "Go to Anya."

He nudged at my hand without budging and I patted his head before taking off again, needing to get farther away or find somewhere to hide. The forest was a horrible hiding spot, or at least this one was.

Gizmo was following me but then growled, causing me to hide behind another tree.

"Omega! We can smell you! We don't want to hurt

you!" The same woman who had been talking to Anya was headed right for me.

I looked around, my hope fading away when I realized I had nowhere to go. Even if I could have climbed one of the trees, they'd be able to smell me. I was perfuming like crazy, and my scent was strong anyway from being in heat.

"Is this really necessary? She's safe with me." I could barely hear Anya. "She's in heat! You can't just take her!"

Gizmo growled again, standing right next to the tree. He was baring his teeth, his hair bristling as footsteps moved closer and closer.

"We know you're scared. We want to talk and make sure you're safe." The woman was way closer now, but I think she stopped. I'd have stopped too if a dog was growling at me. "What's your name, hun?"

So, they didn't know who I was. It was a little bit of a relief that it hadn't been someone I knew that had called it in. Had someone seen or smelled me? It couldn't have been Anya with the way she was acting, but could it have been Jonathan?

No. He wouldn't do that to the pack.

"Don't do this," Anya pleaded with someone. "It will break them. They love her and she loves them!"

I bit back a sob as tears spilled down my cheeks. We hadn't even gotten to say the words to each other yet. I wished I could now. I wished I could scream it into the forest and it would travel to them.

"If they loved her, they would have followed proper

protocol," a man bit out with a growl. "They really had us fooled."

A branch snapped off to my right and my head turned in that direction just as a female officer lunged for me.

I screamed, my feet slow to get moving. The woman wrapped a hand around my wrist a little too tightly, causing me to whimper.

Gizmo was there in an instant, grabbing onto the woman's arm and yanking her off me.

"Gizmo! No!" Anya yelled.

The woman grabbed her baton, and I grabbed onto it before she could swing it at Gizmo. Another officer appeared, shoving me out of the way.

I fell back onto my ass, pain shooting up my tailbone. Anya rushed to me, helping me stand.

Gizmo yelped and then was standing off to the side of us, slightly in front. He didn't seem to be injured, but boy, was he pissed.

"Gizmo. No." Anya was trying to be firm but was also sobbing.

"Call off your dog!" The male officer that had pushed me had his gun drawn, pointing it at Gizmo's feet.

The agent from OPS moved forward a few steps and held up her hands in one of those calm down gestures that did nothing to calm me down. "Let's just all take a few deep breaths and go back to the house to talk."

There were two men and another woman behind

her. I didn't need to smell the men to know they were alphas; I could tell just from the way they stood.

"They're my pack. I won't leave them." I had somehow found my voice and stood a little taller. "Anya is right. We love each other. I want them as my pack."

"We'll see what we can do." She was lying. I knew she was, and everyone else knew too. She moved closer, her hands still raised in that placating way that was pissing me off.

It happened fast. One second, Gizmo had been off to the side, growling but not moving. The next, he was heading straight for the OPS agent.

The officer raised his gun.

I lunged for Gizmo, my fingers touching his fur.

Anya lunged for me, her hands shoving me.

The gun went off.

CHAPTER TWENTY-THREE

Avery

I could feel happiness radiating through our bond as we relaxed in our dressing room—another locker room—an hour before our show. I was pumped to perform and even more pumped to go back to our omega afterward.

If I had known all the pain would have led us to Kara, the last several years would have been so much more enjoyable. I hadn't enjoyed the journey we'd been on because I'd been so inside my head.

"She's not texting me back." Cal threw his phone on the couch cushion between us.

"Probably taking a nap." I didn't look up from my

phone where I was playing a game. "She said she and Anya were working on a surprise dinner for us."

"Well, what are they doing? Hunting down a wild turkey?" Cal picked up his phone again. "I wish we could video chat with her before the show."

"Not a good idea with so many people coming in and out." I glanced over at him and snorted at his pout. "She's fine, bro."

"Bro?" He looked at me in shock. "You haven't called me that in forever."

I shrugged and went back to my game. "Well, you did lick my dick. It's only fitting." I saw him flinch out of the corner of my eye and laughed. "Although, I guess a real brother wouldn't do that."

"Let's just forget that happened." Cal grabbed his water off the coffee table.

The locker room we were in was set up very similarly to the last one we'd been in. It was spacious, with comfortable lounge areas. It also had arcade games, which Alvaro and Tate were playing the crap out of.

"It's nothing to be embarrassed about. I would have probably done the same thing." I used my last life on my game and turned off the screen. "I can't wait until this tour is over."

The locker room door opened, and our two managers strode in with Tate's dad. This couldn't be good.

"Shit," Cal muttered and crossed his arms over his chest.

"Boys. Where are Alvaro and my son?" Marcus Carter was dressed in an expensive-looking navy-blue pin-striped suit, and his shoes probably cost more than my phone. Our pack had a lot of money, but we didn't wear it.

Alvaro and Tate popped around the corner from the area where the games were. The mood in the room had shifted from content joy to annoyance and unease.

"Have a seat, boys," Marcus said, gesturing to the sectional where Cal and I were already seated.

Alvaro sat down between me and Cal, and Tate sat on the other side of me. This was a common arrangement of ours; Alvaro close to both me and Cal and Tate next to me for added emotional support. I don't even think they realized they did it, but I did.

Our managers moved to stand behind us, which was comforting at least. If they felt like something was wrong, they would have probably stood with Marcus.

We'd had our managers since the beginning. One of them had been fresh out of college, just like we were, and the other had twenty years of experience managing some of the biggest names in the music industry. They ran our career like a well-oiled machine.

"What brings you to our neck of the woods?" Alvaro sat back and crossed his ankle over his knee, cool as a cucumber. I was glad at least one of us was.

Marcus started to walk along the other side of the coffee table, his fingers rubbing his clean-shaven chin. "We're going to be adding an extra concert to your tour two nights from now at Levi's Stadium. The demand was so high we decided it would be in our best interest to add another show."

"We weren't consulted on this," one of our managers added. "Tickets went on sale an hour ago."

Tate growled. "You can't just do shit like that. We're fucking human beings."

"Son, you're an alpha. You have plenty of stamina to do another concert. To make up for the short notice, we've booked you hotel suites for the duration of the tour."

I stiffened, and my heart went somewhere, but it wasn't in my chest anymore. "We'll stay on the bus."

"Well, that's another reason for the hotel rooms. The bus-"

"What the-" Alvaro jumped up from his seat just as the locker room doors burst open.

Jonathan ran in, looking like someone had punched him in the stomach. His face was pale and his eyes... something was wrong. His phone was gripped so hard in his hand I was surprised it hadn't broken to pieces yet.

We all stood, ignoring Marcus telling us to sit back down.

"I..." Jonathan looked at Marcus and then at our managers. "I need to speak to my pack alone."

Marcus crossed his arms. "They are going on stage in an hour. If you're worried about the bus, don't be. The

Pack Health agents said they were taking it for a routine inspection since the pack went MIA for a few days."

"What did you do?" Tate grabbed his father by the tie and walked him back into the wall.

Marcus held his hands up. "I did nothing, son. They were looking for you boys last night, and you weren't with the other buses."

My heart had returned and was beating violently in my chest. We'd cleaned the bus and doused the back room in de-scenting spray, but what if that wasn't enough?

Jonathan was staring off at nothing. "We need to go. Now."

That wasn't all he wanted to say. Whatever Alvaro felt coming from Jonathan sent worry through our bond. I was grateful our pack bond wasn't strong enough yet that I could feel Jonathan because I was struggling enough with the three.

As if sensing I was about to lose it, Cal grabbed my hand. "Cancel the show." He started toward the door, where Jonathan was still standing.

Marcus growled. "We are not canceling the show. There are twenty five thousand fans out there!"

Tate let Marcus go, and we followed Jonathan out into the hall, shutting the door behind us. The hallway was mostly empty and those that were in it were rushing about preparing for us to perform.

"They're in the hospital." Jonathan spoke so quietly I

thought I heard wrong. "Anya's in surgery to remove..." He choked up and put a hand over his eyes.

"To remove what?" Alvaro growled, his whole body vibrating with an anger I'd never seen from him before.

I could feel everyone's intense emotions, and I quickly threw up my mental blocks. It was too much. We needed to go to our omega and make sure she was okay.

Jonathan swallowed and shook his head. "A bullet. They wouldn't tell me anything about Kara. They just said Anya was brought in with another woman."

The locker room door opened, and Marcus walked out, his phone to his ear. He stopped and seemed to be processing the looks on all of our faces. "Can one of you tell me what the fuck is going on?"

Tate and Alvaro exchanged glances, and Alvaro nodded. "Dad, we need a ride to the hospital."

EVERYTHING WAS NUMB. I couldn't let myself feel anything other than nothing as we sat in the back of an SUV on the way to the hospital.

Marcus had insisted on coming with us but was giving us space by sitting in the front with the driver. He was on his phone anyway.

I didn't understand Tate's dad at all. One second, he was all alpha asshole, and the next he seemed to get it completely without asking any more questions. We didn't have to tell him. It was like he just somehow knew. I guessed it made sense given he was in a pack himself.

Cal's leg was bouncing non-stop next to me, occasionally hitting my leg and making me jump out of the thoughts I'd buried myself under.

"Kayla and her pack aren't answering their phones." Alvaro had been trying to call them since we'd gotten into the SUV.

"Airplane," Tate mumbled.

"What?" Alvaro was texting Kayla now instead of trying to call.

"If Kara is in the hospital, they would have called her family who would then have called her. They are probably on a plane coming here." Tate was worrying even me. He was usually the strong one, keeping the rest of us from falling apart. I needed him not to fall apart.

"Why would they shoot Anya?" Jonathan had asked that a few times, but none of us had an answer for him.

Marcus turned in his seat. "I was able to get ahold of my contact in Pack Health. When the agents couldn't locate your bus last night, they looked into your credit cards, including your betas'. They found credit card purchases on Anya's credit card and had enough reason to trace her phone location. There was an incident with the dog and that's all he could tell me."

I bit the inside of my cheek so hard to stop myself

from losing it that I tasted blood. Our omega. Our beta. Our dog.

We could lose them all. In one night. Everything.

Cal grabbed my hand for the second time. "It's going to be okay. It has to be."

"Sir, we're just about there. Where would you like me to drop you off?" The driver put on his turn signal, and as soon as he turned right, I could see the hospital down the street.

"The back. I arranged for us to use the staff elevator." Marcus had the phone to his ear again.

"Why are you doing this?" Tate finally tore his gaze away from the window.

"It's your pack, son. Am I happy we have to cancel the show? No, but if you went out there like this..." He shook his head, not finishing his thought. "You're my son."

He hadn't said a word about our omega, but probably because of the driver. I still wasn't a hundred percent certain that Marcus hadn't put all of this in motion in the first place, but then, why would he be helping us?

We stopped outside an employee's only entrance at the back of the hospital and scrambled out, not sure where the fuck we were headed, but knowing we needed to get to Kara.

An employee opened the door, and we followed him to an elevator. "Do you know what floor you're headed to?"

"Surgery." Jonathan looked terrified. Anya was his

world, and she was upstairs somewhere having a bullet dug out of her.

Was Kara having the same thing done? I growled at the thought and Cal squeezed my hand that I didn't even realize he was still holding.

Please be okay.

I'd already lost one omega, and before that, I'd lost my parents because they believed alphas and omegas were abominations.

I sure felt like one now as the elevator flew upwards. We couldn't protect our omega and now she was in a hospital bed, possibly dying.

"We need the seventh floor," Marcus said as the elevator stopped on the second.

"Go. I'll text you once I know more about Anya." Jonathan quickly got off the elevator.

"Need special clearance to go to the seventh floor." That was all the man had to say for us to know that's where any omegas were.

Marcus turned toward him. *"You'll take us to the seventh floor."* His bark was strong enough that I was even tempted to take us there myself, even though I had no clue how.

"I... I... I can't." The man gulped, his hand trembling as he lifted his keycard toward the panel on the door while fighting the barked command. The man was a beta, but a strong one if he was resisting a bark as strong as Marcus's.

The elevator doors slid shut but the elevator didn't move.

Tate grabbed the man's wrist and raised it to the electronic pad and pressed the button with a seven on it. The man made a strangled kind of whimpering noise, sweat breaking out on his forehead.

The elevator took off again, and I felt like I might vomit. She had to be okay. She just had to be. It was a good sign if Marcus knew she was on the seventh floor and not in surgery or the ICU.

As soon as the doors slid open, I caught a hint of her scent that hadn't been scrubbed from the air yet and was out the door before someone could stop me.

But they weren't running after me to stop me; they were running with me.

We passed a nurse's station and then there it was. Her room. The door was shut, but the faint scent was a little stronger here.

I stopped outside the door and turned the handle.

Locked.

I tried again, and again.

"Code Gold. Code Gold," a robotic voice said over the PA system.

I prowled toward the nurse's station where the nurses were scrambling. "Open the door!"

"Sir, we're going to have to ask you and your friends to leave," an older nurse said calmly. "We have to protect them, and we won't be letting you into any rooms under any circumstances."

"She's our omega!" I wanted to grab her by the front of her scrub top and drag her to the door. *"Open it right now."* My voice was deadly, and she paled.

"Avery, let's go." I wasn't entirely sure who grabbed my arm and tried to tug me away from the nurse.

"Open the fucking door!" My bark wasn't as strong as Alvaro's or even Tate's, but at that moment it sure as fuck felt like it.

"Freeze!"

The nurse put her hands in the air and slowly backed away, her face a mixture of fear and sympathy. I didn't want her sympathy, I wanted her to open the damn door so I could get to my omega.

"We're just here to see their omega," Marcus said to the footfalls quickly coming down the corridor. "There's no need for weapons."

I turned back to the door, ignoring my pack mates' pleas from behind me to freeze. I wasn't going to freeze. I needed her. I needed Kara.

"Tranquilize him," I heard someone say.

"Is that really-" Marcus started before I felt a stab of pain in my arm.

I looked down to find a fucking dart sticking out of it. I yanked it out, throwing it to the ground as my vision started to swim. We weren't animals; we were human fucking beings.

"Kara! Open the door!" My voice was already fading along with the sound of Alvaro telling someone not to hurt me. "Kara..."

I leaned against the door, my body feeling both heavy and like it was floating up, up, up.

My knees collapsed, and my hands squeaked as they dragged down the door. "Kara..." Her name died on my lips, just like the last thread of my sanity.

CHAPTER TWENTY-FOUR

Kara

Blood.

There was so much blood. Blood on my hands. My shirt. Gizmo.

Anya.

"Kara? Wake up." A soft hand touched my cheek, the owner smelling like a jar of Nutella.

"Kayla?" I croaked, trying to open my eyes, but my eyelids felt like they were glued shut. Why did my body and mind feel so heavy? It felt like I hadn't slept in days, and there was this bone-deep soreness like I'd never experienced before. "Where's Anya?"

"She's alive and had to have surgery. She's probably out now, I'm not sure." Kayla was on the bed with me, and I managed to open my eyes just as she raised the bed so we weren't lying down. "How are you feeling?"

I lifted my left hand and it felt like a hunk of lead. There was an IV in my forearm and I was hooked up to a monitor that was on but was silent. "What happened? Surgery? Where am I?"

Kayla shimmied out of the bed and grabbed a pink cup and pitcher from a rolling table. "You've been asleep for at least twelve hours. Here, drink some water."

I was still a little out of it, and I appreciated her being here. It was keeping me calm when I should have been freaking out. Why wasn't I freaking out?

OPS, Pack Health, and law enforcement had shown up at the cabin. *They knew.* They knew and had tried to come and take me away from my pack.

My pack.

My stomach turned with nausea, and I took a sip of the water Kayla handed me. It tasted funny, but my throat and mouth were dry, so I drank the rest.

She went to the window and opened the curtain, revealing a morning sky. "I got here only a few hours ago and my pack is working on finding out more information. They aren't allowed in here, though, so they're in the waiting room on the bonded side of the floor."

She'd come all the way from Los Angeles with her pack? I felt my head, looking for any bumps. "Did I hit my head? My brain is a little... fuzzy feeling and nothing makes sense. Where's Anya? My pack?"

I was oddly calm and relaxed, and it almost felt like I

was having some kind of out-of-body experience. It felt a little like having too much wine, but a notch past that. I'd never done drugs, so I wasn't sure if it was what being high felt like.

Kayla came back to the bed and sat next to me. There was just enough room on it for both of us. "They have you on some medicine that stopped your heat and also something to keep you calm. You were freaking out when everything happened, and they sedated you."

My eyes widened. "They tranquilized me, you mean."

She rolled her eyes in true Kayla fashion, and it made me smile just a little. "They told our parents they used a syringe and didn't shoot you with a tranq gun, but that doesn't matter. What matters is you're safe."

All agents and law enforcement carried tranquilizers with them because both alphas and omegas had extreme emotions thanks to our biology. I thought it was barbaric, especially when they used tranquilizer guns like we were animals. I'd never heard of an omega needing it since we were kept under lock and key, but alphas? That was really why they had them.

Kayla sighed and took my hand. "We're on the secure side of the omega floor at the hospital. Anya was shot in the lower abdomen or stomach—it wasn't very clear—and had surgery to remove the bullet. That's all I was able to find out. They called our parents, but because Mom's heats are crazy from omegapause, they wanted to wait and see if you needed them to come or not."

Part of me wanted my mom and dads surrounding

me for comfort, but another part of me didn't want to see the disappointment on their faces when they found out I wasn't following omega regulations.

"And Gizmo? My pack? What is going on? Just tell me, Kayla." I knew she was telling me everything else first because there was only bad news where my pack was concerned.

"Gizmo is fine. You were trying to stop him from getting to the agent right as that fucking idiot sheriff tried to shoot him. Anya apparently has fast reflexes because she dived for you and the bullet hit her. I think she was in the process of falling to knock you out of the way."

It sounded like something out of a movie, but it was starting to come back to me now. It had happened so fast, and I'd hit the ground right as the gun was finishing going off. It wasn't a movie at all, it was my personal nightmare that I was going to have to live with for the rest of my life. They had been there because of me. Anya was shot because of me.

I squeezed Kayla's hand for comfort because everything could have been a lot worse. "I need to find out if Anya is going to be okay. She's my beta. They should tell me, right? Or Jonathan. He's here, isn't he?"

"I'm sure he is." She sighed and scooted closer to me. "They took your pack into custody, Kayla. They came... and they tried to get to you."

Whatever shit they had me on was strong because all I could do was let tears fall down my cheeks, even though I wanted to run out and find them. "It's not their fault, Kayla. I went on their bus."

She handed me a tissue just as there was a knock on the door. The lock tumbled and two women in suits walked in.

Omega Protective Services.

"Good morning." The OPS agent who had tried talking me into coming with them smiled tightly at me and then looked at Kayla. "I guess you really are identical, aren't you?"

I didn't say anything, because I couldn't. There was a giant lump in my throat, and I just knew they were here to take me back to the compound; that's why they had gone to the cabin.

Kayla put the bed up even more, so we were sitting all the way up instead of reclined. "Can we get my sister off of all this stuff messing with her emotions?"

"They'll be in to remove the IV and monitor when we're done here. The doctors would like to keep her a few hours after that just as a precaution." The agent pulled up a chair next to the bed and sat down. "I'm Lena Clarkson, and this is Mary Lee from Omega Protective Services."

Kayla snorted. "Enough with the pleasantries. My sister wants to return to her pack immediately."

I put my head on Kayla's shoulder. There was nothing worse than feeling helpless, and that was exactly how I felt all drugged up. What would I have done if Kayla hadn't come to be by my side?

Lena pulled out a tape recorder and pressed a button. "Right now, we need to follow protocol and that includes recording all conversations from this point forward."

Kayla and I both knew the drill when it came to OPS. Everything was documented to make it easier for their agency and us. I knew they were just doing their jobs, but that didn't mean I had to like it.

"Do I have to go back to the compound I was at? Can I move to the one in Los Angeles so I'm closer to my sister?" I somehow managed to string those two questions together, but it felt like I'd written an essay.

"That wouldn't be a good idea." Mary paced at the end of the bed. This whole thing made her nervous, probably because she was a bonded omega. I could see the silver scars of her claiming bites peeking out from the collar of her shirt. "If the Estrada pack is released and knows you are there..."

"But the match is soon, and when I match to them..." I didn't finish because the looks on their faces told me everything I needed to know.

"As you know, and have been taught, one of the many reasons Omega Match is in place is so that omegas can be free to make their own decisions without their hormones or other people making the decision for them." Lena was a beta, so she just didn't understand.

"It *is* my decision. What does it matter if we're together now or during an authorized matching time? We're only going to put each other on our match lists.

They're mine and I'm theirs." I was starting to become a little more focused, but I already felt like I could sleep another twelve hours.

Mary stopped at the end of the bed, concern written in her eyes. "They were practically feral a few months ago. Pack Health was ready to put chips in them to monitor their every move and keep any and all omegas away from them. Two in particular would have needed time in a facility."

"That's ridiculous!" Kayla couldn't sit still next to me any longer and stood on the opposite side of the bed from the agents. "They were around me and I was unbonded! They were perfect gentlemen. So what if they have an *alpha* reaction to scents? They don't act on them!"

"You put yourself at great risk. Anything could have happened. All it takes is one hit of an appealing scent and they could have attacked you and gone into a rut without consent." Lena looked at my sister like she was insane for putting herself in that situation.

"But nothing happened because they're amazing alphas! Nothing happened to my sister either, and trust me, they were into her scent." Kayla crossed her arms defiantly. "Kara is a four-time *Omega of the Year* award winner. Do you really think she'd pick a pack that was bad for her?"

Lena kept her eyes on me the entire time my sister was fighting my battle for me. "There's a reason they aren't in Omega Match."

"I know why. It's such a ridiculous reason. It's not their fault an omega couldn't handle the situation a little better. How many times do children get lost in the store and there are no consequences? She could have just gone in after them." I put my head back against the bed and wondered if the girl regretted acting irrationally.

"She didn't feel safe, and maybe things would have been different had they noticed she was missing sooner. She wouldn't have been able to get into that club as crazy as it was. They should have never made the decision to take her there when they had no connection with her yet." Lena glanced at Mary and then back at me. "Did you mate with them?"

My cheeks heated, and I looked down at my hands clasped in my lap. "I think you know the answer to that question. Just seeing them step on stage after building a connection with them over the last few months sent me into a breakthrough heat."

My sister was back on the bed, patting my arm to comfort me. If it had been any other omega, I would have smacked her away. What I needed was the comfort of my alphas' purrs.

"How did you meet them? Through Kayla?" Mary asked, genuine curiosity and support in her voice. She wanted me to have my pack. The problem was convincing those that didn't understand.

"No. Well, sort of. I... I borrowed someone's car and went to visit my sister. The first night I was there I went back out to the car, which I'd parked down the street, and..."

I told them everything. From being chased by Gizmo, to falling into the pool, to how they took care of me. One of the hardest parts to share was how we made the decision to do the match the right way and we were separated for months.

"You can't blame them for this. I was the one that went to their bus. I wanted them for my heat. I was selfish and now-" I took a sharp breath to stop the sob welling in my chest. "Now, they might never be happy or have the love they deserve."

The room was quiet besides sniffling from me and my sister. I had to give the two agents credit for keeping their composure because they both looked ready to cry too. Even Lena, who I had pegged for a hard ass with no heart.

"I think we've heard enough for now." Lena turned off the tape recorder and leaned forward in her chair to put her hand over mine. "I know I come off as uncaring and detached, but my job is to make sure all omegas are safe with or without a pack."

"I'm safe with them," I whispered, my eyes burning as new tears continued to well up. "They're going to take time off once we match. I know exactly what I'll be facing with a famous pack, so please just... fight for me."

Kayla sighed. "It would be an absolute shame if everyone found out about the dangers of Omega Match and how they are keeping an omega apart from her pack."

Lena finally looked over at my sister with raised eyebrows. "If Omega Match fails, then we go back to arranged matches or something even worse. Is that what you want?"

"We know Omega Match isn't ideal for everyone, but it's the safest and easiest way for omegas to find a pack right now. There are some things that need to be fixed, and maybe with all the technology there is now, there can be a little bit more to it than meet and greets or speed dating." Mary looked at her watch. "We'll be back in a few hours to take you back to the compound."

What she really meant was she'd take me back to my prison.

CHAPTER TWENTY-FIVE

Cal

nkle monitors.

They'd put fucking ankle monitors on us like we were some kind of animals. Maybe we were deep down, and that's why we were treated like royalty one minute and trash the next.

If alphas weren't so motivated and ruthless when it came to being the best of the best, I was sure betas would have had us locked away by now. And who knew, maybe that would one day happen. They outnumbered us plain and simple.

I propped my foot on the coffee table and stared at the solid green light that let me know I was within the range they'd laid out. We were allowed within a twenty-mile radius of our house but couldn't go anywhere near the academies or compounds here. Like we were interested in any omega other than Kara.

Alvaro came down the stairs, his own ankle accessory also glowing green, and sat next to me with a heavy sigh. "Avery's playing video games."

Thank fuck. I thought we were going to have to lock him in a room or tie his ass to a chair. He kept saying he was going to go find Kara, and we believed he would.

Avery was a mess and had been since we were detained the night before. We'd been questioned all night, gone through assessments all day, and now we were home after a short flight from Oregon.

The rest of our tour was canceled—not by choice—and so now we awaited our hearing in a few days to find out what the next steps were. For now, everyone thought we were sick, and in a way, we were, and hopefully it stayed that way.

That was really wishful thinking on my part.

"Do you think they're going to put him in a facility? He doesn't seem feral to me. More like... heartbroken." I leaned my head back on the couch and stared at the ceiling. "I think I'm going to go for a ride."

Alvaro grumbled and leaned his head back too. "Now is not the time to go pick up women."

I growled and sat up, smacking his chest with the back of my hand. "I would never do that. Not now. Not ever again. If we don't get Kara back, I'll... I'll... cut off my dick and send it to her."

Alvaro shut his eyes and sighed. "I don't even feel like laughing at that."

"I'm not joking. This dick is never touching another pussy, ass, or mouth again. As soon as I have the balls to do it, I'm tattooing her name down the side of it." I sat back with a huff, knowing I was being a bit dramatic, but also not caring.

I was dealing the best way I knew how, just like the rest of them were dealing in their own ways.

Alvaro was holding himself together by a thread; I could see it in his eyes and the tension in his neck and shoulders. He'd been occupying himself with Avery and making sure he was settled.

Avery had woken up from being tranq'd with a growl so vicious I was half tempted to sedate him myself. I don't know how the agents managed to interview him or do assessments, but they didn't keep him, so he'd clearly snapped out of it. Besides muttering he needed to go get Kara, he'd been silent since they let us go.

As soon as we got home, Tate had gone straight out to the backyard and parked his ass in a lounge chair. He was usually rock solid, and it worried me he was retreating from us.

Alvaro's phone rang, and he answered it on speaker. "Hey, man. How is she?"

I still could hardly believe that Anya had been shot pushing Kara out of the way. It made my blood boil that someone had a real gun out, not just around our omega but our beta and dog too.

"She's doing really well. They are probably going to release her tomorrow and we'll stay in a nearby hotel for a few days just to be on the safe side. How are you four doing?" Jonathan had a lot to deal with, and the last of his concerns should have been us.

"We're hanging in there. Glad to be home but still processing everything that happened." Alvaro rubbed his forehead like he had a headache. "I'm sorry you two got dragged into this."

"Why are you apologizing? It's not your fault a broken system can't let you guys find your happiness. They interviewed me earlier today and I told them as much." Jonathan must have been outside the hospital room, but now the beeping of machines could be heard. "Anya is awake. I'll check in tomorrow when we're released."

"Sounds good. Love you, man. Tell Anya we love her." Alvaro hung up, and we sat in silence for a few minutes.

Anya was going to be fine, but the bullet had come close to really messing her up. Luckily, they'd been able to get the bullet out.

"You know what?" I jumped up, wincing as the movement made the monitor pinch my skin. "You should all come with me to blow off some steam. It's like ten miles away."

"We don't have motorcycles."

"We'll take a car instead. It's where I go when I need to let my alpha out, and you just assume I'm fucking around." I went to the sliding door and opened it. "Hey, we're going to my top-secret spot. Want to come?"

Tate sat up and looked back at me. "And where's that?"

"Wouldn't you like to know." I left the door open, knowing Tate wouldn't be able to resist having his questions about where I went several times a week answered.

Alvaro went to the kitchen and opened the refrigerator. "I'll pack us some drinks."

"I have drinks there." I usually started my nights with a few beers when I went and had a fully stocked fridge.

I ran up the stairs and jogged down the hall to where Avery should have been playing video games. The TV was on, but Avery and Gizmo were nowhere to be found.

My eye caught on the slightly ajar door to the primary bedroom and my chest started to pound. What the hell was he doing?

We'd spent countless hours preparing the room for us and Kara. If he was messing it up, I was going to fucking kill him.

"Avery?" I pushed the door open, and Gizmo made a sad whimper from the bed.

The bed he shouldn't have been on. I rolled my eyes and grabbed his collar, pulling him off the custom-made mattress that was big enough to fit all five of us comfortably. The thing had cost a small fortune.

"Where's Avery, Gizzy? Did he climb out the

window?" If we had to chase his ass down, I was not going to be happy.

Gizmo went to the French doors leading into the nesting area and looked back at me. I couldn't say I was surprised Avery had come in here; I'd been tempted to as well. But it wasn't like it smelled like Kara; Pack Health had taken all of her nesting stuff as evidence.

Fuckers.

I knocked gently and opened one of the doors. The area had once been a small sitting area that was part of the main bedroom, but we'd walled it off and put doors in. The ceilings were high, just like the bedroom, and we'd constructed a tent-like structure to hang lush draperies from.

Right inside the doorway was a little area where there was a half-sized refrigerator and freezer and a cabinet to keep things we might need.

I pulled back the curtain door and peered inside. Avery was lying in the dark in the center, the Squishmallows and pillows surrounding him.

"Hey, man. Can I come in?" I wasn't sure if he was going to be irritated by me or not. We'd just started to heal our bond with each other when shit had hit the fan.

"No." He grunted, rolling to his side and hugging the Squishmallow he'd picked out. "Leave me alone."

"Well, too bad." I looked back to check that Gizmo wasn't about to come into the nest, but he was back on the bed again. Damn dog, but I guess he deserved some comfort after trying to protect our omega and beta.

I let the curtain fall shut and we were bathed in darkness. The area was about the size of two full beds, and I flopped down to the right of where I'd seen Avery.

"So, what's up? Just hanging out in the dark?" I itched to turn on the fairy lights we'd strung with the drapery, but I was already pushing it with Avery.

He didn't respond, and I reached over and poked him in the back. He let out a low growl but didn't move or speak.

"We're going to my secret spot. Want to come? It'll be good to get out some of that angsty alpha energy." I poked him again.

"Stop fucking poking me!"

I poked him in the ass, and that was apparently the line I shouldn't have crossed. He growled and grabbed my wrist, his grip brutal.

"Ow!" I sat up and tried to yank my arm away. "I was just playing around. Fuck!"

He shoved my arm away. "Get the fuck out of here before I make you."

I sighed and rubbed at my wrist, which would probably have marks. "Maybe Pack Health is right and we shouldn't be around omegas."

"*I* shouldn't be around omegas." His voice was muffled like he had his face buried in a pillow. "Just leave, Cal."

"You know what? No, I'm staying right here until you agree to come with us." I reached over and pressed the button to turn on a strand of lights.

The nest was just as epic as it had always been, but seeing it now made me sad. We'd been so sure things would work out for us.

"Then you'll be waiting there forever. I'm not leaving." He grabbed a pillow and threw it at me.

I caught it before it could hit me in the face. "Well, what if you have to pee? Or take a shit?"

He didn't respond, and I sat quietly for a few minutes, collecting my thoughts before speaking again in a soft voice like I was talking to a wild animal... which wasn't too far from reality.

"From the moment we all met, we had this connection. This brotherhood that grew into the best thing that has happened to me... to any of us, I think. It brought me three brothers who push me to be a better person, even though I sometimes might not act like it. We formed a pack, bonded... we worked our asses off to create a name for ourselves in an industry that even the best of the best might not make it in.

"And then we let an immature omega take the only thing that really mattered away from us; our bond with each other. Our family. It fucking hurt. Every day I watched you suffer, Alvaro worry, and Tate ignored it. It's a miracle our career is what it is when we were merely roommates."

Avery turned over to his other side, his lips in a tight line and his eyes intense. I had to look away as I continued.

"And then Kara showed up. The hope we had for her

being our omega brought us back together—not to how we once were as a pack, but it was getting there—and everyone was so damn happy. We were healing. *She* was healing us. And then she showed up on our bus and..." I shook my head, suddenly feeling ridiculous that I was detailing everything Avery already knew.

"Keep going," Avery rasped.

"I thought, this is it, this is the defining moment of my life. Our omega was with us, and we were taking care of her. Nothing else mattered but her... and then they took her from us. It sucks ass, but if we give up now when we are so close to having everything we could ever want? We can't give up on her. She's ours, and if we have to spend the next twenty years fighting for her, then that's going to have to be okay. Kara is worth every sleepless night and every tear. We have to keep trying and that means being a pack and fighting like our lives depend on it to get her back. She deserves that much, doesn't she?"

He shut his eyes and took a deep breath before letting it out, causing his cheeks to puff out. "I'm tired of never being good enough, Cal."

"We are good enough. Don't let people who don't even know us or Kara dictate if we're good enough for each other. Maybe if we all started believing that, so would they."

"How did you go from going crazy and licking my dick like it was an omega popsicle to being so... rational?" Avery sat up and ran his hands through his messy hair as I chuckled about him calling his dick an omega popsicle. "You said you have a place to get out angsty energy?"

I got to my knees and rubbed my hands together. "The more I think about sharing it, the more excited I am."

Maybe a few months ago they would have been worried about me, but now? Not a chance.

TWENTY MINUTES LATER, I pulled off the freeway and drove toward the warehouses. I could feel the tension in the SUV as my pack mates wondered where the fuck I was taking them.

Most of the buildings were dark, but a few had late shifts. I turned into a parking space of a darkened building and shut off the SUV.

"Is this where we find out you moonlight as a serial killer and you have a freezer full of bodies?" Alvaro peered out the window, trying to see where the fuck we were.

"This is where he's manufacturing omega popsicles," Avery said, deadpan.

Tate snorted. "What the hell are omega popsicles?"

"Alpha dicks coated in slick." Avery opened his door and got out before anyone could respond.

Alvaro looked over at me. "What did you say to him?"

I shrugged. "Just told him that Kara deserves for us to try."

We got out of the car, and I walked to the door where Avery was leaning against the wall, a thoughtful expression on his face.

The alarm beeped in warning as I opened the door, and I quickly entered my code before flipping on the lights.

"Holy shit." Avery walked in first, his eyes widening. "I don't know whether to be mad you've never brought us here or excited you finally did."

I let the three of them take in the five thousand square feet of old cars, furniture, appliances, electronics, and other breakable fun. "I went to a place one night where you could destroy shit, and well... I wanted more. The only things off limits are the sound system, the refrigerator, and the couch over in the corner."

I headed toward the opposite corner we entered from. "Beers?"

"Fuck yes, I want a beer." Avery followed me, excitement in his voice.

I had a feeling he'd like this place. Was it healthy to beat the shit out of inanimate objects? Probably not. But it was a hell of a lot better than letting my anger and unhappiness fester.

And besides, destroying stuff was fun.

After we all had beers in hand, I handed them safety glasses that had conveniently come in a pack of four.

"Where do you get all this stuff?" Tate took a sip of beer after putting the safety glasses on.

"I pay someone at one of those junk hauling places to bring me stuff. The cars I have another guy gets me from auctions. My favorite thing is to stand on the top of a car and beat the windshield in. Makes me feel like I'm a badass."

Avery grinned and grabbed a sledgehammer I had leaning against the wall. "Let's show these inanimate objects just how strong a pack we are."

And we did just that.

CHAPTER TWENTY-SIX

Alvaro

The hardest part of what we were going through was that we weren't allowed to contact Kara or her sister. It felt like a slap in the face to not even be able to ask Kayla if Kara was all right.

We couldn't ruin our chances, though, so we sucked it up and went to Cal's smash warehouse nearly every day to take out our aggressive energy.

But now, the day was here, and our driver dropped us off at the rear entrance of the building that the World Pack Health Organization operated from. A few days before, news broke about our situation, and so much love and support —as well as some hate—poured in.

That also meant our privacy had gone out the window and there were already people gathering in front of the building, hoping to catch a glimpse of us.

We were led up to the fifth floor and put in a conference room to wait for the agents and our lawyers to arrive. With the media coverage, we'd been asked to arrive earlier to ensure we weren't held up in the chaos.

"I feel like I'm going to vomit." Cal stood and paced by the windows. "Does anyone else feel like they're going to vomit?"

"Sit down, Cal. We don't need them to think we're losing it." I pulled out my phone and checked it for the hundredth time, hoping to see a text from Kara.

I knew there would be no text, though. She wanted this just as badly as we did and wouldn't jeopardize the chance. I stared at the last text from her telling us she had a surprise for us after our concert.

We'd certainly had a surprise. It had just come before the concert and wasn't a good one.

Without thinking about what I was doing, I clicked over to my favorite social media app and wasn't surprised to see my notifications maxed out.

"You shouldn't be on there." Avery nudged me with his elbow.

"It's mostly positive stuff, and all the negative things are shit we already thought about ourselves. We're at the top of the trending list." I snorted and clicked it to see what was said about us.

NPactRocks: *Why should alphas and omegas not have another chance at love? Betas do. Look at our divorce rate.*

SharkyMcShark: *I can't believe they had an omega and she called OPS on them for something out of their control. I hope this new one is better.*

Beta4life69: *They couldn't handle an omega and now they can?*

OmegaGirl: *I'll be their omega if this doesn't work out for them.*

RealKaylaSterling: *We are protesting outside of Pack Health headquarters at ten! Bring signs!*

ChickenLover: *@RealKaylaSterling. OMG, I'm fangirling so hard right now. Will your pack be there?*

DarkHeart22: *@ChickenLover if they let @RealKaylaSterling come alone, then maybe OPS needs to separate them.*

RealKaylaSterling: *@ChickenLover they'll be there. @DarkHeart22 they're my pack, not my babysitters.*

I exited the app and went to the window. "Holy shit."

We'd come in the opposite way, so we didn't see the front of the building. The entire street out front was flooded with a sea of people holding signs. I couldn't read what any of them said, but I hoped it was in support of us.

"Guys, come look." This was the boost of confidence we needed to get through this.

"Woah. That's at least a thousand people, don't you think?" Avery stood next to me and put his hand on my shoulder. "This isn't going to hurt us, is it?"

I hoped not. I could see it going either way, though.

On one hand, the number of people on social media saying we should be allowed to do Omega Match again was overwhelming. But on the other, the crowd below was no place for an omega, and we were constantly dealing with crowds like that.

"Look!" Tate pointed. "Kayla's standing in the bed of a truck with her pack. She's pointing to us!"

Kayla had a megaphone and was saying something I couldn't quite hear through the thick windows. But I didn't need to because soon the entire sea of people was chanting, *"Let them match."*

"This is amazing!" Cal waved, and the protestors waved back. "Looks peaceful... right now."

Even if things didn't go well today, I hoped things didn't get out of control on the street. The last thing I wanted was for any fans or my omega's sister to get hurt.

The conference room door opened, and our legal team came in. We had the best of the best, a pack of three ruthless unbonded alphas who were devoted to representing alphas tied up in the legal system.

"Gentlemen, let's get our game faces on. We don't want anyone to get any ideas about you four being responsible for the protests outside." Hudson, the pack's leader, was a bit cold-hearted, but he knew his shit.

We sat down in our usual arrangement, although I was less concerned about Avery and Cal after the week of pack bonding we had smashing shit to pieces.

The three alphas sat across from us, leaving the other

chairs at the opposite end of the table empty for the OPS and Pack Health representatives.

Everett took a small stack of papers out of his briefcase and placed them on the table. "We're hoping this will be a quick decision in your favor, but if it's not, we are prepared to take this to court based on Omega Match's history of match mismanagement and what transpired at the cabin."

Tate ran his hand down his tie. "They won't want to take this to court. Omega Match has been good about keeping their fuck ups out of the limelight."

"Even if they don't allow you to match, there are other options." Jace grinned slyly and then cringed when Hudson growled. "We'll talk later if it comes to it."

There was a soft knock on the door, and we all turned to watch the head of Omega Protective Services and a Pack Health official and lawyer file into the room.

I could feel the anxiousness in my pack bond and tried to turn my own into something more positive: optimism. There weren't Pack Health agents, which was a good sign. Of course, they could have been waiting on standby down the hall to take us if things got bad.

I grabbed Avery's hand and then Cal's, hoping the contact would keep them calm. Avery reached for Tate's hand, and we were connected. One pack to face whatever decision was made.

Tape recorders from both parties were turned on and the head of OPS started the meeting off. "This has been a very complicated matter for my organization.

After our evaluation of the assessments, interviews with those close to the pack and the omega, their previous match, and Kara, we feel Pack Estrada is fully capable of welcoming an omega into their pack."

I squeezed the guys' hands. One hurdle down, one to go.

The representative for Pack Health spoke next. "This decision will set a precedence for all other packs excluded from Omega Match for very serious reasons. Ignoring that they mated with an unbonded omega during her heat opens our communities to more widespread abuse."

No.

"Two consenting parties doesn't equate to an abuse of any kind. It is a barbaric practice to let omegas suffer through heats without a pack, even if the pack isn't the one that they intend to bond with." Hudson took a paper off the top of Everett's stack of papers. "Here we have a study done by the leading doctors in omega medicine that details that even during suppressed heats, omegas are ten times more likely to have a cardiac or psychological event and have pain the equivalent of a heart attack."

The Pack Health lawyer took the paper and skimmed through it. "There are medical interventions in place to support omegas during their heats."

"Even with those medical interventions, heats are painful. As was the case with Kara, she was on suppressants and had a breakthrough heat. Our bodies do not take kindly to medicines that go against our very nature." The head of OPS, who was a bonded omega, sat a little taller in her seat. "While I don't think it should be a free for all with packs, I think Kara and the pack were in a situation where there was no choice."

"Precisely. The omega didn't have a choice whether or not to mate with them. They could have very easily called OPS to come and get the girl." The Pack Health official gave me a disapproving look that made me feel like the worst alpha in the world.

"They were already in a long-distance relationship." Hudson handed another piece of paper to the lawyer. "This shows the long history of communication between the omega and the pack. Unlike with Omega Match, they got to know each other for months before Ms. Sterling decided to go to them during her heat. This is how things should be; not a five-minute session and a profile with a scent card."

They looked over the paper, and the impassive looks on their faces were not giving me any indication of whether what our lawyers were presenting was helping our case. "We'd have to see the actual conversations to know if the omega was being manipulated."

"I've reviewed the text conversations. They are in line with what an omega and a pack should be discussing." The omega turned the faintest shade of pink. She was a middle-aged omega, probably already having gone through omegapause, which was most likely why she'd come into a room of alphas with no guards.

Our lawyers had reviewed the conversations too, but with omissions, and we'd mutually decided not to share them unless it was absolutely necessary. We didn't want other alphas seeing our omega sexting us and vice versa.

Jace took the next piece of paper on the stack. "I have a statement here I'd like to read from the omega the pack matched with who later decided to reject their match."

My eyes widened and I gave Hudson a *what the fuck* look. He hadn't discussed talking to Jenna. Avery shifted in his chair, and I gave his hand a reassuring squeeze.

"The day an omega joins her pack is supposed to be one of the best days of her life. I'd been looking forward to matching with a pack on my list and was excited that Alvaro, Avery, Cal, and Tate were paired with me. I didn't know much about them outside of the ten minutes we mingled at an event at my academy but was attracted to them and liked that they were into the arts.

"Things didn't go well, though. We were all young. They were fresh out of college, and I was an anxious omega who needed my hand held for everything. One would think I'd be excited to match with emerging superstars, but the second we stepped into the crowd, I knew I wasn't going to be able to handle the life they were about to fall into.

"It takes a special omega such as Kara Sterling, who is well known in the omega community, to meet the demands of a superstar pack. While it was heart-breaking to reject the match so soon, I have found my own amazing pack that meets my needs. It just wasn't a good match, and the Estrada pack should not be made to suffer any longer for something that happened three years ago. By denying them, you are denying nature."

Jace handed the paper down the table. "What she says is absolutely true. The Pack Health Organization claims to be working in the best interest of alphas, but right now you are preventing them from fulfilling their alpha nature."

"Our organization is working in the best interest of all alphas. The second an omega is mauled or killed, we'll face more oversight. None of us want that."

Everett had the last piece of paper in his hands. "I'd like to read a statement from Kara Sterling."

Our pack collectively took a breath. We must have been a sight in our custom suits, holding hands and sweating bullets. I knew I could handle hearing what Kara had to say, even if in a statement, but I didn't know if Avery or Cal could.

We were about to find out.

CHAPTER TWENTY-SEVEN

Kara

My wine glass sat empty on the coffee table as I stared at the black screen of my phone on the couch next to me. There should have been a decision by now and either I'd get a call from my pack or the lawyers. One meant we'd be able to match, and the other…

I stood from the couch, taking my wine glass to the kitchen to pour another half a glass. Yes, it was before noon on a weekday, but I didn't care. I wasn't working for obvious reasons, and I needed some kind of support since Ella couldn't take the last few days of her employment off.

She'd decided to enter the match this fall after her

visit to her parents' house over the summer. I had a feeling she'd met a pack, but I couldn't get her to tell me anything.

I went back to the couch and checked my phone just in case I'd missed a call. Kayla hadn't texted me in over an hour, but she might have also been arrested.

I couldn't stop my smile as I took a sip of wine. Kayla had sent me a picture one of her alphas had taken as she screamed into a megaphone. My sister was badass, and I loved her to pieces for being outside of Pack Health headquarters supporting my pack when I couldn't be there myself.

I clicked over to my documents and pulled open the letter I'd written for the pack's lawyers. It had flowed straight from my heart but left me an emotional wreck.

Dear Omega Protective Services, *World Pack Health Organization, and Omega Match,*

I was once the type of omega that followed the rules and lived with the fear of not being perfect. My entire being was consumed with the need to be the best I could be, and then Omega Match happened.

On the morning that spring match results were sent, I was so excited, only to have every hope and dream I'd had taken away. I had no matches. While I don't know if I'll ever know what truly happened to my match results, I am glad it happened because I met my pack.

Growing up, I had the privilege of watching a strong and loving omega be surrounded by equally as strong and loving alphas. With six fathers, I was no stranger to how alphas should treat and take care of their omega, each other, and their offspring. It wasn't just a pack with an omega, but a partnership of seven amazing parents.

When one of my fathers passed away suddenly, I thought everything was going to fall apart. My mom was a mess and my fathers had just lost an essential part of their pack bond. What could have easily destroyed the pack didn't because of the strength they had together.

Every pack must face tragedies and overcome obstacles to their happiness, but it's how they come out on the other side that shows their true strength.

Alvaro, Tate, Cal, and Avery have faced a lot in their short time as a pack. From rejection, to fame, to navigating it all without an omega that they so desperately wanted and needed. By all accounts, the pack should have fallen apart and turned feral, but they didn't. Their bond, even when weakened, was able to withstand intense pressures other packs would have crumbled over.

It's cruel to stop a pack that does nothing but bring joy to others from having their own joy. They've jumped through every hoop imaginable and yet are still told they can't have the only thing they really want: me.

We met under interesting circumstances where they could have very well taken advantage of my fragile state of mind, *but they didn't. They tried to return me to my sister's house, but I stopped them. It was ultimately them who decided to do things the right way when all I wanted were their bites on my neck, consequences be damned.*

Over the last few months, I have gotten to know the pack better than I ever could have through Omega Match. I know what hardworking and compassionate men they are. Their bond has only strengthened, and when I showed up on their bus in heat, they worked as a pack to make sure I was comfortable and taken care of. Not once did I feel they were taking advantage of me or feel they would force a bond with me.

I do not take choosing a pack lightly. My entire being knows that the Estrada pack is mine. They will always be mine, and if it takes years to be allowed to match with them, then I will wait.

My biggest regret is I never had the chance to tell Alvaro, Tate, Cal, and Avery that I love them before I was ripped away from them. I hope you find it in your hearts to let me have the chance to say it every day for the rest of my life.

Sincerely,
Kara Sterling

I put my phone on the arm of the couch and finished my wine. My nerves were shot and there was a slight tremble in my hand as I put the glass on the table.

Maybe they wouldn't be allowed to talk to me afterward, even if things went well. My sister hadn't been able to contact her pack after matching because of their celebrity status. But I had their numbers and they had mine, so why was no one calling me?

I grabbed my Squishmallows and pulled them to my chest. "What are we thinking, girls? Are we going to be packing or opening a new box of tissues?"

"Don't be such a downer! We can still run away to Mexico with them," Jane Doe squeaked.

Princess Leia smooshed against the deer. "But if we run away, we can never come back! Plus, people can be extradited, and N'Pact are pretty recognizable. Although, maybe they could grow bushy beards."

"Not bushy beards! They remind me of hunters! Ahhh!" I threw the deer across the room. "Run!"

I sighed and lay down. If they didn't approve them to do the match, I honestly didn't know what I was going to do.

My phone rang and I nearly knocked it off the arm of the couch grabbing it. Breaking it was the last thing I needed.

Alvaro flashed across the screen, and I burst into tears as I pressed the *accept call* button. This was it. He was either going to break my heart or give me the best news ever.

"Sweetheart, what's wrong?" Concern filled Alvaro's voice as I struggled to even say hello. He was quiet for a minute. "I love you too. It's all going to be okay. We're doing the fall match and we can finally be together."

His voice cracked, and now I really wasn't going to be able to talk. I wanted to be there with them and go home with them. I wanted to make love to them and have them give me their marks and then mark them.

"I... really?" I laughed through my sobs because it felt like a dream, or maybe that was just from having a few glasses of wine.

"Really. Your letter helped immensely. We'll have to do weekly check-ins with OPS and Pack Health for the first few months. We hope that's okay with you. It's a bit intrusive."

"I don't care." I grabbed a tissue and wiped my nose. "Three weeks..."

"Three weeks." He sniffled, and I heard someone whisper in the background. "We have to go and sign some paperwork now and then deal with the crowd in front of the building. We'll call back when we're home and can video chat, okay?"

I didn't want to hang up the phone or wait. Why couldn't we be together now? What if Omega Match deleted my matches again and I was left packless?

"Kara? It's going to happen. We have it in writing, so even if something did fuck up the match, it's a done deal." Alvaro's voice was all alpha and it made all negative thoughts vanish.

It was actually going to happen. It had all been worth

it, and now I just had to be patient for three more weeks.

TIME MOVES SO SLOWLY when you're waiting for something. I had a countdown on my phone and found myself staring at it more than was healthy. Talking on video chat just made the yearning ache so much worse.

By the time matching was done and I was cleared to leave the compound, I was a ball of omega nervous energy and kept letting whimpers free as I rode to the airport.

I was bringing the most important stuff with me, but everything else I owned was packed in boxes and shipped to the pack's house in Los Angeles.

We turned off the highway and headed for the private plane entrance. In just a few short hours, I was going to be home with my pack.

The driver passed the small parking lot and turned down a driveway running along the side of the building.

"Um, ma'am, I think you're supposed to park in that lot back there." I thought the drivers knew where to go since they drove so many omegas back and forth to this very same airport.

"Special clearance to drop you off by the plane." She rolled down her window as we came to a gate manned by two armed guards. "I have Kara Sterling."

One of the men looked past the woman and into the

backseat. "Follow the arrows next to the building and stop at the stop sign. Someone will direct the car out to the plane."

"Oh, well this is fancy." I pulled out my cell phone and sent a text to the group chat.

> Me: Did you guys arrange for me to be treated like a celebrity?

> Cal: Only the best for our omega.

> Tate: We didn't want you to be bothered by anyone.

> Avery: Can't wait to hold you in my arms again...

> Alvaro: The whole world has been watching this since news got out about us. We just don't want you to be overwhelmed.

I smiled and put my phone in my purse, planning on texting them again once I was settled on the plane. Since newly matched omegas weren't bonded, we had to use private planes to get to our pack if they were far away. I'd offered to drive but was met with four very growly nos.

The driver stopped at a stop sign and we waited. There were a few private planes parked, but I didn't know which one I'd be on.

A pilot stepped out of one of the planes and waved to

us to drive up. I was vibrating with excitement as we stopped near the stairs leading up to the plane.

The pilot opened my door. "Good morning, Ms. Sterling. I'll be one of your pilots today."

"Good morning." It was a great morning, and I slid out of the backseat and slung my backpack and purse on. The other pilot waved from the cockpit window.

"Go on up and I'll get your bags all squared away. There isn't a flight attendant on this flight, so get settled anywhere you'd like." The pilot shut the back door and went to the trunk to help the driver with my two large suitcases.

"Don't mind if I do," I said to myself, practically skipping to the stairs and then climbing them carefully. I'd seen enough videos of people falling down plane steps to go slowly.

I stopped at the door, my stomach suddenly in my throat because the delicious scents of my mates whacked me in the face.

Was this their plane? They hadn't said anything about sending their own plane for me. I knew they had one but thought I'd be taking one in the fleet for omegas.

If I had to smell them the entire way home, I was going to be out of my mind by the time we landed. I'd just have to not breathe through my nose and really practice my olfactory management skills.

I walked on board and turned the corner, a cry

bursting from my lungs as I came face to face with my pack.

Alvaro, Tate, Cal, and Avery were all waiting for me on the plane, and my world blurred as I ran the short distance to them, falling into Tate's arms since he was the closest. They surrounded me, stroking my hair, my back, my cheeks, and any other part of me they could get their hands on. For once, we didn't have to worry about anyone seeing us or about crossing any boundaries.

They were mine forever.

CHAPTER TWENTY-EIGHT

Kara

It felt like I was floating on a cloud the entire flight to Los Angeles. We'd had to break apart to take off, but as soon as we got the go-ahead, I took turns in each of my alpha's laps, kissing them and basking in their purrs and soft touches.

If the flight weren't a short one, I would have suggested them marking me right then and there, but we all deserved better than a mile-high bonding. I was anxious to make them mine forever, and although we hadn't discussed it yet, I was sure they were too.

We landed around noon, and another surprise was waiting for me on the tarmac. Jonathan and Anya stood outside an SUV, flowers in hand and smiles on their faces.

Anya and I had talked or texted nearly every day since she got out of the hospital, and she'd quickly become a close friend. She was almost completely healed from the gunshot wound but still had a few weeks of rest before she started working for the pack again.

We arrived home twenty minutes later, and Jonathan parked in the driveway. It was weird coming back here after all that had happened. I was seeing it in a new light and was excited to see the rest of the house.

"We stocked the fridge with food and have Gizmo at our house. Let me know if you need anything." Jonathan pulled my suitcases out of the back as we got out and wrapped his arm around Anya. "Don't have too much fun."

Cal and Tate grabbed my bags and we walked to the front door as Alvaro used his phone to turn off the alarm system. Why was I nervous all of a sudden? I'd been here before and been with them before. But all of that felt like a dream compared to now. This was real.

"You aren't having second thoughts, are you?" Avery held my hand tightly in his like he was scared I would run.

I stopped him as Alvaro unlocked the front door. "I'm here to stay." I cupped his cheek and he shut his eyes. "I'm yours."

He gave me the smallest nod, a tear falling down his

cheek as he opened his eyes. "I didn't think this day would ever come."

I wrapped my arms around him, laying my head against his chest. "I would have done anything, Avery. That's how much I love you." I pulled back enough to kiss him.

He groaned, or maybe it was a growl, his hands moving to my hips and grabbing them tightly. The kisses from him—and all of them—on the plane had been tender and sweet, but this kiss was all-consuming.

"Guys, let's take this inside, or did you forget the paparazzi out on the street?" Tate was always the voice of reason.

I didn't care if they saw us, but as heated as the kiss was, it was probably best to go inside before clothes started getting removed.

I started to pull away and Avery lifted me, my legs naturally wrapping around him. "What are you doing, sir?"

"Can't an alpha carry his omega?" He kissed me again, and I threaded my fingers into his hair.

We somehow ended up inside and the door shut behind us. I wanted to look around but also wanted him to ravish me and make me his.

Alvaro moved behind me, his hand stroking my arms, and then his fingers brushed across my neck. "Tell us what you want, Kara."

My entire body broke out in goosebumps and Avery

kissed along my jaw to my ear, and then to my neck. I was already tingling with need for them.

"I want to bond." I gasped as Avery nipped at my neck and then sucked the spot. "Please, make me yours."

Alvaro growled and gathered my hair in his hand, lifting it off the back of my neck so he could kiss there. I wanted all of their mouths on me, covering me in their scents.

Tate and Cal came to join our entryway make-out session. Tate grabbed one of my arms and started kissing my inner wrist. It sent a jolt of lust straight to my core and I squeezed my legs around Avery, trying to relieve the ache.

Cal guided my face toward him and kissed me, his tongue immediately finding its way into my mouth and tangling with mine. All of my senses were overwhelmed with their scents and their touches.

I had thought my heat was amazing, but this was even better. There were no crazed hormones driving us to fuck. It was just us, wanting to be together.

Alvaro growled again, letting my hair fall back over my neck. "Take her upstairs to our bedroom."

He didn't have to bark for Avery to comply, but the bonding was already starting, and he was letting the lead alpha in him take charge.

An honest to God purr rumbled out of me and I put my hand over my chest as it continued. I'd never purred before and was a little surprised by it.

"Already making our girl purr." Cal stroked my cheek.

"She's really going to be purring here in a minute." Tate kissed me quickly just before Avery walked toward the stairs.

I hadn't seen the house during the day and was surprised by how bright it was with all of the windows along the back. The house was fairly clean considering Anya wasn't able to help out.

Alvaro brought up the rear as we reached the top of the stairs. His eyes were locked on me, serious as can be. I stuck my tongue out at him as I was carried down the hall and he fought a smile, but ultimately, his grin lit up his face.

They were all so handsome before, but the lightness in their eyes and the happiness I could almost feel made them even more attractive. I'd never realized just how much sadness they carried with them because that was how I'd always seen them.

We walked through the gaming and sitting area, and I turned my head just as the double doors were opened into the primary bedroom.

My jaw hung open, and to say I was surprised at how it was decorated was an understatement.

There was a gigantic bed with a blush pink headboard big enough to fit all five of us. The bedding was white, gray, and pink, and the walls in the room were a light gray. It was the perfect blend of masculine and feminine but was definitely decorated with me in mind.

"This is..." I shimmied out of Avery's arms and went to the bed, running my hand over the soft comforter.

"If you don't like it, we can redecorate it. We wanted everything to be perfect for when you came home." Cal wrapped his arms around me from behind. "Welcome home, Kara."

Tears sprang to my eyes and Cal's purr rumbled against my back. "It's perfect."

My mind instantly went to where my nest was going to be, but I could worry about that later. I would have loved to bond there, but the beautiful bedroom was as good a spot as any.

I turned in Cal's arms and kissed him before lying back on the bed, propping myself up on my forearms. "Take your clothes off, Alphas. I'm ready for you."

"Fuck, yes! Let's do this." Cal eagerly started removing his clothes, and I caught Tate rolling his eyes.

"You too, Tate. Let me see what's mine." I bit my lip, hoping they weren't going to get all growly on me for being a little dominant.

"You heard our omega. Strip." Alvaro winked at me, and I relaxed as he pulled his shirt over his head, revealing his glorious abs. At some point, I planned on licking every divot.

By the time the last article of clothing was shed, and I had a pair of boxers thrown at my head, I was panting. I was so incredibly lucky, and not just because they were gorgeous men, but because their hearts were just as beautiful.

"We have a big problem, Kara." Avery ran his hand over his tattooed stomach, and I added licking every line of his tattoos to my list of things to lick.

"Oh?" I looked down at their erections. "I wouldn't say they're problems, but they are certainly big."

Avery stalked forward from the line of alpha deliciousness they'd all been standing in, grabbed my ankle, and pulled me to the edge of the bed. "You have entirely too many clothes on."

"Just how I like it." I giggled as he lifted my leg and took off my shoe and sock. "Are you going to help me undress, Alpha?"

Avery's jaw clenched and his cock twitched. He liked the little bit of sass I brought. It had always been there, but they brought it out in me more than ever before.

I'd already toed off my other shoe, and he yanked that sock off. I couldn't wait for them to see what was underneath my clothes. I hadn't known when we were going to bond but had prepared for at least sex.

"Stand up." Alvaro barked, his voice growly and strained. "Let us watch you undress."

Avery backed up into the line, his eyes ablaze with desire. They were all gazing at me like I was a feast just waiting to be eaten.

I stood, unbuttoning my jeans and pushing them down to step out of them. My shirt came next, and I stood before them in red lace cheeky panties and a bra.

"Fuck." Tate ran his hand down his face and then wrapped his hand around his cock. "So beautiful."

"Turn around for us." Cal was rubbing his bottom lip, his eyes on my breasts.

"Yes, Alpha." I loved calling them alpha just to hear the pleased growls. I slowly turned around, pausing when my back was to them and looking over my shoulder. "Do you like what you see?"

The red lace in the back was cut higher up, revealing most of my ass to them. I put a knee on the bed and their growls filled the room. I felt like the sexiest omega to ever grace the Earth as I crawled onto my hands and knees, presenting myself to them.

Alvaro was the first to break rank and ran his hand over my ass and then bent down and bit it. I whimpered, wiggling my ass at him, egging him on.

He hooked his fingers around the waistband and pulled them down before sliding the side of his hand through my slick folds. "Fucking soaked, but I want you dripping and begging for our bites and my knot."

"Yes." I pushed back but he moved away. "Please, give me your knot." It was a pitiful beg, but I had to start somewhere and them just staring at me was getting me all kinds of worked up.

"Take her to the nest." Alvaro brought his hand to his mouth and licked my slick off it.

"The nest?" I whimpered in anticipation as Tate wrapped an arm around my waist and pulled me to my feet. "You made me a nest?"

"Of course we did. And if there's anything you don't like, we'll fix it." He kissed my cheek and moved me in front of him, putting his hands over my eyes. "Don't cry."

I couldn't help it. I was just so happy and full of love for these men. It had been well worth all the heartache to get to this point.

We didn't go far, and I could feel the shift in energy and air. My body knew our nest was near, and I was itching to get inside and fill it with our scents, although it already faintly smelled of all of them.

Tate moved his hands, and I gasped as I noticed a little nook of the room that had been hidden behind doors. They'd draped heavy dark purple fabric from the ceiling and walls to create a tent of sorts in the small area.

Avery held open a strip of fabric and inside was lit faintly with fairy lights. There were the nesting mattresses put together to make a bigger nest, tons of pillows, and four Squishmallows.

Cal was already lounging inside against the mound of pillows and gestured for me to come to him. I started forward and Tate grabbed my wrist, stopping me.

"One last thing." His hands danced along my lower back and then up to my bra clasp, unhooking it and letting it fall down my arms and to the floor. "Perfect."

I ducked into the nest and lowered onto my knees before crawling into Cal's open arms.

He kissed me with every ounce of emotion he had in him and then pulled away, panting. "I love you." He pushed my hair behind my ears.

"I love you too." I rubbed myself on his hard cock. "I want you inside me."

"Not yet." He sat us up. "Turn around and sit back against me."

It was so difficult being ready to go but having to wait on Alvaro's commands. I turned around and sat back against him. He grabbed the backs of my legs and lifted them over his, spreading me open.

Oh, sweet baby Squishmallows, the other three were in the nest, the flap shut, their eyes glued to me spread out in front of them.

"Avery, get your mouth between her legs, and don't come up for air until I tell you to." Alvaro's order sent a shiver down my spine. "Tate and Cal, I want to see those nipples hard enough to cut glass."

Alvaro squatted down so he didn't have to hunch because of the drapery, his balls hanging heavy between his legs and his cock straining toward me.

Avery kissed up my leg and growled before he licked me from ass to clit. He was taking Alvaro's directions very seriously, his whole face pressed into me as he began ravishing me with his tongue.

Cal kissed my neck and ear, one hand cupping my breast and running his thumb over the nipple. Tate knelt on the other side of me and took my nipple into his mouth.

"Yes... oh, this is so good. So, so... Avery!" My hand went to his hair, grabbing onto it as he sucked my clit.

Cal pinched and Tate bit me gently, making my fingers and toes start to burn. "Oh!"

I lifted my hips, moving my pussy against Avery's mouth, and Cal's hands both slipped under me, grabbing my ass and helping me. I was going to come, and I was going to come hard.

Fingers pushed into me, two then three, sending me spiraling into bliss. I cried out as my orgasm hit, my walls squeezing around nothing as the fingers disappeared and so did Avery's mouth.

My entire being was shaking, and I whimpered as Tate moved away, and then Cal moved out from behind me.

"Hands and knees, omega. Center of the nest." Alvaro's bark made the last tendrils of my orgasm linger a little longer.

With rubbery feeling arms and legs, I rolled over and crawled to where he directed. He moved in behind me, his cock pressing against my crack.

"One day, this ass will be mine to take first." He kissed the center of my back. "I love you, Kara, and now you're going to be ours forever."

He lined up with my soaked cunt and slammed into me with a groan that made my clit feel like it had a heartbeat.

"I love you," I managed to pant out. "All of you. Make me yours forever. Give me your bites."

Alvaro pumped in and out of me and one of the

hands that had been holding my hips moved around my waist and pulled me up against him. *"Avery, bite her."*

Avery walked on his knees to me. He ran his fingers over my neck, stopping in the spot he'd always given more attention to. *"Mine."* He bit me, his teeth sending a blissful pain and pleasure through me and wrapped around my heart. "I love you more than you can even imagine."

He licked his bite, stroked my cheek, and backed away. My teeth ached to bite into his neck and leave my mark, but I had to wait.

"Cal, bite her." Alvaro's bark was starting to sound strained as he got closer and closer to release.

Cal moved in, his mouth hovering over a spot right next to Avery's. *"Mine."* He bit me, the sensation running through my veins growing stronger.

"Tate, bite her." Alvaro's fingers dug into my skin, and he alternated between a few punishing thrusts and a few gentle ones. He was struggling to hold himself back.

"I love you, Kara." Tate's eyes moved from mine to my neck. *"Mine."* His bite was right next to the other two, overlapping with them both a little.

They were marking me so anyone would clearly be able to see I had four alphas. My clit throbbed and Alvaro pulled out. I opened my mouth to protest, but he was already in front of me, kissing me as he laid me on my back.

He thrust back in and reached between us, sliding

my clit between his fingers. His lips hovered over my neck where the other bites were.

"Mine." He thrust one final time, exploding inside me, his knot filling me and locking me in place at the same time he bit me.

My mouth opened in a silent scream as the most intense wave of pleasure wrapped around my entire body.

After licking my neck so it would heal faster and leave beautiful silver scars, he tilted his head to the side. "Claim me as yours, omega."

It was instinct as I bit into him right where I intended to mark all of them. Right above the curve where the neck connected to the shoulders; visible to all. The faintest taste of blood hit my tongue and the bond between us snapped into place.

The others moved in, Alvaro leaning his torso to the side a bit so they could offer me their necks. Later, they'd knot me one by one, and then our bond would be complete.

It already felt so amazing, I could only imagine how strong our pack would become and I couldn't wait.

Our journey might have started a mess, but now everything was exactly like it should be. *Perfect.*

CHAPTER TWENTY-NINE

Avery

I'd always felt like I'd been missing something from my world, and when Alvaro, Tate, and Cal came into my life, some of the void inside me was filled. For a while, the three of them were enough, but my heart craved an omega.

We were young when we did Omega Match the first time, barely able to take care of ourselves, let alone an omega. While other alphas made sure they had a secure foundation before even entertaining the idea of welcoming an omega into their fold, we were barely making enough to afford a decent-sized rental.

Maybe all the pain from that mess-up was a necessary step to get where we were now, bonded to an omega who made me feel like I'd finally found home. We were more than prepared to take care of our omega, and hopefully a baby or two soon.

I'd thought about babies more and more since meeting Kara, and I couldn't wait until we decided to expand our family. There was no rush, though. We were all still young, and Kara probably wanted to enjoy her freedom after spending the last six years stashed away.

Thoughts of Kara filled my mind, and I stirred awake, ready to wake her up with my face between her legs. Unfortunately, the narrow spot between me and Tate was empty, and the mattress was cold. I could sense Kara though, like a warm caress in my chest. She was nearby, and our bond thrummed with contentedness.

We'd had a long afternoon of completing our bonds, and everyone else was still asleep. It was just supposed to be a nap, but judging by the hunger pang in my stomach, it was well past dinner time.

I carefully crawled out of the nest and stood, going into the bedroom to find my omega. I needed to wrap my arms around her and take in her delicious scent. Four piles of clothes were carefully folded on the end of the bed, and I grabbed mine, bringing them to my nose when I caught her scent wafting from them.

She'd scented them.

My skin broke out in goosebumps at how perfect it was, and I quickly pulled on my boxers and lounge pants, tossing the shirt back on the bed. I didn't plan on keeping my clothes on for very long.

As I walked out of the bedroom and down the hall, I could hear our music coming from downstairs. It was always weird hearing it when we weren't singing it ourselves.

Kara came into view as I descended the stairs, busy in the kitchen and shaking her ass to the upbeat song. She was wearing the blush pink satin robe we'd hung in the bathroom for her, and it clung perfectly to her curves and stopped at just the right spot on her thigh to leave me drooling.

She turned with a mixing bowl and jumped a little when she saw me. "Don't sneak up on a girl like that. I almost dropped the bowl."

"What are you up to? You should be resting." I padded into the kitchen, looking at the pile of dishes in the sink and then at the clock on the microwave. It was nearly eight o'clock. "You didn't have to cook, Kara. We have pizza on speed dial."

"I know, but I wanted to." She smiled and poured brownie batter into a pan. "I enjoy cooking and now that I have this amazing kitchen and a pack, it makes it even better."

She shook the glass pan to even out the batter and slid it into the oven, setting the timer. Brownies were my favorite, even more so now that their smell reminded me of her.

I couldn't resist wrapping my arms around her and pulling her back against my chest, burying my face in her neck. "I was hoping to have you for dinner and dessert."

She leaned back against me, her hands going to my arms and stroking them. "We have all the time in the world for that, but if we don't eat, we'll perish, and there won't be any more orgasms."

"We can't let that happen." I kissed where I'd marked her neck, happy to see my bite was already healing. "Do you need help finishing?"

"Everything is cooking. Just have to wake everyone up in a few minutes." She flicked on the light in the other oven, and I spotted a lasagna. "This is what I was cooking as a surprise when everything happened. Anya said it's your favorite."

"I'm so sorry you had to go through that. We should have canceled our concert." There were a lot of things I regretted about how we handled her heat, and leaving her miles away from us unprotected was unacceptable. "It will never happen again. I promise you that."

"There was no other choice. None of us could have known they would find out and come after me." She turned and looped her arms around my neck. "You took perfect care of me given the situation."

"But that shouldn't be the situation. Life on a tour bus isn't the best, even for us." I kissed her forehead and swayed to the ballad that had started playing from her phone. "We have one more album and tour under this contract."

"I'll just be on suppressants when we're about to go on tour. I would love to travel around the country or the world with you. Don't think you have to give up your music career for me." She put her head on my shoulder, one of her hands sliding from around my neck to trace around the empty space just left of the center. "Your whole torso is covered except this spot."

I covered her hand with mine. "I wanted to save the place right over my heart to put your portrait."

She lifted her head, her blue eyes swimming with tears. "Avery…"

"I know, it's corny as fuck, but-"

She kissed me, her fingers digging into my skin right where her face would soon be. I couldn't stop myself from lifting her onto the counter. Her lips broke from mine, a gasp and a tiny squeal coming from her reddened lips. "The counter is cold!"

"Mm." I grabbed one of the ties of the robe. "You don't have anything on under here?"

"Just underwear." She shivered, her nipples peeking through the thin fabric. "It feels nice against my skin."

"You know what else would feel good against your skin?" Just as I was about to yank on the tie to open her robe her stomach growled so loud that her sister would have been able to hear it down the street. "We need to get some food in you first."

She wrapped her arms and legs tightly around me. "Can we just cuddle on the couch for a bit? The lasagna will be ready soon and we'll wake the guys up."

Who was I to deny my omega such a simple pleasure?

I carried her to the living room and lowered onto the couch with her still wrapped around me. "I'm so glad thinking about babies woke me up."

She lifted her head from my shoulder and looked me in the eyes with such a serious expression I thought maybe I'd messed up. Tears sprang to her eyes, and she brought her hand to my face. "You're serious?"

"I am. I wouldn't joke around about having babies. You do want them, right?" I leaned into her touch and fought the urge to shut my eyes.

"Yes, but maybe not for a year or two." She ran her thumb back and forth across my cheek. "We all need some time to adjust, and you four are going to be a bit protective once I'm pregnant."

I snorted my amusement. "Whenever it happens, I'm ready."

There were a few moments over the past few months where I never imagined I'd see the day I'd be holding my omega. I was a bit lost, but now I knew right where I belonged.

CHAPTER THIRTY

Cal

Kara had become the center of our world, and life with an omega was better than I could have ever hoped for. It had been a week since we'd bonded, and with each day, our individual connection grew stronger, and so did the entire pack's.

Now that we were settled and had security protocols in place for when we went out with her, I was ready to take her out for a ride. It was self-indulgent of me to want her wrapped around me and holding on for dear life when she'd already been lavishing us with affection. She had never been on a motorcycle before, but she'd reluctantly agreed to at least try around the block a few times.

"I'm scared." Kara held the helmet I handed her and looked from it to my bike. "What if we crash?"

"I mean… the possibility is there, but I'm the best driver and would never put you in danger." I took the helmet from her and put up the visor. "Trust me."

She bit her lip and gave me a quick nod before I put the helmet over her head. I'd had it specially made for her in the hopes she'd enjoy going for rides with me.

"My dads have motorcycles, but I've always been too scared to ride with them." She looked at the motorcycle again. "You'll go slow?"

"We'll go around the block a few times and then you can tell me if you still want to go. If it's too scary, we'll take a car." I threw my leg over the seat and patted the spot behind me.

"That's not a whole lot of space, Callum." Fuck, I loved when she used my entire name, no matter the reason.

"It's plenty of space. Throw your leg over and scoot all the way against me. Your feet go on these pegs." I reached down and touched one of them. "You keep them here the whole time."

She sighed and grabbed onto me as she got situated behind me. The heat between her legs felt amazing as she slid flush against me and wrapped her arms around me. "I can't believe I'm doing this."

"The second you feel uncomfortable, pinch my stomach, and I'll pull over." I started the motorcycle and put on my helmet. "Ready?"

"I suppose." She had a death grip on me, and her thighs squeezed so tight against me I worried that they might cramp up on her.

I knew that once we got out on it, she'd love it, but right then, she was shaking slightly and scared we were going to crash. My purr rumbled through me, adding to the rumble of the bike, and she relaxed slightly against me.

"Here we go." I took off slowly out of the garage to the gate, which opened automatically as it sensed the vehicle. "You okay so far?"

"I'm good so far. It's just really weird. Do I put the visor thing down so I don't get a mouth full of bugs?"

"We'll wait. We're only going fifteen to twenty miles per hour in the neighborhood. Plus, I want to be able to hear you. Here we go. Just do what we talked about." I pulled out of the gate and was happy to see there were no paparazzi staked out since we'd done a quick interview on video call the day before.

They'd all wanted the first pictures of us with our omega, but Anya and Jonathan had taken some of us and posted them on our social media, thwarting that plan. There was always the chance they'd follow us, but it wasn't worth the worry.

I circled the block a few times and could feel Kara becoming more and more relaxed with each passing minute. Stopping outside our house, I put my hand over one of hers. "We good?"

"Yes!" Oh, fuck yes. She was enthusiastic, and excitement filled her voice.

"Put your visor down and hold on." I waited until her hand was back in place and put my own visor down.

It was a gorgeous day and traffic was decent enough that we didn't have to stop at all. I hadn't told her where we were going because one of my favorite things was to see her surprised expression when one of us did something she wasn't expecting, like the impromptu living room concert in our underwear or when Tate scooped her up from a patio chair and jumped right into the pool with her.

There was this joy and lightness that we hadn't felt for a while as a pack, and it made me both ecstatic and a bit angry that we were being kept from it. A lot of changes were needed to the World Pack Health Organization and Omega Match, and hopefully we could help bring that change.

I parked outside my warehouse and took off my helmet, waiting for Kara to get off the bike. I missed the press of her body as she carefully dismounted and pulled the helmet off. She walked forward, gaping at the building.

I grinned and couldn't wait to see her take out some of her pent-up aggression on something. "How was the ride?"

"Amazing. What is this place?" She turned to look at me, her face flushed from wearing the helmet.

"You tell me what you think it is." I led her to the door and unlocked it but didn't open it.

"I honestly have no clue… unless this is your evil workshop." She wiped at a drip of sweat on her forehead. "Do they have helmets with fans or air conditioners?"

I laughed and opened the door, gesturing for her to enter. "No, they don't. You just have to get used to it. After you, my lady."

She gasped as she walked in and turned to face the inside of the warehouse. "You have an indoor junkyard."

I shut the door and locked it, chuckling. "It's kind of like one, but this is where I come to get out my aggression or just when I need time alone." I took her helmet and put it with mine on a table next to the door. "Do you want water, beer, or soda?"

"Water." She walked farther into the room, her eyes taking in everything. "So, you destroy these things?"

I grabbed two water bottles and handed her one. "Yup. I thought you'd like to see it and watch me break a few things."

She took a long drink of water, her eyes narrowing slightly. I just grinned because if there was anything I'd learned about Kara in the last week it was that she liked challenges. "If you think I'm just going to sit on that junky couch over there and watch, you have another thing coming."

"Hey, that couch is not junky." I went to the storage

cabinet and pulled out gloves and glasses. "Do you want a jumpsuit? You're covered up, so you should be safe."

"No jumpsuit." She walked over to where I kept different sizes of sledgehammers and picked a lighter one. "I can smash anything I want?"

"Yes." I handed her the glasses and gloves and put my own on. "Except in this corner where we hang out."

She practically skipped out into the junk, looking for her first casualty. I had a feeling she was going to go for a car, and sure enough, she stopped by one and looked back at me. "This one is pretty beat up, but it still has some windows. Can I smash them?"

I joined her. "Have at it."

She squealed in delight, swinging the hammer at the back passenger window. It shattered on impact, and she ran to the other side to smash the other.

There was something so sexy about watching her swing the hammer, and I pressed my palm against my crotch as my cock started to come to life. It seemed to constantly be hard around her.

"My arms are already burning." She swung her hammer and knocked off the side mirror. "I'm going to need a massage later."

"Anything and everything you want is yours." I wanted my omega to have everything her heart could ever desire because she had already given me everything I'd ever dreamed of.

CHAPTER THIRTY-ONE

Tate

Over the past month with Kara, I'd realized there wasn't a single thing I wouldn't do for her or with her. She was so excited to experience everything and try new things, including golf.

On the rare occasions I could get the guys to come with me, all they wanted to do was drink and complain it was boring. I found it relaxing and peaceful being away from the world, especially when I booked all of the other reservations that were an hour after mine and could take my time.

And we definitely required extra time with as many swings Kara needed to hit the ball. She'd only been to the driving range with me twice and had been more than willing to be my companion.

Kara pulled to a stop at the tee of the third hole and hopped out of the golf cart. She was dressed in the cutest white skirt and a pink and purple polo shirt. Her curly hair was pulled into a high ponytail and a purple visor kept the sun out of her eyes.

"How many hits do I get to get a birdie?" She selected a driver from the golf clubs I'd bought her.

"A birdie? Don't you mean a par? You get four swings." I grabbed my own driver and was amused as she struggled to get her ball to stay on the tee. "Need some help?"

"Nope. Okay, so if I want a birdie, I get… three swings." She looked over at me. "Why are you smiling like that?"

"Just enjoying the view." I blatantly looked her up and down. "You're going to wear that for me later."

"Am I?" She bent over again, purposely flashing me the short little shorts under the skirt.

Before she stood up, I dropped my club and moved in behind her, grabbing her hips. "Or we can go right here, right now."

She laughed and stood up straight, rubbing her ass against me. "We shouldn't disturb the turkeys."

I stiffened—and not in the way I wanted to—and looked around. "Where?"

"It's just too easy with you." She turned around and

patted my cheek. "I'll protect you if they come after you."

My relief was instant; she was just poking fun at me. "You sure know how to kick a man when he's down."

She snorted and lined up at the tee as I backed up out of the way. "They can sense your fear. Now, quiet, so I can concentrate."

I adjusted myself and picked up my club, watching as she swung once, twice, then finally hit the ball on the third time, taking a chunk of grass with it. She watched the ball and then did a little happy dance that it stayed on the green.

"Good job, babe." I gave her a quick kiss as we switched places. "Now, watch the pro."

"You have the bigger advantage of having muscles and years of practice." She put her driver away and crossed her arms. "But let's see you beat the perfect hit I just had."

I picked up the chunk of grass she hit and wiggled it in the air before putting it back where it had come from. "So perfect."

My swing was a little off from the hard-on I was sporting and seeing Kara in my periphery looking like a snack. I hadn't anticipated her being so flirty and distracting. I managed to get the ball on the green, barely.

"Not too bad, Carter. A career in the NBA is in your future." She climbed back in the driver's seat as I laughed and put my club away. "I really do appreciate you bringing me golfing. A few of my dads golfed, but I could never get up early enough to tag along."

"My dads golf at least once a month. Well, at least they did before they got too busy." I sighed and climbed into the passenger seat, holding on as she took off toward her ball.

"Maybe you should invite them to golf with you and make a rule that business talk isn't allowed." She stopped rather abruptly, and I was glad I was holding on. As soon as she got out, I slid over to the driver's seat.

"We'll see. I'm still not happy about how my dad added another concert without consulting us first." I knew my dad meant well from a business standpoint, but he was an idiot when it came to what was best for us as human beings.

Kara hit the ball on the first try, not taking any grass in the process. I clapped, grinning as she did some kind of jig on her way back to the cart.

"I know your one dad can be frustrating at times, but I think you should just talk to him and tell him how you feel." She got in the cart, and I headed for her ball again since mine was still farther from my first swing. "I don't want you to regret not having a relationship with him because he's an overbearing record exec."

She was right, and I knew we just needed to talk it out during a time when he wasn't being a VP. Sometimes I just needed a reminder that he was family, despite his role in my professional life.

"Thank you." I pulled to a stop next to her ball and kissed her cheek.

She turned toward me and put her hand on my chest. I couldn't help but purr, and she sighed, her blue eyes brighter than I'd ever seen them. "It just keeps getting better, doesn't it?"

"I never knew it would be like this, Kara." I brought her hand up to my lips and kissed each knuckle. "I didn't just get a new best friend, but I got my old best friends back too."

I entwined our fingers, and she squeezed my hand, her cheeks flushing. God, she was beautiful, and I wanted to kiss her so badly, but her hat was in the way, so I did the next best thing and kissed my mark on her neck.

She groaned. "We're supposed to be golfing, not getting frisky."

"Can't I just kiss my mark?" I did it again and then pulled back. "Go hit your ball, Tiger. You need to get this in the hole if you want a birdie."

She rolled her eyes and jumped out of the cart. "You doubt my skills. Just watch."

I planned to watch her for the rest of my life.

CHAPTER THIRTY-TWO

Alvaro

My pack was stronger than ever, and every day when I opened my eyes, I felt a lightness that had been missing for a long time. After our bonding, we'd had frequent check-ins from both OPS and Pack Health for two months, but they'd finally decided to leave us alone.

Thank fuck, because I was tired of worrying they'd pop up at really inconvenient times, like when I just wanted some alone time with Kara. It would have been hard to have agents tag along on a drive to look at Christmas lights.

Growing up, one of my favorite things to do in the days leading up to Christmas was to pile into the car with my family with Christmas music playing and sip hot chocolate while cruising through neighborhoods all decked out for the holidays.

I put a new blanket in the passenger seat of my car, two travel mugs of hot chocolate in the cupholders, and a container of snickerdoodles on the dash. I'd been able to sneak out of the house for a while and go to Jonathan and Anya's to bake Kara's favorite cookies.

"Alvie?" Kara stood at the garage door. "I'm ready to go."

I turned and grinned at her standing there in red buffalo print pajama pants and a snowman-face hooded sweatshirt. "You look adorable."

She stepped into the garage and looked me up and down with a smile. "Matching pajamas? Now that I know you're into this, we're all going to have them for Christmas."

"Already have it covered. I just haven't told them yet." I gestured to the open passenger door. "Your chariot awaits."

"Where's their Christmas spirit?" She climbed into the passenger seat and a purr rumbled from her.

I shut her door and went around the driver's seat. "It's there. We just haven't had much of a reason to celebrate." The thought saddened me a bit, but as soon as I smelled her delicious scent in my car, I decided not to dwell on the past.

"Are these snickerdoodles?" She grabbed the container and opened it. "Did you bake these?"

"Yes." I pulled out of the garage and took a sip of my hot chocolate as I waited for the gate to open. "Want to put some Christmas music on?"

She closed the cookies and used the mousepad on the dashboard to find a Christmas pop station. "I wish you guys had a Christmas album."

"Maybe after our contract is up." There were a lot of maybes I'd been thinking about lately. "We can record you your own special album."

"You'd do that for me?" She rested her arm on the center console.

"I'd do anything for you." I turned out of the driveway before taking her hand and placing it on my thigh. "If you wanted us to record a death metal album, we would."

"I appreciate the sentiment, but I'm going to have to pass." She squeezed my leg. "Where are we going exactly?"

"It's a surprise." I turned off our street and headed for the freeway. "It's about a thirty-minute drive unless traffic is crazy."

She laughed. "Traffic is always crazy here. I don't think I'll ever get used to it."

"Where would you want to live if you could live anywhere?"

"I like the weather here, just not the air and all the people. Somewhere with lots of trees, but not a forest. Maybe the coast? I honestly haven't thought much about it because it was kind of pointless thinking about." She moved her hand off my thigh to grab her mug.

"It's not pointless to think about. Would you still want to live near your sister?"

"I love living near my sister." Out of the corner of my eye, I could see her examining her pink custom cup with her name and small pictures of her favorite Squishmallows all over it. "Oh, this is so fancy with my name. Did you make this too?"

I snorted. "I can bake, but I can't say I'm into crafting."

"That's too bad. An alpha who crafts is so unbelievably sexy." She sipped her drink.

I filed that nugget of information away for later use. Making Kara happy was one of the most incredible feelings in the world and gave me a high unlike anything else, even a venue full of tens of thousands of screaming fans.

About thirty minutes later when I turned off the freeway and wove my way into a neighborhood, her squeal of delight was all I needed. We'd done decorations inside the house, but nothing besides a wreath on the front door on the outside. What was the point when it was all hidden behind bushes and fences?

"This is amazing!" She clutched her blanket in her lap like if she didn't, she'd start clapping. "Maybe next year we can decorate the fence with lights."

I cringed and tightened my hand on the wheel. Even

if we decorated our house, it would be hard to enjoy our own lights. "Maybe next year we'll have a better house."

Her head snapped in my direction. "I didn't mean…"

I took her hand, keeping my eyes on the cars in front of me. "I know you didn't mean you wanted a new house. I always want you to have the best of the best, and I don't know if our house is the best. Especially here in a few years if we decide to have babies."

"Anywhere that you, Tate, Avery, and Cal are is the best." She brought my hand over to her lap, clutching it between both hands. "You *are* my home."

I glanced over at her looking out the windshield, her eyes sparkling from the lights outside. A warmth spread across me, settling in my chest.

She was right. It didn't matter where we were. All that mattered was that we were together.

EPILOGUE

Kara

Life was a whirlwind, and I was smack dab in the middle of it. I'd been bonded to my alphas for two years now and I didn't think I could love them anymore, but each day, I did.

After a much-needed break, they'd jumped right into the recording studio and recorded their best album to date. Fans drooled over the more mature sound they'd gone with, and now they were wrapping up their world tour with a final performance in Los Angeles.

Their contract was done, and they hadn't resigned, but I didn't think they would stop making music. Now, they would do it on their own terms and when they wanted instead of having a record label ordering them around.

Tate's dad still played a major role in their career, but when it came to me, he completely backed off. I didn't know if it was his omega knocking some sense into him or because he could see how much happier the band was with me in their lives.

Anya sat next to me in the suite as N'Pact took the stage for their final song of the night. I hadn't been at all of their shows, opting to stay on the bus and get work done, but I had attended at least half of them, and it never got old seeing them come alive on stage.

God, they were perfect, and I couldn't wait to get them home and finally tell them my secret.

I didn't mean to project my feelings to them, but I did, and four heads turned our way even though they couldn't see us very well.

"I don't think I'll ever get used to the weird telepathy thing you five have going on." Anya laughed and glanced over at me. "What was that about? I don't see anyone adjusting themselves, so it clearly wasn't a dirty thought like usual."

I shifted in my seat. "Yeah, well… I've been struggling to keep my feelings to myself lately."

"Is everything okay?" Anya looked at me with concern. "I know you've been stressed. The party tomorrow is going to go great."

I squirmed in my seat again; it was so hard for me to keep things from everyone when my scent had changed. "I know that... we're going to miss their last song."

Anya continued to stare at me as I looked back at the stage. "Oh my God, you're-"

"Shh." I gave her a warning glare and darted my eyes over to my sister and her pack. "I haven't told anyone. Not even Kayla."

Her eyes widened and she put her hands over her mouth, tears springing to her eyes. She was going to attract Kayla's attention. I wanted to tell my sister so badly it hurt, but I wanted to tell my alphas first. Plus, it was still early in the pregnancy.

"Go cry in the bathroom or something..." I bit my lip, my own eyes watering a little. "I just found out yesterday, okay? I haven't figured out how to tell them yet."

It had only been two heats since I'd been off birth control, and I hadn't got my hopes up since the first one didn't result in a pregnancy. But I should have guessed the last heat I had four weeks ago was different. It was more intense. I'd been the neediest I'd ever been, and not just because we were on tour.

"This is so exciting." Anya was practically bouncing in her chair. "When are you going to tell them?"

I shrugged. "Tonight? Last night they were too tired, and I didn't want to affect their last show." I looked back at them singing their hearts out. "They've been worried about my scent because it's a little different."

"Oh, I know. They've asked me and Jon to keep an

eye on you because they think you're stressing too much about your business and Omega Match."

"There's nothing to worry about. I'm not stressed. Maybe just a little tired." I'd been working quite a bit on an app where alphas and omegas could communicate before matches even happened.

My pack had been worried when I agreed to start helping Omega Match restructure and improve on top of the consulting business I'd started. I loved doing both and couldn't see myself giving either up.

I'd thought about teaching at one of the omega academies nearby, but that would not have worked with as much travel as my pack did. I wanted to be with them most of the time, and being away for weeks or months was not going to work.

Of course, Kayla had come up with the idea, and in true sisterly fashion sent me a mock-up of branding the same day we'd talked about it.

So far, it had been well received, and I had a waitlist that was months long. Packs who struggled after they first matched—and sometimes even well after they matched and bonded—hired me to give them an objective look at what was happening and suggestions for fixing it. The best part was that I set my own schedule and did everything from home, which meant I could do it while on tour.

As the show ended and we were escorted by security out to our SUV, I grew nervous about telling them. We'd talked about having children a lot—going off birth control had been a mutual decision—but now that it was going to happen, I didn't know if they'd have the same enthusiasm.

I had a good hour to mull over how to tell them while I waited in our living room for them to get home. Things were always crazy after shows, so hanging around their dressing room wasn't something I normally did, and now with a baby on board, I had to be extra cautious.

My eyes were growing heavier when Gizmo lifted his head from my lap and let out a yip of excitement. He stood, lording over me like the true protector he was. I wasn't sure if I believed dogs could sense pregnancies, but he sure had become extra clingy the last few weeks.

"Honey, we're home!" Alvaro announced, coming in the front door first. He kicked off his shoes and dropped a bag by the door.

I greeted them with kisses and hugs. Tate was watching me carefully, but if he noticed I was sweating, he didn't say anything.

"Let's have a toast." Cal grabbed a bottle of expensive champagne from one of the bags they'd put by the door.

I bit my lip, walking with them into the kitchen, where Avery grabbed five champagne flutes from a cabinet. Was this how I told them?

My mind was on how exactly to say it while they chatted excitedly and poured the drinks. There should be a manual on how to tell your pack you're pregnant, especially on such a momentous night. I didn't want to take away from their accomplishment, but tomorrow there'd be alcohol at the party to celebrate the end of a successful tour.

"You all right, sweetheart?" Tate handed me my glass. "You're really quiet."

"I'm… perfect." I looked at each of them, my heart filling with so much joy at seeing their happiness. I raised my glass and so did they, falling silent to hear what I had to say. "To eight months of freedom."

They looked so confused, and if it wasn't such an emotional moment, I would have laughed at their expressions.

"Eight months?" Alvaro brought his drink down but didn't drink it yet. "What's in eight months?"

I set my glass down on the counter and put a hand on my stomach. "When you become fathers."

"I knew it!" Tate put his glass down and wrapped his arms around me, picking me up and spinning me around. "I knew you were, and they didn't believe me."

I burst into tears, burying my face against Tate's shirt. I was just so happy and overwhelmed by it all. They jumped into action, surrounding me, their purrs and scents comforting me.

"Don't cry, Kara. We're here." Avery was stroking my hair just how I liked.

"Always." Cal kissed my arm. "We can't wait."

Alvaro's purr was strong against my back, and he kissed the shell of my ear. "This is the perfect way to start the next chapter of our life."

"Let's go to the nest." Tate scooped me up in his arms and the champagne was forgotten.

"But what about celebrating the end of the tour?" I wrapped my arms around his neck and rested my head against his shoulder, breathing in his scent and being comforted by his purr.

"We have something even more special to celebrate tonight." Avery was beaming, and I reached one of my hands out to him. He squeezed it before we started going up the stairs.

It was moments like these that made me feel loved and cherished by the most perfect pack an omega could ever ask for.

The End

Manufactured by Amazon.ca
Bolton, ON